Kind of a Dirty Talker

A BAD DOG ROMANCE

THE MCGUIRE BROTHERS

LILI VALENTE

All Rights Reserved

Copyright **Kind of a Dirty Talker** © 2024 Lili Valente

All rights reserved. Without limiting the rights under copyright reserved above, no part of this publication may be reproduced, stored in or introduced into a retrieval system, or transmitted, in any form, or by any means (electronic, mechanical, photocopying, recording, or otherwise) without the prior written permission of the copyright owner. This romance is a work of fiction. Names, characters, places, brands, media, and incidents are either the product of the author's imagination or are used fictitiously. The author acknowledges the trademarked status and trademark owners of various products referenced in this work of fiction, which have been used without permission. The publication/use of these trademarks is not authorized, associated with, or sponsored by the trademark owners. This e-book is licensed for your personal use only. This e-book may not be re-sold or given away to other people. If you would like to share this book with another person, please purchase an additional copy for each person you share it with, especially if you enjoy hot, sexy, emotional novels featuring firefighting alpha males. If you are reading this book and did not purchase it, or it was not purchased for your use only, then you should return it and purchase your own copy. Thank you for respecting the author's work. Editing by Sandra Shipman. Cover design by Bootstrap Designs.

❀ Created with Vellum

About the Book

Seven nights, one bed, and the last dirty talker I should want to share it with...

Wesley McGuire is a gentleman in the streets and a filthy beast in the sheets.

He's also my best friend's brother, which means he's part of the found family that's come to mean so much to me. I refuse to put that at risk, especially when I know from experience that dirty talking men always let you down.

That night with Wes was a mistake, one I'm determined not to make again.

I hold strong until one cursed night, when I accidentally ignite a feud with the biggest troublemaker in Bad Dog and wind up on Wes's doorstep in a tattered bridesmaid's dress, needing to get out of town...fast.

Soon, Wes and I are on the run in a borrowed camper van, accompanied by my pet ferret and enough sexual tension to launch us all into outer space.

Even worse?

With every passing mile, he's proving he might be my dream guy.

But will he still want me when he realizes he's not the only one with secrets?

Chapter One

TESSA MARLEY GRAY MARTIN

A woman having the worst second date ever.
And maybe...her last second date ever?

Eighteen months earlier...

I'm freaking out over nothing.

I've listened to too many true crime podcasts at work while chopping vegetables.

That's all this is—my morbid imagination running away with me.

Carl isn't a bad guy! He's an accountant and accountants are never bad. People who get turned on by spreadsheets and tax codes aren't built for murder and mayhem. That would be way too much excitement for such an orderly brain.

To be frank, Carl is, well...

Carl is boring.

Dull as rocks. About as much fun as watching paint

dry. If televised golf and the line at the DMV had a baby, it would still be more exciting than Carl.

But Carl is also a forty-year-old man looking for a woman close to his own age—a rare creature in my current dating ecosystem. He's in great shape, owns his own home a few towns over, and thinks it's "cute" that I've skipped Botox and let the smile lines around my eyes run wild. He doesn't mind that I'm fifteen pounds overweight, even though I jog four days a week after work, and best of all?

He loves hiking as much as I do.

That's how we came to be here, nearly eight miles into a national forest on a lovely, crisp fall afternoon, all alone, without another soul in sight. The trails closer to the parking area are always busy, but out here, in the backwoods, the vibe is different. The words I would usually use to describe it are "peaceful" and "uplifting."

There's nothing I love more than being on a trail with the breeze in my hair and the sun on my face. Out in nature, all my problems feel smaller. *I* feel small, but in the best way.

But the usual peace isn't with me today. There's been something…off with Carl since we reached the ridge overlooking the valley. His tepid attempts at conversation have grown stone cold, he's stopped looking over his shoulder to nod or smile, and when I asked him if he thought we'd taken a wrong turn, he ignored me completely.

Even though I repeated myself.

Twice.

Run, the inner voice hisses between my ears. *Turn around and run and don't look back until you reach the ranger's station.*

I chew my bottom lip, pulse thready as I glance down at the map again. But the slick brochure from the trail entrance hasn't magically rearranged itself in the past five minutes. It still says we should have turned left, not right, at Walrus Rock, a hunk of granite that looks just like a Walrus, right down to the spiky "teeth" formations on its front.

When we stopped to take in the view by the landmark, I caught Carl running his fingers over the sharp, stone "tusks" in a way that set my stomach to churning. And that was before he insisted the smaller trail was a shortcut that would lead us back to the parking lot before it gets dark and took off into the woods, refusing to stop and look at the map.

Run! The inner voice screeches again.

But I can't run.

That would be bizarre! Carl would think I was insane. He hasn't done anything to threaten me. He's been perfectly polite, if a bit...mute.

But maybe he's practicing for ghosting me as soon as we're off the trail. Men on dating apps love to ghost people. It's probably one of the top three things they enjoy after cradling fish for pictures and talking about how ready they are to start a family now that they're forty-two.

And that will be fine! I don't care if Carl ghosts me.

I've been ghosted by far superior men, including Nate, my stone-cold fox of an ex, who slept in my bed for the better part of six months before abruptly ending things after I dared to ask where the relationship was headed. Now, he pretends his eyes no longer function when fixed in my direction. When our paths cross downtown near his bar, he breezes past me with no sign of recognition, ignoring my friendly "hello, Nathaniel," every damned time.

Ditto with my texts asking for a reason for the breakup and my email offering to let bygones be bygones if we can just be civil in public.

If I didn't have friends and family members who acknowledge my existence on a regular basis, I might think I really *was* a ghost. Just a specter haunting the Bad Dog dating scene, only visible a few days a month, when the moon is full.

It's going to be full tonight.

I mentioned that to Carl when we started our hike, joking that if we got lost, at least we'd be able to see the trail after sundown.

He'd huffed in response—the closest I've gotten to a laugh from the man—and replied, "Don't worry. I don't get lost. You can leave that map for someone else."

But I didn't leave the map. I've never been this deep into the reserve and wanted to be prepared in case Carl and I became separated. Or if his sense of direction turned out not to be as fantastic as he believed.

In my experience, men believe a lot of things about themselves that don't turn out to be true.

My ex-fiancé, Xavier, believed he was the most talented guitar player (and lover) of all time, and that the music industry would eventually come running to rural Minnesota if he posted enough stoned strum-sessions to social media. (Spoiler alert: No one came running and Xavier could rarely maintain an erection or hold down a job, leading to my breakup with the "most talented guitarist/lover of all time.")

Once I ended our six-year relationship, I dove into

serial monogamy with a long line of similarly deluded men.

Christoph was a tattoo artist whose "world famous" pet portraits looked like zombie puppies from hell. Pete was a chef with a drinking problem who yelled at his customers from the kitchen. Farley was another guitarist, this time in a wedding band. He refused to play mainstream music at his gigs. So, the gigs eventually dried up, leading him to relocate to Detroit, where he was certain people would appreciate death metal as wedding reception fare.

And then, there was Nate, a sculptor turned bar owner who swore he was a settle-down-with-one-woman kind of a man.

He was perhaps the most deluded of all, I realized after our breakup, when I heard through the grapevine that he'd been sleeping with one of his art students, a girl young enough to be his daughter, the entire time we were together.

I figured an accountant might be a nice change of pace from deluded artists with egos the size of Walrus Rock. And yes, a part of me thought seeing me on the arm of a tall, fit man with a nicely trimmed beard might make it clear to Nate that I'm over him, and he can stop pretending that I don't exist.

I didn't intend to use Carl, exactly, I just...

Okay, fine, I planned to use Carl!

But not in a mean way! He seems to enjoy my company. There's no harm in going for a few public downtown dates where my ex would be likely to spot us together. I even offered to buy a Sunday beer bucket and pizza special at Riff's tonight after our hike.

Which gives me a brilliant idea!

"Hey, Carl," I say, keeping my voice as breezy as possible. "How far do you think we are from the parking lot? If we want to grab the special at Riff's we need to get there before six o'clock."

But he only continues to trudge, slowly, methodically forward, moving deeper down the narrowing trail.

Run, run, run! the inner voice warbles, her fear intense enough to make my footsteps slow.

"Carl?" I repeat, louder this time. I stop dead, gripping the straps of my daypack tight as I add, "I need you to stop and talk to me. I'm not going another step until I'm sure we're on the right trail."

Finally, Carl slows, stops, and begins to turn. But he moves so slowly, it's like he's moving through honey. I suppose his sudden snail impression should make me feel better—I'll surely be able to outrun him, if I have to—but it doesn't.

It's terrifying, and by the time he's lurched around to fully face me, my heart is in my throat and my inner voice is running in frantic circles in my head.

Because this isn't Carl, at least not the Carl I met at the bar last week or hugged in the parking lot in front of the ranger's station. He has the same neatly trimmed beard and broad shoulders, but his dark brown eyes are... dead inside.

"Carl?" I croak, telling myself he's had a stroke or something. There has to be a logical, non-terrifying explanation for why he looks like he's been body-snatched by a hostile alien.

But he doesn't clutch his head or pass out in the fall leaves. He takes a step forward that I mirror with a quick step back.

"Carl?" I squeak again, but there isn't a flicker of recognition in his eyes.

It's like he can't hear me.

Or like he's listening to a voice that isn't mine, a voice deep in his head telling him it's okay to let his real personality out for show-and-tell now that he's lured me so far out into the woods, no one will hear me scream.

He may be right about that, but that doesn't mean I'm not going to holler for all I'm worth.

I pull in a breath, calling on all those singing lessons from junior high to engage my diaphragm as I bellow, "Help! Someone, help me! Help! Please!"

Before I'm halfway through the second "help" Carl is on the move, running impressively fast for a man his size. He isn't chubby per se, but he's a thick human, from his wide shoulders to the muscled thighs that strain the seams of his jeans, the kind of guy who ambles or lumbers.

But he isn't lumbering now. He's sprinting toward me so fast that by the time I turn to run, I barely make it five steps before his big arm locks around my shoulders, dragging me back against his chest.

"No! Let me go! Help!" I scream before his wide hand closes over my lips. His palm is warm and dry and smells pleasantly of evergreen needles, but that does nothing to ease my terror as he rumbles softly in my ear, "Quiet."

I scream into his palm, sucking in air through my nose and crying out until my eyes start to ache and water. I kick and thrash, but Carl doesn't seem to feel the heels of my hiking boots slamming into his shins.

He doesn't seem bothered by my screaming, either.

He doesn't tell me to be quiet again. He simply shuffles slowly backward on the trail, bound for...I have no idea what.

I only know it's nowhere I want to be.

I scream and whimper and thrash even harder, clawing at his arm with my nails, but his denim jacket is thick and my nails are barely a centimeter long. I work with my hands, preparing food all day. I can't afford to have long nails in the way when I pull on my latex gloves or need to chop vegetables at the speed of light.

My thoughts race, trying to remember if I have anything I can use as a weapon in my daypack. I brought a flashlight, but it's a tiny thing, tossed in on the off chance I got turned around on a trail and needed help staying on course after dark.

Otherwise, all I brought is lunch, snacks, gum, water, and—

Water! Since we were aiming for close to fifteen miles round trip, I brought my extra-large Hydro Flask. It's as long as my forearm and heavy enough to do damage if I aim it at a vulnerable area.

If I can just get away from Carl, I can grab it and swing it at his head like a baseball bat.

I stomp down hard on his instep, but his hiking boots are as sturdy as mine, and again, he doesn't even seem to notice my attempts at self-defense. Gritting my teeth and calling on all my strength, I ball my hand into a fist and slam it back behind me, aiming for Carl's balls.

This time, I get the reaction I've been hoping for.

He groans and doubles over, his arm loosening around my shoulders just enough for me to wiggle free and start running again.

I hurl my body down the trail, screaming as I run

faster than I've run in years, "Help me, I'm being attacked! Help me, someone, please! He—"

My words end in a choking sound as Carl's arm goes around my throat this time, gagging me as he drags me back against him. His hand returns to my mouth as he says in that same, chillingly calm voice, "Be quiet or I'll gag you. Just be good and play nice, and I won't hurt you."

My scream turns to a sob, tears slipping down my face as he begins pulling me backward again.

Because I know this story.

I've listened to a hundred variations of this tale on a dozen different true crime podcasts. When the bad guy says he "isn't going to hurt you," he almost always hurts you.

And most of the time?

Most of the time, he does a lot worse than hurt...

Chapter 2

TESSA

I howl and screech and kick, but his hand is too big. I'm barely making any noise at all, and my hope is swiftly slipping away. There's no one around to hear me anyway. We haven't seen another soul on the trail in close to an hour.

Please, I sob, begging the universe for mercy with everything in me. *Please let someone have heard me scream. Please, please, please. Please, don't let it end like this. I have so many things I still want to do. So many dreams I want to make come true. So many adventures I haven't had the chance to take. Please. Please!*

At that exact moment, just as a sunbeam cuts through the leaves, blinding me for a second, I hear a deep voice ask, "Hello? Is someone back here?"

Nerves electrified with sudden hope, I scream louder, but Carl's hand tightens at the same time, muffling the sound.

"Shut up," he hisses into my ear. "Be quiet or I'll break your arm."

Trembling, I sob and wail even harder, snot spilling

from my nose onto Carl's hand as I frantically shuffle my feet in the leaves beneath us, making as much noise as possible.

And then, something miraculous happens...

A man appears around the bend in the narrow trail, and not just any man.

It's someone I know! It's Wesley McGuire, my boss, Melissa's, older brother, who just happens to be a lawyer. And sure, he's a divorce attorney, not a criminal prosecutor, but he's a goddamned *lawyer*, a man sworn to upholding the law, which somehow makes me certain everything is going to be okay.

The fact that he's as tall as Carl, with equally broad shoulders, doesn't hurt. Wes might be a little less girthy through the thighs, but he's strong and intimidating, a fact I can tell hasn't gone unnoticed by Carl.

When Wes's gaze lands on us, taking in the scene with obvious horror, Carl freezes like a murderous deer in the headlights.

"Tessa?" Wes says, sending my heart soaring. He remembers me! We've only met a few times at holiday parties for the catering company, but he remembers!

And aren't all people more inclined to stick their necks out for people they know than complete strangers?

I whimper against Carl's hand and nod, begging Wes with my eyes to get me out of here.

His gaze going black with rage, Wes shifts his focus to Carl and says in a soft, menacing voice that lifts the hair on my arms, "Let her go. Right now."

"We're okay," Carl says. "Go away. We're on a date."

"Let her go," Wes repeats, dropping his large backpack on the ground as he steps forward, his hands curling into fists. "This is your last chance. Let her go and run that way as fast as you can." He points over Carl's shoulder before letting his arm fall back to his side. "If you don't, I'm going to make sure you won't be walking anywhere for a very long time. The police will have to airlift you out of the forest on a stretcher."

The way he says it, so calm, but so completely confident, is chilling. It leaves no doubt in my mind that he's capable of crippling another man without hesitation.

Apparently, Carl is equally convinced. A beat later, the pressure around my throat eases and the repulsive heft of Carl's body vanishes from my back.

I lurch forward, choking and sobbing as I hurry toward Wes. I glance over my shoulder as I go, so grateful to see Carl hauling ass up the trail that I start crying even harder.

"Are you all right?" Wesley asks, gathering me against him, his strong arms comforting and safe, the opposite of Carl's crushing grip.

I nod, but I can't stop sniffling and snotting all over the place. I suck in a breath, swiping my sleeve across my dripping nose as I pull myself together enough to say, "Yes, thanks to you. Thank you so much. Thank you." I snatch at the sleeve of his brown canvas coat. "But we should run. We have to run. He might come back."

"If he does, I'll take care of it," Wes says, adjusting his belt.

I glance down, my jaw dropping as I spot a serious-looking knife in a brown leather sheath at his waist. "You have a knife."

"I have a knife," Wes confirms calmly. "Is your friend armed?"

I shake my head, but almost instantly second-guess myself. "I don't know. I don't think so. I didn't see anything in his pack when we stopped for lunch, but I could be wrong." I glance anxiously over my shoulder again, the urge to run punching inside my stomach. "So, we should go. Now. Fast. Please?"

He nods and grabs the strap of his large camping pack. "Let's go. You first. I'll follow behind and watch our backs."

Trembling with relief, I snatch my daypack off the trail a few feet ahead and hurry toward the ridge. I scurry forward in silence for several seconds before glancing back over my shoulder to whisper, "And Wes?"

"Yes?" he rumbles, in that same calm, confident voice that's like a balm to my frazzled nervous system.

"Carl isn't my friend, not even close," I say. "He's basically a stranger and that was the worst second date of my life."

His lips curve in a grim smile. "Good. That will make it less complicated when we file a report with the police."

A report with the police...

The thought is shocking at first, but of course, Wes is right. We have to go to the police. Carl didn't technically do anything awful to me, at least nothing awful enough to land him in prison, but if Wes hadn't shown up...

I shudder and walk faster, not wanting to think about what would have happened if Wes hadn't shown up. If we hurry, we can be back at the parking area not long after dark and at the police station at a decent enough hour that they might be able to question Carl tonight.

But by the time we reach Walrus Rock, the sun is already slinking behind the ridge on the other side of the valley.

I skid to a stop, my stomach dropping. "Shit. It's so

late. I had no idea." I guess I was wandering that trail and wrestling with Carl way longer than I thought.

"Yeah, and the trail back to the ranger's station won't be safe in the dark," Wesley says. "But it's okay. We can find a secure place to hole up for the night and hike out in the morning."

"We're going to spend the night out here?" I squeak, my terror at the thought obvious enough that Wesley's hand settles on my shoulder.

"It's okay. I doubt Carl is dumb enough to come after you again, but just in case, I know a hidden camping spot. In five years of camping out here, I've never seen another soul there." He squeezes my shoulder gently. "Come on. If we hustle, we can get everything set up before nightfall and I'll make you a nice dinner."

My ears perk up at that. Even when life is dark and scary, the way to my heart is apparently still straight through my stomach.

"Okay, thanks," I say, a shiver of something different than fear working through me as I meet Wes's steady green gaze. God, he's dreamy. All the McGuire brothers are gorgeous, but Wes is...more than that.

He's strong and kind and not as easygoing as everyone seems to think. When shit gets scary, so does Wes, and something primal inside me finds that very interesting.

I remind that primal part of me that Wes is six years younger than I am and my boss and best friend's brother. Even if he were interested—which I'm sure he isn't after seeing me covered in snot—he's romantically off-limits.

Off-limits, off-limits, I chant silently as we make our way to a hidden fork in the trail a bit farther up the ridge.

But the primal part of me isn't so easily silenced. And

when she realizes that Wes and I are going to be sharing a sleeping bag?

Well, let's just say she's excited enough to banish the last of the fear from my encounter with Carl, setting my body to humming in a much more pleasant way as we gather firewood and settle in for a night in the woods.

Chapter 3

Wesley Preston McGuire

A man who never
gives in to temptation.
Well, almost never...

For the hundredth time since Tessa ran to me on the trail while her attacker lumbered off into the woods, I want to pull her into my arms and hold her.

Hold her, kiss her forehead, and promise her I'll cut Carl's heart out if he dares come near her again.

I have a reputation for being a calm and easygoing guy, but I have a dark side. Everyone does. I just keep mine under tighter wraps than most. Growing up, I witnessed volatile behavior from my brothers on more than one occasion—especially from Matty and Christian—but I never felt safe letting the wilder side of my own nature out to play.

Somehow, even as a child, I sensed that *my* dark side, once unleashed, wouldn't be so easily reined back in. I was simply born with a little more rage than the average person. The unfairness in the world, the injustice in so many of our systems, and the way innocent people suffer while billionaires and corporations get off scot-free for their sins—affect me on a visceral level.

That's why I became a lawyer. I wanted to do my part to ensure that the good guys won and justice was served. It's also why I'm careful about who I choose to represent. I've passed up my fair share of paydays because I knew the client was in the wrong.

Living in a town as small as Bad Dog, everyone hears the hot gossip. I know who's been cheating on whom, who's hiding marital assets from a chronically ill spouse, and who yanked his kid from the baseball field by his hair after a Little League loss. None of those people are going to make it onto my busy schedule.

I loathe a liar and a cheat. I remind myself of that fact as Tessa tidies up in the tent and I start the stir-fry on my camp stove.

Yes, things have been awful with my girlfriend lately.

Yes, my head-clearing hike today convinced me we aren't long-term-commitment material and I intend to end the relationship once I'm back in town tomorrow.

But we haven't broken up yet. We're still technically together, which makes how much I want to spill blood on Tessa's behalf, then go to sleep curled around her curvy body, even more morally wrong.

But something came alive inside of me when I saw

that man's hand over her mouth. Her wide, tear-filled blue eyes met mine and, in that moment, I knew I would happily rip Carl limb from limb for her. I would destroy him with my bare hands, tear out his throat with my teeth, like some savage throwback to humanity's caveman days.

It was primal...as primal as the attraction that pulsed through me every time my gaze drifted down to Tessa's ass as she walked ahead of me on the trail.

And I'm fucking ashamed of myself for it.

I'm not this guy. I don't ogle women. I don't engage in fantasies about how hot it would be to drive my fingers through a near-stranger's thick hair and tug her head back while I kiss her senseless. And I especially don't have to fight an erection simply because a pretty woman sits down next to me in a tank top that shows her cleavage and a pink-and-blue flannel that brings out the turquoise in her eyes.

"Better?" I ask as Tessa settles onto the log next to mine beside the fire.

She sighs, tossing her impossibly thick hair over her shoulder. I swear, the woman's golden-streaked chestnut hair hangs all the way to her waist, and I'm here for it. "Yes. Amazing what a wet wipe and a little ChapStick can do for a person's morale." She extends her hands toward the fire with a smile. "This is so nice. I always struggle to get a fire going when I camp."

"Boy Scout," I confess. "One who was really obsessed with s'mores and wasn't about to miss a chance to get sticky before lights out."

"Cute." Her smile widens, making the dimple in her right cheek pop and smile lines crinkle around her eyes.

Fuck, her smile...

It lights up the dark every bit as much as the fire. It's such a nice change.

I haven't seen Darcy smile in so long. No matter how hard I try, it seems my girlfriend is always upset with me. Mostly because I'm not ready to move in together, and I'm especially not ready to let her twin sister come along for the ride.

Daria is, to put it nicely, *difficult*. Very difficult. After spending every day fighting for my clients, the last thing I want is conflict in my home. But Darcy refuses to see her sister's shortcomings or admit that we haven't been having fun together for a long time.

Bottom line, Darcy and I aren't meant to be. We're too different. I should have ended things in August when she announced she wasn't up for Thanksgiving with the McGuires. She said it would be too overwhelming and she'd prefer to spend the holiday with her more "reasonably sized" family instead of dividing our time between her parents' house and mine.

But my family is my family. Yes, there are a ridiculous number of them and they're loud and nosy and we're packed in like sardines at every holiday, but they're mine, and I love them. A woman who can't embrace my family isn't the woman for me.

My mind involuntarily turns back to Tessa and how much she clearly enjoys a big, crazy McGuire family gathering. Last summer, she dove into the fun at our annual lake party with the same abandon as the rest of my siblings, and she and Melissa are so close, they're already like sisters.

"So, what do we have here?" Tessa asks, shooting a suspect look at the pot and pan in front of me.

"Stir-fry and rice," I say, motioning to the small plastic container of brown liquid I'm reserving until the end. "And a homemade honey sesame sauce I made myself. There should be plenty for both of us. I always overpack when it comes to food. My eyes are bigger than my stomach."

"And my stomach is a spoiled brat," Tessa says, shifting closer and nudging my hip with hers. "Scootch, mister. Let a professional take over before you burn the rice and ruin that stir-fry pan."

I surrender my spatula with a soft laugh, not minding her sitting this close. Not minding it one bit. "Just like Melissa."

Tessa sighs and shrugs. "Sorry. We're chefs and control freaks. We can't help it." She turns back to the rice pot. She scrapes at the bottom and turns down the heat on the stove, muttering something beneath her breath.

"What was that?"

"Nothing," she says, her dimple popping again.

"No, you have to tell me. If you mutter it, you have to repeat it if asked. Those are the rules."

"Oh yeah?" She laughs. "Good to know. I just said that I've also heard that you're a terrible cook."

I huff. "I am not."

"Mel said you've given her food poisoning three times."

My jaw drops. "I have not. And she comes over for fancy grilled cheese at my place at least once a month. She loves my grilled cheese."

"She lets you cook grilled cheese because it doesn't have any raw ingredients that might kill her if you don't cook them properly." She winces sympathetically. "Sorry.

I'm a truth-teller. It's a problem. Part of the reason I have very few close friends."

I frown. "I doubt that."

"No, it's true. Most people don't like a truth-teller." She wrinkles her nose. "And I'm so busy with work and plotting my epic hike summer after next, I don't have a lot of time to get out and socialize."

Intrigued, I ask, "Epic hike. Sounds exciting. Where are you headed?"

"The Appalachian Trail on the East Coast. I've wanted to hike it my entire life, ever since I read about it in my dad's nature books when I was a kid. I'm not going to do the entire twenty-two hundred miles, obviously, since I can only take two weeks off, but I figure I'll get a good chunk of it done." Her smile fades. "Though after today, hiking alone doesn't sound like the most fun."

"I'll go with you," I hear myself say, the words surprising me as much as they clearly surprise Tessa.

Her head jerks my way and her brows shoot up her forehead. But she's smiling when she says, "What?"

I exhale a breathy laugh. "Sorry. It just came out. I've always wanted to hike it, too, and I really hated seeing that man's hands on you. I don't like to think about you running into someone else like that while you're alone in the woods."

Her grip tightens on the spatula as she flips the vegetables. "Yeah. Me, either." She sighs. "Isn't it sad? That I'm more afraid of people than I am of bears or mountain lions or catching a nasty case of poison ivy?"

"Not people. Men," I say, my jaw clenching. "I'm so sorry. I hate that the women I love don't have the freedom or safety I do. Humanity should be ashamed of itself."

Her gaze settles on my face, searching for a long beat, until I ask in a softer voice, "What?"

She shakes her head. "I don't know, I just... It's nice to hear that. Nice to know there are still good men out there, after all."

"Not always so good," I murmur, a husky note in my voice.

Her lips part. When her gaze meets mine again it's with the same awareness I've been feeling every time her thigh brushes mine. "Why do you say that?"

"Because if he'd given me the excuse, I would have hurt him. Badly," I say, confessing to one of my sins, the one less likely to end in me betraying a promise to my girlfriend. "A part of me wanted to teach him what it feels like to be powerless and afraid. And that's not nice. Not even a little bit."

Her expression sobers, but her eyes remain locked on mine as she whispers, "Fuck nice."

My lips twitch and my traitorous cock thickens behind my fly. "Yeah?"

"Yeah. I'd rather be a brave, ballsy person who stands up for the underdog, any day." Her pretty mouth hooks up on one side as the wind gusts through camp, sending strands of silky hair sliding into her face. "I don't like *being* the underdog, as much. But into every life a little underdog must fall, I guess."

I reach up, tucking her hair behind her ear, enjoying the moment when my fingers slide over her soft skin way too much. "We'll get you a whistle and some mace. I can teach you a few self-defense techniques, too, if you'd like."

"I'd like," she whispers, transforming my semi into a

full-fledged problem that makes me grateful for the shadows slowly closing in on our campsite.

Clearing my throat, I turn to take in the view across the valley. "Then we'll make it happen."

"Thanks," she says. "And if you were serious about wanting a trail buddy, you're welcome to join me. It could be fun. Even as a big, strong guy, it can be nice to have someone around to watch your back."

"Yeah, it can," I agree, turning back to her. Just meeting her gaze is enough to make the urge to kiss her almost irresistible. "And nice to have someone around who can cook, I guess."

She arches a wry brow. "You guess?"

"Well, I haven't eaten any of your cooking yet," I tease as her chest puffs up at the challenge.

Fuck, her chest... I will myself not to glance down, but my stupid eyes have a mind of their own.

So, I glance.

And because she isn't blind, Tessa notices.

She goes still and I go still, until there's nothing but the soft hiss of the vegetables in the pan and the rustle of the leaves in the trees.

The tense moment stretches on, electric and loaded. I'm about to apologize for being a pig who can't keep his roaming gaze in line when she whispers, "Well, then, you'll just have to give me the chance to prove my culinary skills to you. Dinner? My place? Tomorrow night? This meal doesn't count because I didn't prep or plan it myself, and you burned the rice a little before I intervened."

I smile. "Sorry about that. And yes, dinner sounds amazing," I say, refusing to think about all the reasons I should say no.

I don't want to say no. I want to say "yes," more than I've wanted to in a long, long time. Besides, a lot of things can change by tomorrow night.

It isn't the classiest thing in the world to break up with my girlfriend in the morning and go out on a date with another woman the same day. But my problems with Darcy are the reason I'm out in the woods, camping alone on a Friday night. I needed some space to breathe and think. And even if I'd asked her, Darcy wouldn't have come with me. She's afraid of the woods and finds camping an exercise in torture.

Which makes me wonder, "Do you think you'll be more afraid now? Of the woods?"

Tessa seems to mull that over as she turns off the heat on both burners. Finally, she says, "Maybe, a little. But that won't stop me. Cooking is my passion, but hiking and camping..." She gazes out over the twilight-kissed hills with an appreciation I feel in every bone in my body. "This is where I feel most alive. It feels like where I'm supposed to be, you know? And I'm not going to let a twat like Carl take that away from me."

"You're pretty amazing," I murmur.

She shifts her focus my way. "You, too. So, do you want my honest evaluation of your sauce before I decide whether or not to pour it over our stir-fry?"

I smile. "Could I stop you?"

She returns my grin. "I mean, yeah. You probably could. If you asked very bravely."

Catching her call back to our "nice vs. brave" conversation, I laugh. "Nah. I save my bravery for bigger battles. I defer to your expertise. If you say the sauce isn't up to snuff, I trust you."

I watch, trying my best to keep a neutral expression as

she opens the small container, squeezes a few drops onto her finger, and brings it to her lips. But when her tongue sweeps across the pad of her fingertip, my breath catches and for a second, I forget how to breathe.

Then, she looks up and whispers, "That may be the most disgusting thing I've tasted in recent memory, Wesley McGuire," and the urge to kiss her grows almost unbearable.

"Ever been told you're a little bit of a brat, Tessa Martin?"

A big, bright smile blooms across her face. "You know my last name?"

"Of course," I say. "I pay attention to interesting people."

She traps her bottom lip between her teeth, making me ache to do the same. "Me, too. Shall we debate the benefits of hiking the northern stretch of the Appalachian Trail versus the southern while we eat? I mean, if we're considering joining forces, we should see if we have similar ideas about what constitutes a good hike, right?"

"We should," I agree, but I already know I want to join forces with this woman.

I'm not usually the kind to fall headfirst into a crush like this, but there's something about Tessa. Something that keeps me hanging on her every word as we devour our simple dinner and the stars flicker to life in the clear sky, promising a beautiful night ahead.

It's the kind of night that a person doesn't forget.

The kind that has the potential to change things, forever...

Chapter 4

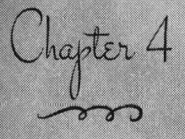

TESSA

I can't make out with my best friend's brother.
I really can't!
I also can't drag him into that tent and ride him like a prancing pony all night long.

That would be bad. Very, very bad!

But it would feel so good. There's no doubt in my mind about that. And the way Wesley's been looking at me since we settled around the fire makes me pretty sure he'd be up for a little hanky-panky in our shared sleeping bag.

Maybe it's the fact that we survived something terrifying that's drawing us together like the opposite ends of a horny magnet. Or maybe it's our shared love of nature, hiking, and planning grand adventures that lit this fire smoldering between us.

Or maybe it's just that spark of magic a person's lucky enough to stumble upon every now and then, that instant connection with another soul that makes your mind and heart (and libido) sit up and take notice.

I can't remember the last time I laughed so much

during dinner. Or the last time my panties were damp without a man having so much as kissed me.

But Wesley's eye contact is...next level.

When he looks at me, I feel it *everywhere*, from my tingling lips to my aching thighs. And when I actually caught him staring at my chest?

Well, forget about it. My cool was a thing of the past.

My nipples have been hard ever since, silently begging Wes to touch them, even if it's just for one stolen night. I have no idea what his romantic status is, but he's never brought a girlfriend to any of the McGuire parties. I've always assumed he's the kind of guy who's married to his work and doesn't have time for a relationship. That's true of a lot of people in their early thirties. It takes so much effort to establish yourself when you're first starting out, especially when you're a lawyer who didn't even finish school until you were in your late twenties.

And as for my romantic status? It's obviously at rock bottom.

If nothing else, Carl proved that it can always get worse than falling for flaky commitment-phobes or men who don't want to get serious if I can't give them a baby. Serious bodily harm (or worse) is also on the menu for the intrepid lady dater.

But not tonight...

Tonight, I'm having a damned good time, even if all Wes and I do is talk.

"Okay, but what if we run into a moose in Vermont or Maine?" I ask once we've established that we both think the northern stretch of the Long Trail is the superior choice for views and staying cool on a summer night. "I've heard they're way more aggressive than black bears. I mean, assuming you've properly stored your food."

He shrugs. "I'm not worried about moose."

"They kill people every year," I say, though I'm forced to amend, "Mostly in Alaska, but still. Mama moose can be dangerous."

"Not as dangerous as ticks," he counters. "Tick-born illnesses are on the rise and some of them are incurable at this point."

I hum around my last bite of stir-fry. "You're right. We're going to need good bug spray."

"And to do a thorough tick check before we roll up for the night," he says, his eyes dancing in the firelight. "Which could get tricky. You can't search every inch of yourself without a mirror."

I set my plate on the ground beside the camp stove and shift to face him with a flirty smile. "You're right. We'll have to bring mirrors."

He exhales a soft laugh. "That wasn't what I was thinking." He leans across my thighs, setting his plate on top of mine. On his way back, he hesitates, his mouth inches away from my lips as he adds, "But that could work."

"Or we could just check each other, I guess," I whisper, my nervous system flashing like the giant holiday lights my cousin Nancy hangs on her Christmas tree every year. "Might be more efficient."

He hums low in his throat, not making any move to shift farther away. "Efficient is good. And we could practice tonight. Deer ticks are active in Minnesota until November."

My lips part, and my heart thumps harder. "I know. I put spray on my boots when I got to the parking lot, but I..." I trail off, mesmerized by the way the firelight caresses his face. After a beat, I realize I'm being a spazz and hurry to add, "But yeah. I totally forgot to reapply."

"Turn around," he murmurs, his voice a physical caress that does further damage to my panties. "I'll check your neck and you can check mine."

"Sounds good," I say, sounding as flustered as I feel.

But I don't know the meaning of "flustered." Wesley teaches me that as he sweeps my hair to one side and tugs my flannel down far enough to bare the top of my shoulders. He brushes warm fingers over the back of my neck, sending lightning bolts of awareness ricocheting through my body with such force, that it takes my breath away.

My jaw drops and I try to suck in oxygen, but my lungs no longer remember how to perform that function. My eyes slide closed and my world narrows to his touch, the rough pads of his fingers dragging over my skin, the rumble in his chest as he performs a very thorough check of my exposed flesh.

"Well, nothing so far," he murmurs, "but you know what ticks like."

Forcing my lungs to draw in air, I wheeze, "What's that?"

"Tight places," he says, his mouth so close to my skin, that I can feel his breath on the nape of my neck. "Would you mind if I lifted the straps on your bra and looked underneath?"

"Sure," I say, not bothering to tell him that it's a tank top with a built-in support shelf, not a bra.

Hopefully, he'll find that out for himself soon enough...

I don't know when I became this scandalous woman intent on having my way with a man that I absolutely shouldn't have my way with. But thoughts of what my bestie might have to say about me having co-ed naked fun times with her brother are suddenly the furthest thing from my mind as Wesley slides my tank top straps down my shoulders.

My nipples immediately celebrate the development with a contraction that makes the ache between my thighs even worse. And then Wesley utters a sympathetic sound, beginning to rub the grooves left behind by the straps, and I melt into a simmering puddle of lust.

"Ouch," he murmurs. "This looks like it hurts."

I hum as his big hands curve over my shoulders, kneading gently. God, his touch is...magic. "Just one of the many trials of being a woman with a large chest," I practically purr. "You should see the shoulder grooves after a run."

"I would like to see that," he says, sounding a little breathless himself.

I glance at him over my shoulder, my heart swooping in my chest at the rapt expression on his face. "Yeah?"

His focus shifts my way, building the tension between us until it's almost unbearable. "Sorry. I didn't mean that. I just meant..."

"What did you mean?" I whisper after a moment.

"I meant that...you're beautiful," he says, sending the swooping, spinning feeling spreading through my entire body, until I feel like a bird about to take flight. "And I like touching you way too much."

"Or maybe just enough," I say, following the magnetic pole in my chest sucking me inexorably toward this man.

Before I know what's happening, I turn and lean in, pressing my lips to his.

Chapter 5

WESLEY

I shouldn't do this. *We* shouldn't do this.

I'm still technically in a relationship—at least for a few more hours—and Tessa is best friends with my sister. A failed fling could make things very awkward for both of us moving forward.

But just thirty seconds into this kiss, I already know Tessa isn't "fling" material. There's nothing casual about the way I feel when she straddles me, moaning her approval as I grip her ass in both hands. Nothing casual about this kiss that sets every cell in my body on fire.

Speaking of fire…

"Can I take you inside?" I say, breath coming fast as I kiss my way down her neck. "I'd like to touch you without worrying about campfire smoke in our eyes."

"You can take me anywhere you want to take me," Tessa says, her words banishing the last of my hesitation.

She starts to shift backward on my lap, but I grip her tighter, holding her in place as I stand and start for the tent, her in my arms.

Her eyes widen as her hands loop around my neck. "Impressive display, Mr. McGuire. I'm not a dainty girl."

"No, you're a sexy as hell woman, and I can't wait to have my mouth all over you."

She bites her lip, her eyes glittering. "Yes, please."

I set her down by the tent, pulling aside the flap for her to enter first. Once she's inside, I join her, zipping the opening shut so we're not surprised by anything else that might want to blow or crawl in to join us.

When I turn back to her, she's already stripped off her boots and flannel and is reaching for the bottom of her tank top.

"Should we finish that tick check?" she asks, heat in her gaze that makes my already throbbing cock twitch behind my fly.

"Absolutely." I chuck my own boots and reach for my shirt, cursing beneath my breath as her breasts bob free of her top. They're each an overflowing handful, topped by pale peach nipples that I need my mouth on. *Now.*

Right fucking now.

I'm across the tent in seconds, my hand diving into her hair and fisting there as I pull her close. I crush my lips to hers, kissing her with all the hunger she's summoned to the surface as I cup her breast in my other hand, teasing her pretty nipple until it's hard beneath my fingers.

"Jesus, Wes," she pants when we finally come up for air.

"Too much?" I ask, a flicker of uncertainty tightening my ribs. She hasn't given any sign that she isn't enjoying this as much as I am. But Darcy didn't either, not until we'd been dating for a few months and she confessed she found me too "aggressive" in bed, leaving me feeling terrible for not sensing her discomfort earlier.

Tessa shakes her head, her blue eyes wide. "No. Not even close. You just... You make me feel things. Things I haven't felt in a long time."

"Good things?" I mold her breasts with my hands, loving the heavy weight of them. Loving the way her gaze fills with hunger as I tease her nipples between my fingers even more...

"So good." She braces her hands on my chest as I lay back, pulling her on top of me. Her breath hitches, a moan wrenching from low in her throat as I bring my mouth to her flushed skin, showing her nipples how happy I am to meet them. "We probably shouldn't do this, but damn...I don't want to stop. Please, don't stop."

"Never," I say, continuing to attend to her gorgeous breasts as I reach between us, popping the button on her hiking pants. My hand dives down the back of the now gaping fabric, discovering silky panties and the delectable curve of her ass.

"God, Wes, you make me so wet," she murmurs.

"Yeah?" I reach farther down and around until my fingers skim over the soaked cotton panel of her panties. I drag the fabric aside, groaning as I explore every perfect slick fold between her legs.

"Clothes," she pants, squirming on top of me. "We need fewer of them."

"Right now," I agree, wrapping an arm tight around her waist as I flip us over, reversing our position on the sleeping bag.

A moment later, I've ripped her pants, panties, and socks down her legs and am kneeling between her thighs, admiring a tantalizing glimpse of her pussy.

"Spread your legs," I tell her as I work open my pants and pull down the zipper on my fly. "I want to see you."

"I like your bossy side," she says as she obeys, her gaze devouring me as I drag my pants and boxer briefs down and toss them to the side of the tent. Her lips part on a rush of breath. "I like that even better."

"My cock?" I grip my swollen length, stroking myself up and down.

She nods loosely. "Hell, yes. Get over here and do bad things to me." She reaches for me and I go into her arms without a beat of hesitation.

It just feels so right, so easy and comfortable and hot as fucking hell. Tessa doesn't feel like a new lover. Even the way we communicate—the way she asks for me to suck her clit harder when I'm making her come on my mouth, how quickly she says "yes," when I ask if I can pull her hair while I fuck her from behind—it's all so simple and...beautiful.

She's so fucking beautiful, back on top of me now, her breasts bouncing as she rides me to her third orgasm of the night. I drag her lips back to mine and lift my hips, giving her even more to grind against as she takes me every bit as fiercely as I'm taking her.

"Oh, Wes. Oh, God, Wes, I'm almost there," she says. "So close, I'm so close."

"Then come for me, baby," I say. "Come all over my cock." Her spine arches and ridiculously sexy coming sounds coo and moan and whimper from her throat. "Good girl," I pant as I pump harder into the slick, clutching silk of her pussy. "Good girl, fuck you feel so good. So good, Tessa."

I come so hard the pleasure is almost painful. I grimace into her hair as my cock jerks inside her and my release moves through me in fierce, wrenching waves. It feels so good, so fucking good, I should have known there was something different about this aside from the fact that Tessa is absolutely delicious in bed.

As I finally come back into my body, I register the wetness all over my thighs, and tense beneath her, cursing softly.

"What's wrong?" She props up on one arm, staring down at me in the thick shadows of the tent.

I run what I hope is a comforting hand down her back to rest on the curve of her ass. "Nothing. I just... We didn't use a condom."

"Oh, don't worry." She relaxes with an easy sigh. "Birth control isn't an issue and I was tested after my last relationship. I found out Nate was cheating after we broke up, so I wanted to be sure I was okay. And I am."

I hug her closer. "Nate is a fucking idiot and the rest is...good. I'm safe, too. I've only been with one person in the past year and we were both tested."

She brushes my hair from my forehead. "Good to know."

A hint of guilt worms through my belly again, but I push it away. I should come clean with Tessa about Darcy and...I will. But not now. Not when she's kissing her way down my chest and this night has been so perfect.

Nearly an hour later, after Tessa's sucked my cock back to life and I've fucked her slow and deep, holding her gaze as I move inside her, we lay side by side watching the stars come out through the netting at the top of the tent.

We talk about everything and nothing—our families, our careers, growing up in Bad Dog, and the way Nate ghosted her like an emotionally stunted chump.

The mention of her ex again prompts thoughts of my soon-to-be ex, but I don't mention Darcy until the next morning over coffee.

I do my best to deliver the news with a light touch, assuring her the first thing I'm going to do when I get to town is end things with Darcy.

"Oh my God." Tessa sits down hard on the log beside the dead fire, shaking her head numbly back and forth. "I can't believe this. I'm the other woman. You made me the other woman. I'm a cheater."

"No, you're not," I assure her. "And I'm not either, not really. Honestly, Tessa, I had decided to end things before we ran into each other yesterday. Darcy and I aren't good together. Not anymore. We never were, honestly, not like you and me. We never had a night like last night."

She shakes her head harder, her eyes squeezing closed. "No. I don't want to hear about your girlfriend, Wes. Last night was really special to me. I thought..." She opens her eyes with a sigh. "Never mind what I thought, but I—"

"It was special to me, too," I say, crouching down in front of her and taking her hands in mine, grateful when she allows it. "Please, Tessa," I say, waiting until her troubled gaze meets mine. "I'm going to end things this morning. I swear to you. And then, can we talk more about this? About what comes next, for us? Please? I don't want this to be a one-night thing."

Her gaze softens and there's a hint of hope in her voice when she says, "We could meet for second breakfast at the diner by the lake. Great pancakes and a decent amount of privacy if you eat at one of the outdoor tables."

"That sounds perfect," I say, my heart lifting. "I'll text you as soon as I'm free."

We pack up camp and hike out to our cars.

The vibe between us is more guarded than it was last night—at least, on Tessa's part—but still warm and friendly and so damned good. A wild part of me starts to think maybe this is it, the relationship I've been hoping for since being single started feeling stupid a few years ago.

And then I get to Darcy's place and everything goes to shit.

By the time I text Tessa that evening to try to explain, she's blocked my number.

Over the next several months, I try—and fail—to reconnect with the woman I can't get out of my head, but she turns avoiding me into an art form.

I start to despair, to think there's no hope...until one night in April, a year and a half after that night in the woods, when Fate conspires to give me one last shot at the one who got away.

Chapter 6

WESLEY

Present Day...

Weddings are fun. I love weddings.

Or at least I always have...until tonight.

It's been over a year since that night with Tessa in the tent.

Eighteen long months of avoiding eye contact at family functions and exchanging polite smiles when I stop by Melissa's catering company to fetch food for office parties.

You would think the awkwardness would have faded by now, but it hasn't. If anything, it's grown more intense, along with the attraction I feel for this incomparable woman.

She fucking haunts me.

Watching her dance at Melissa's wedding in my parents' barn is torture. In a sky-blue bridesmaid's dress the same color as her eyes and a flower crown topping her chestnut hair, she's the most beautiful woman in the room. Her smile, her curves, the way the dimple pops when she laughs... they all send an ache twisting through my chest. Every graceful sweep of her arms, every swivel of her hips reminds me of that night I can't forget, no matter how hard I try.

I close my eyes for a beat and see Tessa silhouetted by the moonlight streaming through the tent, her full breasts bare as she leans over me, whispering, "We shouldn't do this."

But we did.

Boy, did we.

And it was filthy and lava hot and so damned wrong. Far more wrong than Tessa realized at the time.

The disappointment on her face the next morning, her shock as I explained my plan to exit my current relationship with as much haste as possible, made me feel like the lowest form of scum.

I wasn't just scum; I was scum skimmed off a puddle of toxic waste filled with dog shit and chunks of soggy oatmeal cookie.

Opening my eyes, I set my slice of wedding cake down on one of the bar tables on this side of the barn, suddenly losing my appetite for sweets.

I showed Tessa I was a cheater, proving to her before we even got started that I wasn't a man she could trust. It didn't matter that I'd never cheated before and had no plans to do so again. Or that there were very real, very valid reasons I didn't text her until hours later than I promised and had to delay breaking up with Darcy.

But Tessa didn't want to hear my reasons. She didn't want to hear anything from me. Her ears—and her heart

—were closed against me for good. I'd fucked up in a way there was no coming back from. The only thing to do was move on and try to be a better man, using the incredible woman who got away as motivation to live in my integrity.

If I get another chance with a woman like Tessa, I won't fuck it up again.

But there's one problem with that plan.

There *is* no other woman like Tessa. I've been looking, believe me, but I haven't met a woman I've wanted to take on a second date, let alone bring home every night. Tessa's special, a unique mix of impulsive, playful, and sweet, with a lust for adventure that calls to the deepest part of me.

I don't want to hike the Appalachian Trail with some other woman, I want to hike it with Tessa. That's why I postponed my trip last summer.

And it's why I didn't bring a date tonight. I didn't want to share Melissa's wedding with just anyone, I wanted to share it with Tessa. Or at least be free to watch her from the shadows and beat myself up for screwing up my chance with her without interruption.

Which I'm managing to pull off quite well if I do say so myself...

Right until the moment her ex, Nate Spear, sidles up behind her, putting an arm around her waist.

Nate, who ghosted her without so much as a "see you later," break-up text.

Nate, who stares right through her when they pass on the street, acting like she's invisible in a way she confessed drives her absolutely insane.

Nate, who she once thought was her person, the man

who would deliver the happily-ever-after she's wanted for so long…

Before I realize it, I'm on the move. I aim myself for the dance floor and Tessa's now startled face.

I may not be good enough for her, but neither is Mr. Grabby Hands.

I'm usually a peace-loving guy, but sometimes you have to inter-fucking-vene.

So, I do. I inter-fucking-vene.

By the time Tessa turns, shooting Nate an incredulous look over her shoulder, I'm beside them. "Let her go," I say, fighting to keep my voice low. I don't want to cause a scene at my sister's wedding, but I'm not about to let this man get away with touching Tessa without her permission.

Not after everything he's done.

Nate's bleary eyes widen my way, but the arm around her waist doesn't budge as he slurs, "Wassup, McGuire? I didn't know you could dance." He snorts. "Thought you had too big a stick up your ass."

"Let her go," I repeat, prompting Tessa to hiss, "It's fine, Wes. I'll handle it."

"See?" Nate flashes a smug, drunken grin my way as he tugs her closer. "She'll handle it. Tessa can take care of herself." He shoots a pointed glance down to where her bottom is pressed tight to his hips before looking back at me. "She's a big girl."

And that's it. That's all it takes to make me lose my damned mind.

Before I know what I'm doing, Nate's dress shirt is balled in my hands. I charge across the room, dragging him with me until I reach one of the barn's large support beams and slam him against it. I'm dimly aware of gasps of shock from the other guests and the band screeching to a halt, but it doesn't stop my mouth from growling, "You touch her again, and I will destroy you. That's it. That's the message, Nate. Now take your drunken ass home, sober up, and start thinking about all the ways you're going to make sure you stay away from Tessa in the future."

He blinks, his dark eyes clearer than they were before as he sputters, "What the fuck's wrong with you, McGuire? She's my fucking girlfriend."

"We haven't dated for almost two years, Nate," Tessa says, appearing beside me. "You're drunk. Go home and email me an apology tomorrow morning. I'm open to being friends if you are, but the ghosting and grabbing has to stop. You also owe Melissa an apology. She invited you as a favor to her cousin, who is friends with you for some unknown reason, and you abused her trust and generosity."

Nate hangs his head, muttering, "Sorry."

I'm feeling proud of her when Tessa shifts her focus my way, her glare sharpening into a deadly weapon as she whispers, "And you... You're even more ridiculous. I don't need your protection, Wesley. I don't need anything from you, except for you to leave me alone."

My hands release Nate's shirt with a spasm as my jaw drops.

Before I can respond, Tessa points a firm finger at my face and continues in a voice too soft for anyone else to hear, "That's it. Enough of this embarrassing nonsense. I'll stay on my side of the barn and you stay on yours. If you ruin another second of Mel's wedding because of me, I will never forgive you. Never."

She spins and walks away, smiling widely and waving to the band. "It's fine. We're all good. Just a case of too much wine and not enough sense. Play on, guys. We have a wedding to celebrate!"

The lead guitarist nods and lifts a hand, counting the band in for a cover of "Come on Eileen," the anthem of Irish-American people everywhere. Anyone with more than a drop of Irish blood in their veins is helpless against the song, compelled to jump, shout, and belt out the chorus with abandon whenever it's played.

The McGuires, being about as Irish as you can get without having shamrocks growing out of our ears, are easy prey to the tune's magic.

In less than a minute, the party is hopping again, all my nearest and dearest bouncing on the dance floor while the old folks cheer them on from their tables and the various pets run around barking and oinking and... skunking with their happy people.

I have no idea what sound a skunk makes—Bella, Christian's unconventional pet, is a pretty quiet lady—but the rest of the menagerie holds nothing back. Keanu Reeves, the dog, is barking his head off, Kyle the turkey and his family are warbling up a storm, and my cousin Theo's pig appears to be singing along as she prances back and forth in front of the stage.

It sounds like a zoo at feeding time, which I blame for the fact that I don't hear Melissa calling my name until she tugs on my sleeve and shouts, "Wesley!"

I glance sharply down at my sister, who's studying me with wide, shocked eyes. "What on earth? Overreact much?"

"He grabbed her," I say, torn between the feral part of

me that feels completely justified in borderline assault and the part of me that's mortified that I made such a scene.

"Yes, but Tessa could have handled it," Mel says, crossing her arms over her chest as she shakes her head. Even in her lacy maternity wedding dress, swollen belly, and own flower crown, my sister manages to exude the air of a drill sergeant, in control of all she surveys. "She's a grown-up. If she wanted help, she would have asked for it."

I pull in a breath, but before I can apologize, Mel flaps a hand toward the open door at the back of the barn. "Don't waste your apology on me. Tessa went out back to get some air. I suggest you follow her and do an appropriate amount of groveling." I start to speak again, but Mel shakes her head, "Don't worry about it, brother. I'm not mad. You didn't ruin the day." She grins. "It wouldn't be an Irish wedding if someone didn't get into a drunken fight. And Chase is already passed out with Grammy inside on the couch, so he didn't see anything upsetting. Now, go. Apologize to Tessa, make things right, then get another piece of cake. Cake heals all wounds." She pulls me in for a hug.

"Thanks," I tell the top of her head. My shortest, but most badass, sister is always right. "Congratulations again. The ceremony was beautiful. Chase is a lucky little guy to have a stepdad like Aaron."

She pulls back, beaming up at me. "Right? God, I landed a great one, didn't I? He loves me a ridiculous amount."

"An appropriate amount," I correct, making her laugh as she nudges me in the stomach with her fist.

"That's right." She winks. "Don't worry, you'll find a woman to worship someday soon. I'm sure of it."

I arch a brow, wondering if she knows something I don't.

Has Tessa said something? About what happened between us? About maybe wishing it could happen again? This time while we're locked in the bonds of a serious, committed relationship?

I shake my head, dismissing the thought as I head toward the back of the barn. If Mel knew, she would have said something before now. She probably would have read me the riot act for being a dirty cheating asshole who upset her best friend. At the very least, I would have received a stern warning to treat Tessa like a fucking queen.

But I haven't heard a word from my sister. Tessa and I promised each other we wouldn't speak about what happened with anyone else, and Tessa's not the kind to break a promise.

Neither am I, a fact that's made all of this so much harder.

I haven't been able to talk to anyone about my mistake or the fallout or how desperately I wish I could turn back time and do things differently. I knew that night in the woods that the connection I felt with Tessa was special, but I didn't realize *how* special until the chance of seeing her again was off the table.

Since then, I've been plagued by the gut-churning suspicion that she's The One. My One. And I was hers and one stupid mistake on my part ruined that for both of us.

Maybe forever.

I've tried to approach her, to explain myself and talk it out, at least a dozen times, but every time Tessa sees me headed her way, she finds a reason to vanish.

When I step outside in the cool, spring evening, I half expect her to be gone.

But she isn't. She's there, at the far edge of the cluster of fire pits—where my teenage cousins are flirting with the few non-McGuire girls at the reception—beyond the strings of golden lights strung for the occasion, back by the oak tree. She's in the swing my brothers and sisters and I kept busy when we were small, drifting slowly back and forth, her dress fluttering in the breeze like something out of a dream.

I take a breath, my heart racing as I make my way through the campfire smoke toward her, the scent sending visceral reminders of our night by the fire rushing through me. My fingers tingle with the memory of how soft her skin felt beneath my hands, my lips prickle with the need to press against hers again.

I haven't been with another woman since Tessa. I've kissed a few, but it never went further than that. No matter how lonely I've been, I didn't want it to. After that rush, that connection I felt with Tessa, after the way she welcomed everything I had to give, no holding back, all other women seem two-dimensional in comparison.

I'm beginning to suspect I might be in love with her, as wild as that might seem after just one night, and this could be it—my long-awaited shot to turn things around, to convince her that I can be worthy of her, if she'll only give me a second chance.

I'm almost to the swing, close enough to smell her light, floral perfume on the breeze, when it happens. A long, sleek shadow separates from the tree trunk and dashes toward me, flowing gracefully over the rocky dirt like an eel slipping through water.

As it zips closer, I have a split second to notice the big blue ribbon tied around the creature's neck—a ribbon the exact shade of Tessa's dress—before it leaps at my crotch, fangs bared.

Chapter 7

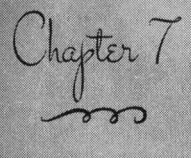

TESSA

One second, Freya is chilling peacefully near my feet, digging at something between the roots of the tree. The next, she emits a clucking battle cry and charges into the shadows behind the swing.

I spin, half expecting to see a drunken Nate coming back for another unwanted cuddle.

But it isn't Nate, it's Wesley. He isn't moving quickly or aggressively—the things that would usually set Freya off—but I've been fostering my cousin Nancy's ferret long enough to know when she's in attack mode.

My lips part in a warning for Wes to back off, but it's too late. Freya is already leaping into the air, her sharp fangs aimed between his legs.

I bolt from the swing as my heart leaps into my throat, every cell in my body electrified with panic. I may be annoyed at Wesley right now, but not annoyed enough to wish harm upon any part of him—especially that part I can't stop dreaming about, fantasizing about, moaning about as I guide my vibrator between my legs and wish he were in bed with me to pull my hair and tell me what an incredible fuck I am.

"No, Freya! Down! Let him go!" I rush toward the scene of my volatile charge's latest attack, praying I can get her dislodged before she does permanent damage. "Wesley, hold still! Don't move."

"Not moving," he says, freezing in a bow-legged position with his arms raised in surrender that has the teenagers behind him snickering. And yes, he looks funny with his legs spread and a long, writhing ferret dangling between his thighs, but it isn't kind to laugh at another person's misfortune, even if you are sixteen and have yet to develop an adult-sized helping of empathy.

Glancing their way, I snap, "You three, go get Barrett. We need a doctor out here, ASAP. Go. Now! If he bleeds to death when she lets go, I'm blaming you for standing there giggling when you should be going for help."

The teens hustle away, and I lower my voice, "Okay, Freya, calm down. We all just need to calm down."

"I won't bleed to death," Wesley says, triggering another round of aggressive dooking from Freya. Dooking is the ferret equivalent to "barking," but it sounds more like a husky chicken cluck than a bark.

"Hush," I whisper. "She doesn't like loud male voices."

"Sorry," he whispers in an almost comically soft tone. "I just meant she didn't break skin. She's hanging from my pants."

I exhale, my shoulders dropping away from my ears in relief. "Thank God," I mutter. "I'm so sorry. She doesn't usually get aggressive unless someone is coming in hard and fast." I reach for the ferret, whispering, "Here now, love. It's all right. He isn't going to hurt us. I promise.

There, now." As her body goes still, I cradle her bottom in one hand and reach for her mouth with the other. "Just let go. That's right." I apply gentle pressure to both sides of her jaw with my fingers and thumb.

After a beat, her small fangs slide free from Wesley's pants, leaving two tiny holes behind.

Rocking her in the crook of my arm, I step back, scratching her scruff until her clucking takes on more of a purring quality. Only when she's relaxed do I tell Wes, "Okay, you can stand up and back away slowly."

"Standing," he says, rising from his crouched position, his hands still raised. "But is it okay if I don't back away just yet? I wanted to apologize."

"All right," I say, my fingers still playing through Freya's fur beneath her ribbon. "You've apologized. Now, you can go tell Barrett that you're not dying."

"Please, Tessa, can't we talk?" he asks, his voice low and soft and every bit as sexy as I remember. God, I love the way he says my name. No one has ever been able to make me shiver with a single word the way he does.

But no one has ever made me so ashamed of myself, either.

This sweet-and-dirty-talking man turned me into a cheater. Or a cheating accomplice, anyway, and that's not something I can forgive. Especially considering the way things played out after our night in the woods.

He didn't end things with his girlfriend that day, the way he insisted he would. He stayed with Darcy for another *two months*.

Two months during which I felt like a monster, torn apart by guilt.

A part of me desperately wanted to tell her that Wes had cheated, but that wasn't my place. And I was a little terrified of what would happen if she found out. My internet stalking led me to believe that Darcy was a sweet woman, beloved by the other dental hygienists in her practice, but her twin sister was another story. Daria seems flat-out terrifying, the kind of maniac who jumps out of airplanes for fun and has a habit of getting hauled into the police station for "brawling" at the local honky-tonk.

I am not a woman who "brawls." I've never even slapped another person. The most violence I've exhibited was while defending myself from Carl.

So, I kept my silence, letting the guilt eat me alive and my resentment toward this very sexy man grow with every passing day. And yes, he finally did end things, but by then, it was too late.

Way too late.

Too late for his apology to make any difference or for there to be any chance for there to be anything between us. Even friendship would be a stretch...mostly because I know I can't be friends with someone I want to lick as much as I want to lick Wesley McGuire.

So, I lift my nose into the air and say, "There's nothing to talk about."

His brows draw together. "You don't believe that. I know you don't. That night was special, Tessa. You felt it, too, I know you did."

"What I felt is irrelevant," I say. "I was feeling things without all the facts, rendering those feelings meaningless." I cuddle the ferret closer. "Now, you should go before you upset Freya again. Like I said, she doesn't care for men."

"Then why did you bring her to an event with literally dozens of men in attendance?" he asks. "Not to be an asshole, but I think it's a reasonable question."

Standing up straighter, I huff, "She isn't dangerous. Yes, sometimes, she'll charge at someone if they're charging at me, but that's only because she's a very sweet, protective little beast. She's never come after someone who was just walking before." I arch an imperious brow. "Maybe she sensed something uniquely awful about you. Ever think of that?"

He winces, almost making me feel bad until he says, "I'm not awful. I made a mistake, but it isn't one I ever intend to make again. Haven't you ever done something you weren't proud of?"

"Yes," I say, my pulse picking up again. "I helped a man cheat and kept quiet about it for two whole months while he strung his girlfriend along, and I've felt horrible about it ever since. Now, if you'll excuse me, I have to—"

He reaches out, catching my elbow as I start past him, triggering another warning dook from Freya. He pulls his hand away as her snout shifts toward him but doesn't step back.

In fact, the ballsy man leans forward, until his lips are only a few inches from mine before he whispers, "I can explain. Please, give me a chance to explain. Let me take you to dinner tomorrow night. Just one night, one meal, and if you still hate me afterward, I'll stay out of your way. I promise. I just...I can't stop thinking about you, Tessa. About that night. It was special to me. *You're* special."

I'm weakening, I can feel it.

Amazingly, so is Freya.

When I glance down—needing a break from Wesley's soul-penetrating breed of eye contact—I'm shocked to see Freya leaning into the fingers Wes scratches gently at her neck.

Freya's hatred of all male beings is the reason I'm fostering her in the first place. When my cousin Nancy's third husband moved in last year, Nancy assumed the two of them would eventually learn to get along. But six months and numerous turds-in-his-shoes later, Allan issued an ultimatum—it was him or the beastie.

Knowing Allan, I would have chosen the ferret, but Nancy was on her way to drop Freya at the shelter when I ran into her at my aunt's house. Feeling sorry for the poor thing, I agreed to foster her for a few months, until the heat blew over at home and Nancy might be able to talk Allan into giving Freya another chance.

With my cousin's luck with men, I figured she and Allan might be separated by then, and she'd be eager to reunite with her pet.

But Allan and Nancy are still going strong, and Freya has quickly become so much more than a foster. Mel calls her my "emotional support weasel," a phrase I've started using myself when we're hanging out around the house, and I need a reminder as to why I'm no longer even trying to date.

I've sworn off men because they're the *real* weasels. After twenty-two years of dating, and only a handful of relationships that were even functional, let alone enjoyable or stable, I've had it. I'm done.

Let the rest of the female race keep fighting the good fight. I'll stay home and bake cookies and grow increasingly pudgy with a pet who would never break my heart or betray my trust. It wasn't a hard decision to make, honestly, and became even easier once I adopted Freya. I knew she would never tolerate a man in my life.

But here she is, falling under Wesley's spell the same way I did.

The sight sends a rush of protective energy flowing through my veins.

I step back, cuddling the ferret closer to my chest, keeping her safe from Wesley's seductive fingers. "I'm sorry, no. I can't. I'm busy tomorrow night and all the nights after."

His lips part, but before he can speak, Barrett calls out from near the fire pits, "Are you okay? Wes? Tyler said you'd been bitten by something?"

As Wes turns toward his brother to explain, I slip away, hurrying back toward the barn, where I hug Mel goodbye and explain I'm taking Freya home before she can castrate any of the McGuire men.

Mel cuts a glance toward the back of the barn before turning back to me. "Are you sure? Mom has spare kennels in the garage. We could tuck Freya into one for a couple hours to decompress if you want to stay."

I shake my head. "It's almost eleven and you know I turn into a pumpkin after midnight. But thank you for a beautiful evening." I lean in to hug her again. "You were a gorgeous bride and the vows were perfect, especially Aaron's." We pull back with a laugh, silently acknowledging that her sexy new hubby is the touchy-feely one. I tuck a stray daisy back into her flower crown with a smile. "I couldn't be happier for you guys. Or Chase. He's a lucky little boy."

"That's what Wes said," she says, glancing toward the open door again. "Did he find you? I was pretty sure he was coming to apologize."

"He found me and he did, but it doesn't matter," I say, pressing on before she can respond. "And I don't need to be fixed up with anyone, Mel. Especially someone I know isn't right for me."

Mel's lips turn down at the edges. "But—"

"No buts," I cut in, forcing a grin as I add. "Remember, I've sworn off men. For keeps. It's just me and Freya from now on, and I feel good about that. Honestly. Sometimes quitting is a good thing. Very freeing."

Mel sighs. "Okay. Well, I hope you and the weasel get home safe. And enjoy your time off. We've both earned two weeks of fun!"

"Have a fantastic honeymoon!" I wave and start toward the opposite end of the barn, toward the even larger doors and the path leading up to the McGuire farmhouse. I'm nearly to the field across the street, now filled with wedding guests' cars, when I catch a whiff of sweet-smelling smoke that takes me straight back to high school.

I haven't smelled a clove cigarette in ages. I'm pretty sure they're illegal in the U.S. in fact…

I turn to see a glowing red dot in the shadows on the front porch. There's just enough light from the lamp by the door to make out the outline of a woman in a long dress with a spiky halo around her head.

"Binx?" I ask, knowing her by the hair.

She shaved her long, gorgeous brown locks into a buzz cut several months ago, an action that scandalized the entire McGuire clan—especially her mother. She's been growing it out ever since, but it's still only a few inches long.

"Hey," she murmurs in her husky voice as I cross to the porch. "Don't tell the clan that you caught me smoking, okay? Especially not my secret stash of cloves. I thought I had time before anyone else decided to leave.

Just needed something to take the edge off." She stubs the cigarette out in the top of a mason jar on the windowsill. "Weddings, right?"

I sigh. "Yeah, but as far as weddings go, it was a great one."

"It was," she says. "I'm really happy for Mel, I'm just...tired. Tired of a gazillion relatives asking me when it's going to be my turn and why a 'pretty girl like me' couldn't find a date to the wedding and Uncle Richard's not-so-subtle offer to hook me up with his laser tattoo removal specialist."

I make a sympathetic sound that Freya echoes, clucking low in her throat. As much as my sweet beast reviles the male of the species, she adores women, Binx in particular. When she squirms in my arms, I release her onto the porch without hesitation.

"Aw, hey there, slinky girl," Binx says, a smile in her voice as Freya hops up onto her lap. "You like my tattoos, don't you?"

Freya clucks in agreement and scampers up the front of Binx's dress to wrap around her neck, like a living mink stole from the 1920s.

"She does and I do, too," I say. "I thought the full sleeve looked beautiful with your bridesmaid dress. The blue made the pinks and yellows in the flowers pop, and I hardly noticed the skull."

Binx chuckles. "You're sweet. My mother noticed the skull, big time. She threatened to drag me into the bathroom and have Dad sit on me while she tried to cover it up with foundation. The only way I escaped without an episode of adult child abuse was by threatening to leave and never come back. And to miss Mel's wedding."

The words connect like an elbow to the gut. In

McGuire-land that's a serious threat, and one I'm sure is going to have ripple effects for some time to come. "Wow."

"Yeah," she says, her tone taking a turn for the melancholy once more. "Now I'm really the black sheep of the family. I'll be getting the silent treatment from my parents, while Mom lights candles for me at church, for the foreseeable future."

"I'm sorry," I say. "I understand the older generation has certain standards for what they deem appropriate, but...you're a grown woman. You're successful and kind and fun and you have the right to do whatever you want with your body."

Binx swipes a hand across her cheek, laughing as Freya leans in to lick her knuckles. "Thanks. But they don't believe that. They think I'm wild and embarrassing and that my body is an extension of the larger, McGuire-family body." She sniffs, confirming my suspicion that she's crying. I've never seen Binx cry. She's the kind who keeps emotions other than joy or anger closer to the chest. "I just want to be myself without losing my family. Is that so wrong?"

"Of course not, sweetheart," I say, my heart breaking for her. "I'm so sorry you're in this tough place."

Freya grips Binx's wrist, holding her hand prisoner for more vigorous, comforting licks.

Binx laughs and sniffs again. "Thanks, Freya. And you, too, Tess. You're a good one. Mel's lucky to have you as a friend."

"I'm *your* friend, too," I say. "I hope you know that."

"I do," Binx says, her voice lifting as she asks, "So... you want to go grab a drink somewhere? Commiserate about being the only single women at the party? Talk shit about Aunt Evie's hideous orange dress?"

"I would, but I have the beastie," I say, motioning toward Freya.

"That's okay. I know a place that doesn't care if you bring animals. As long as they're on a leash. Cute little dive bar with cheap beer and fun mixed drinks. Do you have her harness in the car?"

"I do," I say, not sure if I'm ready to bring my man-hating ferret to a Bad Dog bar, especially not a dive bar where the men are likely to be rough around the edges. "But if a guy gets close enough to hit on us, Freya might rip his heart out. She's protective tonight."

Binx stands, laughing. "No worries. No one will hit on us. I'll scare them off with my short hair and bulging muscles. Bad Dog men like a frail, delicate woman. Not one who's obsessed with weight training."

"They don't like women near forty, either, so we'll probably be safe," I say, warming to the idea of a little single lady time. "All right. Let's do it. Should I follow you in my car?"

"Nah, I'll ride with you," Binx says as she jumps off the porch, juggling Freya easily in her arms. "I'll leave my car here and get one of my brothers to pick it up in the morning. Wesley's always up for a good deed and he's less likely to be hungover than the rest of them. Even Barrett was tying one on tonight. Taking advantage of the fact that his wife's all knocked up and can't drink, I guess."

At the mention of Wesley's name, I hesitate, but then Binx loops her arm through mine and guides me across the gravel road toward the cars. "And on the way, you can tell me all the hot catering gossip. Is it true that Georgia

Devereux threw a cake at her mother during her baby shower?"

I smile. "It was a cupcake, not a cake, but it's true. Then she went wild on the appetizers, pelting her sorority sisters with grilled shrimp and canapes. Mel had to charge her mother an extra five hundred dollars for clean-up. Apparently, third-trimester baby rage is no joke."

Binx clucks her tongue. "I guess. But to be fair, Georgia has always been a wild card. One time, in high school, she set fire to the wrestling mats in the gym because she was pissed that boy sports got more funding than girl sports."

"I get that. Back when I was in high school, Bad Dog didn't even have a girls' soccer team. When my family moved here from Washington, I was so sad."

Binx and I chat about catering gossip and female rage as I guide my tiny Jetta out of the field and onto the road. But when I glance over at the festively lit barn, where so many people I adore are still dancing and enjoying the wedding, I don't feel angry anymore.

I just feel...sad.

If only things had played out differently, maybe I'd be leaving the party with a different McGuire sibling, one I know I could fall head over heels for. But I can't turn back time or arrange to spend a passionate night with Wesley *after* he was a single man.

History can be rewritten, but it can never be changed, a fact that's about to hit home in wild and unexpected ways...

Chapter 8

TESSA

The dive bar Binx guides me to *is* a "lakeside destination," as advertised on the grungy billboard we pass on the way out of town, but it's not in the same class as the bars and restaurants by the marina. It's on the depressed side of the lake, the one once populated by a large trailer park that was, sadly, washed away in the floods a while back.

I'm sure the *Turn Back It's a Trap!* bar and lounge was damaged, too, but the dive bar rose from the dead, like a creepy, clapboard zombie with two, flickering red windows for eyes.

In the glow of the headlights, I see peeling yellow paint on the walls and a spray-painted anarchy symbol near an official sign that reads, "No Firearms, Knives, or Weapons of Any Kind."

"Wow, this is..." I trail off with a little gulp as I shut down the car.

"Creepy as fuck," Binx supplies gleefully. "But don't worry. It's not scary inside. It's actually swanky, in a faded, mid-century kind of way. The clientele is cool, too, mostly old folks from outer bumfuck getting wasted and teenagers scoring cheap beer at a place that doesn't card. Bettie, the owner and bartender, is a doll. She tells the best stories and always cheers me up."

I finish strapping Freya into her harness and cradle her in my arms, still not completely convinced. "And you're sure they won't mind me bringing her in?"

"Not at all, Bettie loves animals," Binx says, swinging out of the passenger's side.

Covering Freya's ears, I add in a softer voice, "And if there are dogs in there, their owners won't let them attack my emotional support weasel and rip her beautiful little body to shreds?"

Binx glances back at me with a bemused grin. "Um, no. Of course not. But you know she's a ferret, right? Not a weasel?"

I laugh—nervously—as I shut the car door. "Yeah. It's a joke. Mel started it. A nod to me preferring an actual weasel to the weasely men around here."

"Aw, got it," Binx says, leading the way toward the entrance. "And I get it. I mean, I'm glad Mel found a great guy, but it's not so easy for the rest of us. Half the men around here are douchebags and the other half...I'm related to." She shoots me a narrow glance over her shoulder as she reaches for the door. "I can't date McGuires, but *you* can. Have you ever thought about my cousin Maynard? Yes, he has a god-awful name, but he's a great guy. Super cool, fun, loves going out on his boat in the summer... And his kids are almost grown, so you wouldn't have to worry about stepmom drama."

I shrug, playing it cool, like I didn't spend most of the past eighteen months fantasizing about her brother pulling my hair while he took me from behind. "I'm on a break from dating right now, but thanks."

"Girl, I hear that." She swings the door wide, calling out as she steps inside, "Sometimes a girls' night is all you need. Isn't that right, Bettie?"

I peek past her, still cradling Freya close as I catch my first glimpse of an old copper bar with a scarred wooden top and the most adorable blue-haired woman behind it. Truly, she's a tiny angel in a fuzzy pink sweater, with turquoise cat-eye glasses and curly turquoise hair to match.

"Binx!" Bettie's eyes widen behind her thick lenses as she smiles. "Baby bird, get in here. We've missed you. What the heck have you been up to?"

My jaw drops as the door closes behind us and the dimly lit bar comes fully into view. Binx is right, it's adorable. From the wood-paneled walls covered in vintage photographs to the doily-covered couches in one corner to the mismatched mid-century tables and chair sets—each topped with a glittering animal figurine and more doilies—it's like your cool grandma threw a party and invited all her friends.

And though I see a cat climbing structure against one wall and several water bowls by the door, there don't appear to be any other animals in the house tonight, aside from an ancient hound dog asleep by a rocking chair in one corner. But he's wearing a leash that's looped around the wrist of his equally sleepy owner, making me feel safe enough to follow Binx down to the empty end of the bar.

"Yeah, Baldy, we missed you," a giant man in a gray flannel says as we pass his stool, offering Binx a fist to bump. "I haven't had a decent dart game in ages. People around here can't see straight, let alone shoot straight."

"I heard that." Another man, as narrow as Flannel Guy is wide, pipes up from his place a few stools closer to the door. "And I'll remember it next time you beg me to play, asshole."

"Now, now, watch your language," Bettie says, still beaming as she leans over the bar to pull Binx in for a big hug. "Oh, sugar, it's so good to see you." She draws back, running a fond hand over Binx's spiky hair, a shine in her eyes. "You're just our miracle worker, that's it. No other word for it."

Red spots rise on Binx's cheeks as she pulls back with a wave of her hand. "Don't start, Bettie. It wasn't a big deal. I'm just glad Sprout got the help she needs. That's all the matters."

Bettie's focus shifts my way. "I bet she didn't tell you, did she? That she pretty much single-handedly raised the money for my grandbaby's surgery? Sprout got her implants last month and heard music for the first time right here in the bar." She motions toward the jukebox. "We put on Blue Moon and she danced and danced. The awe on her face..." Bettie presses a hand to her chest, clearly working through a wave of emotion. "Well, that's something I'll never forget, that's for sure. One of the best moments of my life." Pulling herself together, she claps her ringed hands. "So, what'll you have? Drinks for you and your friend are on me." Glancing back to me, she extends her tiny fingers. "I'm Bettie by the way, darlin. We haven't been properly introduced."

"Tessa," I say, giving her hand a gentle squeeze. "I can't believe I've never heard about your place. It's the cutest."

Bettie beams. "Thank you so much. We're not the fanciest place in town, but when you're here, you're family." She leans down, grinning at Freya. "And so are your critters. What's this lovely lady's name?"

"That's Freya," Binx cuts in, "and I'm paying for drinks, Bettie. I told you, you don't owe me anything. I don't want things to be weird."

"Things aren't weird," Bettie says, cooing as Freya rubs against her scratching fingers. "Now, sit your bootie down and accept your free drink without being a pain in my backside."

"Yeah," Flannel Guy says. "And I'm buying your second round." He tips his beer my way as he explains, "Sprout's my niece. Sweetest kid in the world."

Binx grumbles but settles into a stool at the back of the bar, not far from the cat climbing structure. I'm debating whether or not it's safe for Freya to explore the environment with her leash on when Bettie appears with two waters and whispers, "Go ahead and let her off the lead. It's only Old Blue in here tonight and he doesn't have the energy to chase after anything anymore."

"Thanks," I say, unclipping the leash from Freya's harness and freeing my eagerly squirming girl to play. "She loves exploring things like this," I add, laughing as she slithers into a tiny hole at the bottom only to poke her nose out a hole near the top a second later.

"Well, of course," Bettie says. "Who wouldn't? I'm coming back as a pet in my next life. No doubt about that. So, what can I get ya?"

"I'll have a Doris Day," Binx says, before turning to me. "It's champagne, pomegranate juice, winter citrus spray, mint, and some kind of orange liqueur Bettie keeps hidden under the bar. So fresh and fabulous."

I hum in anticipation. "That sounds amazing. I'll have one, too."

"Coming right up." Bettie sets a 3D card menu with a martini glass popping out in the middle of it between us on the bar. "But be sure to check out the rest of the drinks, too. We have a lot of fun stuff this spring."

"She rotates the menu seasonally," Binx explains as Bettie fetches her cocktail shaker. "But the drinks are always named after famous people from the 1950s. It's pretty cute."

"This whole place is cute," I say, smiling as I spot a row of felt jackalope heads mounted about the liquor display. "Definitely a case of the insides not matching the outsides."

Binx winks. "That's part of the magic. Only the bold make it through the front door. And keeping things quiet keeps the cops away. Bettie would lose her license if they realized how often she sells to minors. But she thinks if you're old enough to vote and die for your country in a war, you ought to be able to order a beer. Can't say I disagree."

I hum beneath my breath. "Makes sense." Shifting on my stool, I check in on Freya, who's still darting in and out of the cat structure, before asking in a softer voice, "So, what's the story, woman? What did you do here?"

She shrugs uncomfortably. "Nothing much, really. I helped spread the word about the fundraiser for Sprout's cochlear implant surgery and agreed to shave my head if we raised a certain amount in ten days. The guys at my gym thought it would be hilarious to see me bald and... the rest is history."

Connecting the dots, I ask, "And you didn't tell your mother this, because..."

She bristles, her shoulders hunching closer to her ears. "I shouldn't have to. If I want to shave my head, for any reason, that should be okay. I'm still the same person, you know? And it's my body." She takes a drink of her water before setting it down a little too hard on the bar. "And she wouldn't have cared if any of my brothers did it. It's pure sexism, it's ridiculous, and I'm sick of it."

I nod. "Valid." I lean in, nudging her shoulder gently with mine. "But I'm sorry. It sucks to be punished for doing a good deed."

"I'm not being punished," she says, brightening as Bettie sets our drinks in front of us. "I'm the luckiest girl in Bad Dog. Damn, Bettie, these smell even better than usual."

"Thank you." Bettie pats her hand. "And watch your mouth. You know my rules. No salty language in my bar, only salty martini rims."

Binx salutes her as she reaches for her drink. "Yes, ma'am. Bettie was in the army, and still has a little drill sergeant in her."

My brows lift as I glance back at the tiny woman. She can't be more than five feet tall and a hundred pounds, if that.

Bettie grins at my reaction. "I was a little taller when I was young, but you're not wrong. The men all laughed at me, until they came into my clinic needing a bullet wound treated, and I was the only one in the med tent who didn't get squeamish. I was one of the first nurses to serve overseas."

"Wow." I blink. "Thank you for your service."

"And thank you for yours," Bettie says with a wink. "I was at the business leader lunch you catered last fall. You do good work. The roasted duck had such a nice flavor, and the cheese puffs were the best I've ever had."

"Thank you," I say, flattered. "That's my recipe. I do most of the bread and baked goods."

"Tessa's a culinary goddess," Binx says, patting my back. "My sister has no idea how she'll keep going if she quits to open her own restaurant."

Bettie's eyes widen. "Is that something you're thinking about?"

I wave a hand. "Nah, not really. I mean, yeah, I dream about it sometimes, but I'm sure the reality would be way too exhausting. Running your own business is no joke."

Bettie nods. "No, it's not. But neither is letting your dreams slip away because something seems scary. We weren't put here to stick to what comes easy, Tessa. We were put here to do the things that scare us. That's the whole point."

"Speaking of things that scare me," Binx mutters, turning from the door and blocking her face with her drink. "Don't look now, but Psycho Twin just walked in."

I look up, gulping as I see Darcy, Wesley's ex swinging through the door.

"What's up, bitches?" she shouts, kicking the door closed behind her with one black boot. "Miss me?"

Scratch that, not Darcy. This is *Daria*, her twin sister, the scary one.

There are some vague murmurs from the two men at the bar, but nothing compared to the warm welcome Binx received when she arrived. But Daria doesn't seem to notice.

She wraps her arms around Flannel Guy, hugging him until his cheeks flush pink. "Oh, I know, me too," she says. "I've missed you at Riff's on Sundays. What the fuck is wrong with this town? How can you ban someone from a bar for life for one fight? It's crazy."

"You're going to get banned here if you don't watch your mouth," Bettie says as she crosses to that side of the bar. "You know the rules, Daria. Now, what can I get you, honey?"

"Give me a Jack Kerouac martini with extra..." She trails off, her brown eyes narrowing as her gaze lands on Binx.

I feel Binx tense beside me, but there's no time to ask about her history with Daria before the woman herself is stomping across the bar.

"You," Daria says, her jaw clenching. "You have some fucking balls. Showing your face on my side of town after what your brother did to my sister."

Binx lifts her hands into the air. "I'm not a part of that, Daria. You stay over there, and I'll stay over here, and we can both have a nice night."

"Nah, I don't think so," Daria snaps, ignoring Bettie's suggestion that she let it go. "I don't have nice nights anymore, not since your piece of shit brother broke my sister's heart. Darcy still cries herself to sleep almost every night, over a year later. Did you know that?"

I press a hand to my cramped stomach, guilt making my insides squirm.

"It was just a breakup, Daria. They happen all the time," Binx says. "And I know Wesley was nice about it. Wes is always nice. It's like...his thing."

Daria snorts. "You don't know jack shit about your brother, do you?"

"Language," Bettie says, but Daria ignores her.

She leans in, stretching across my lap to get closer to Binx as she seethes, "Your brother is a sick fuck, Beatrice

McGuire. He's a pervert who scared the shit out of my sister, then broke up with her when she wouldn't get nasty with him in bed."

My throat tightens until I'm pretty sure I'm going to choke on my tongue. Yes, Wes is bossy in bed, but he isn't a pervert. At least not in my experience.

"My name is Binx," Binx murmurs, her voice cool enough to chill a martini glass. "And I'm not going to talk about this with you, Daria. I told you that the last time you tried to start something. Now, leave us alone."

Daria cuts a sharp glance my way, her face far too close for comfort. My chin slides into my neck as I lean back on my stool, putting some much-needed distance between us. "Who's this? Your lesbian lover? You like 'em old, don't you, gaywad?"

"That's enough," Bettie says, as Binx shouts, "Shut up, Daria. Jesus. You're thirty-four, for fuck's sake. Tessa's only a few years older."

Before I can recover from the shock of being call "old" right to my face, Daria shoots back with an ugly smile, "A few years, my ass, Beatrice." To me, she adds, "You should bail while you can, Wrinkles. Fucking a McGuire's a good way to catch the clap."

"I'd like some space, please," I say, a faint tremble in my voice.

But Daria only leans closer. "Or what? You're going to sit on me with that wide ass of yours?"

Binx comes off her stool beside me. "Seriously, Daria, I'm going to—"

"You're going to what?" She sneers the words straight into my face, not sparing Binx a second glance. "Going to beat me up for talking trash to your fat old girlfriend?"

"I may be fat and old," I hear myself saying, the words

ripped from some previously untapped rage-center in my core. "But Wesley didn't seem to mind. And I thought he was great in bed. Not sure what your sister was complaining about."

Daria's jaw drops, her shock sending a zing of satisfaction through me, followed closely by a fresh wave of fear as she hisses, "You fucking bitch. I'm going to end you."

Binx sucks in a breath and Daria pulls back a fist, but before any blows can land, Freya comes sailing over my shoulder. One moment, she's a streak of gray and white in my peripheral vision, the next, she's hanging from Daria's arm, thrashing and wriggling, throwing my bully off-balance.

"Car. Now!" Binx shouts, grabbing Freya's leash from the bar and pressing it into my hands. "Go!"

"Come on, Freya," I call out as I hurry past Daria. "Come on, girl!" I whistle and my fierce defender comes running, bounding across the floor like a dragon kite in the wind before jumping into my arms.

I'm almost to the exit, with Binx hot on my heels, when the first glass smashes against the wall. Squealing and ducking the flying shards, I wrench the door open and spill out into the dark.

Thanking the universe for my piece of shit Jetta's broken locks, I tumble into the car, tossing Freya into the back and jamming the key into the ignition. By the time Binx jumps in beside me, the engine is already humming. All I have to do is jam the car into reverse and floor it, peeling out seconds before Daria leaps on the hood.

"Drive, drive, drive!" Binx shouts when I hesitate, afraid Daria might try to throw herself in front of the car again.

I put the pedal to the metal again, launching us onto the road with a spray of gravel.

We drive in silence, nothing but the sound of our swiftly indrawn breath until Binx finally says, "Well, well, Miss T. What other secrets are you hiding in that big, beautiful hair of yours?"

I cut a guilty glance her way. "Um, none? Sorry. It just came out."

Binx exhales a shaky laugh. "Yeah, well, I can't say I didn't enjoy seeing Daria's head spin in a circle, but the fallout is going to be nuclear."

I gulp. "She's going to kill me?"

"Possibly," Binx says, making the churning in my gut even worse. "But there's a way to smooth things over. Though I'm pretty sure you're not going to like it. I assume things didn't end well with you and Wes?"

I shake my head. "Um, no."

She sighs. "Yeah, if things were copacetic, I figured I would have heard about it. But he's our only shot at getting through to Darcy, who's our only shot at getting through to Daria." She pulls out her cell. "I'll tell him to meet us at his place in twenty minutes. This isn't something we should leave until tomorrow."

"Really?" I ask, pretty sure I'm going to throw up my one sip of my Doris Day.

"Really." Binx taps at her phone, shooting off message after message. "Daria doesn't sober up and calm down. She sobers up and has more energy to bring her evil schemes to fruition. If we don't nip this in the bud, your yard could be on fire by morning. Or your car. Or your car and your yard and your face." Her phone dings and she lets out a relieved breath. "Okay great, Wes is already home. He says he'll have hot tea waiting for us."

"Oh," I squeak out, regretting every choice I've made tonight. "Okay."

"Better than okay. It's great." Binx tucks her phone back into her purse before shifting to face me. "But before we drink tea, I need you to spill some, woman. What happened with my brother and why aren't you two living happily ever after? As far as I can tell, you two would be perfect together."

And because I'm an honest woman, who got herself into this mess with her own big mouth, I'm forced to tell Binx the truth. Most of it, anyway. I leave out the part about our mad night of tent passion overlapping with his relationship with Darcy by a full eight weeks.

As guilty as I feel about that, it doesn't feel like my secret to tell.

But by the time we get to Wesley's, where the man himself is waiting for us in the driveway in his tux with the shirt open at the top, she has *almost* all the dirt.

She shakes her head sadly at her brother as she passes him by, muttering, "Let's go clean up your mess, bro. Seriously, man, couldn't you have dated someone without a dangerously unhinged relative?"

Wes's gaze darts my way, his eyes wide.

I don't know what to say, so, I say nothing. I just cuddle Freya close and follow Binx into Wes's extremely tidy home, pretty sure this is turning into one of the worst nights of my life.

Chapter 9

WESLEY

"Then Daria threw a glass at us on our way out and is probably plotting Tessa's death as we speak." Binx finishes her wrap-up of the night's events and sits back on my couch, her feet curled beneath her, and her mug clutched to her chest. "And maybe my death, too. That woman has it out for me for some reason." She sips her tea thoughtfully. "Maybe she's secretly in love with me and pissed that I'm not batting for her team?"

My brows shoot up. "Really? Daria's gay? I didn't know that."

Binx rolls her eyes. "I don't know, Wes. I was just talking. But it *is* weird that she's always trying to insult me by calling *me* gay. Like, who cares? Whether I'm gay or I'm straight, she's a bitch, and I hate her, and we will never be friends or kissing friends or anything else." She sits back, propping her feet up on the coffee table. "And this feud is stupid anyway. Your relationship was between you and Darcy, and it's ancient history at this point. She needs to move the hell on."

"Her sister's hurting," Tessa says softly, speaking up for the first time since she indicated that she'd like mint tea instead of passion fruit. She runs a gentle hand over Freya's back, prompting the sleepy ferret to snuggle deeper into her lap. "And Daria's clearly very protective of her sister. I'm guessing she won't be moving on until she knows Darcy's moved on."

I clear my throat, feeling properly ashamed of myself. It's awkward as hell, hearing my ex's name on Tessa's lips, but not nearly as awkward as my little sister knowing I spent a steamy night with the woman in my overstuffed armchair.

"I'm so sorry," I say, apologizing for what feels like the hundredth time since they arrived. "This is my fault and I promise, I'll do whatever it takes to make it right."

"I know you will," Binx says. "That's why we're here. But you'd better call Darcy soon. You know Daria. It's only a matter of time before she escalates this in ridiculous and potentially dangerous ways. Just tell her that you and Tessa hooked up after you two broke up, beg her to talk her sister back from the edge before she does something even stupider than usual, and all will be well."

My gaze shifts sharply to Tessa.

Tessa sighs and shakes her head, answering my unspoken question.

Binx glances between us, her brows pinching closer together. "You two *did* hook up after Wes and Darcy broke up, right?" She looks back and forth again, reading the guilt on our faces loud and clear. "Oh, shit. Guys! This is bad."

"I know, I'm ashamed of myself," Tessa whispers.

"You have nothing to be ashamed of," I cut in. "You didn't know I was in a relationship. This is my fault.

Completely. I'll explain that to Darcy. She hates me right now, but she's a good person. She won't blame you for something I did."

Binx puffs her cheeks before exhaling a long, dubious breath.

I arch a brow her way. "You don't think so? You know Darcy. She's not the vengeful type."

"Well, no, not usually," Binx says. "But you've never confessed that you cheated on her before, either. She has every right to be pissed." She glances toward Tessa. "And maybe she'll realize that Tessa is blameless. Or, maybe she'll join forces with her sister to make 'the other woman's' life a living hell. There's really no way of knowing. These situations make *sane* people crazy, let alone people who are already a little unhinged. It's a key feature of the whole cheating thing."

Tessa sinks lower in her chair with a groan, cuddling Freya to her stomach. "I never should have tried dating again. If I'd just stayed at home and out of the forest, this never would have happened. Wes never would have had to save me from that creep, we never would have shared a tent, and mistakes never would have been made."

"Stop it," Binx says before I can step in. "You're a casualty of war, woman, not a terrorist. The only thing you possibly did wrong is tell Daria things she didn't need to hear, but I can't blame you. If someone had called me a fat, wrinkly old woman—multiple times, *to my face*—I'd probably be in jail right now. Who does that? I mean, where does she get the fucking ovaries to tear another woman down for no reason?"

"She said what?" I ask, heat rushing through my chest.

"She was just picking on me to get at Binx," Tessa says. "She assumed we were together and was mocking Binx for dating an older woman."

"Which is bullshit," Binx says. "If I liked girls and we were dating, Tess, I'd be stoked. You're a foxy snack with gorgeous curves and Disney princess hair. And who cares about age anyway? Love is love."

"I agree," I say.

"Well, obviously," Binx says, rolling her eyes again. "We know you appreciate what Tessa has to offer. You appreciated it so much you acted like a dirty, cheating scoundrel. We don't need your input on how amazing Tessa is. We need you to figure out what you're going to say to Darcy. Personally, I'd recommend lying. I know that isn't usually your style, but it's the most merciful choice. That way Darcy never knows you cheated, Tessa doesn't become more of a target, and Daria will move on to picking on someone else."

"We could just say it happened this past October," Tessa says. "Instead of the one before. That would be... mostly true."

I sigh and drag a hand through my hair. "Yeah. That might be best. I don't want to cause more damage than I have already. I'll work on something and call Darcy in the morning."

"This can't wait, Wes," Binx says. "That's why we're here. Daria is like a ticking time bomb. The more time you give her, the more likely she's going to crawl in Tessa's bedroom window and explode."

"You can both stay here tonight," I say. "I have extra clothes and toothbrushes and—"

"I can't stay here," Binx says. "I have a very important

date with my bed tomorrow. I already have snacks in the pantry and a full season of Masters of Ink ready to binge. I need to wake up in my familiar, cozy place to enjoy my day of sloth." She motions toward Tessa. "And I'm sure Tessa has a life, too. Or work or something."

"I'm actually off for the next two weeks," Tessa says, "but I'd rather get this settled and get home. I know I won't sleep well with the Daria thing hanging over me." She strokes the now sleeping Freya's head. "And I don't have food here for Freya."

I'm about to insist that I have to wait until at least seven a.m. tomorrow—Darcy isn't a night owl and it's already after midnight—when my phone buzzes in my pocket.

I pull it out, my stomach sinking as I see the name on the screen.

"Who is it?" Binx asks.

"Darcy," I murmur, backing toward the door to the kitchen.

"Answer it!" Binx hisses. "Answer it and lie your face off. It's for the greater good!"

I lift a hand, signaling for her to quiet down as I move quickly through the door into the kitchen. I tap the screen to answer, already knowing I'm not going to like whatever Darcy has to say. "Hey," I murmur, willing my heart out of my throat. This is the first time we've spoken since she came over to pick up her things from her drawer in the bedroom after the breakup. "What's up?"

"Daria's here," Darcy says, her voice tight, though I can't tell if she's upset with me or her sister. Daria and Darcy are as close as most twins, but that doesn't mean Darcy doesn't get sick of her sister's antics. There's a reason she never goes out with Daria on weekends. Darcy's as chill and conflict-avoidant and Daria is hot-headed and wild. "She told me you're dating Tessa Martin."

"That's not true," I say, my jaw clenching as I hear Daria yelling in the background.

"Daria stop, I can't hear him," Darcy snaps, proving she's about as excited about this late-night drama as I am. "Yes, I'm serious. Be quiet or I'm hanging up." Once her sister has settled, Darcy asks, "So you aren't with Tessa? And she didn't say I was a prude with a stick up my ass?"

"I'm not seeing anyone right now." I chew the inside of my lip, my conscience prickling too intensely for me to leave it at that. "Tessa and I went camping together once, last October. That was it."

"Camping, your favorite," Darcy repeats wryly. "Well, good for you. I'm glad you're moving on." There's a squawking sound from Daria in the background, but Darcy shushes her. "Truly, I am, Wes. And don't worry about Daria. I've let her know that there's no battle to fight here."

"Thank you," I say, hating that I hurt Darcy, but grateful tonight didn't make things any worse. "I wish you nothing but the best, Darcy. I hope you know that."

"I do," she says, the sadness in her voice twisting the knife a little deeper. "Take care, Wes. And apologize to Binx and Tessa for me. Daria's sorry she ruined their night."

Daria squawks something else—presumably insisting that she *doesn't* apologize because Daria *never* apologizes —but Darcy ends the call a beat later.

I take a moment, stretching my neck to one side and

then the other, releasing the tension in my jaw before turning to see Binx standing in the doorway leading into the living room.

"Sorry, I was eavesdropping," she says. "Sounds like we're good?"

"We're good," I say. "Darcy's called off the dogs and we ended the call amicably."

Binx sags against the doorframe. "Awesome. What a relief. But seriously, someone should put a muzzle on Daria. She's an agent of chaos. Thank God you didn't let her move in with you and Darcy. Can you imagine?"

I shudder. "I can."

"One of you would have been dead in a week. Probably you. No offense, but she's way scarier than you are, even when you're in tough guy mode."

"No offense taken," I assure her.

"Good, now give me the keys to your motorcycle." She holds out her hand, wiggling her fingers. "That way I can drive myself home and you and Tessa can talk."

"I'm sure Tessa doesn't want to talk," I say, pushing on in a hushed voice when Binx tries to cut in, "I tried to talk to her earlier tonight. She made it clear she isn't interested."

"Only because you didn't try hard enough," Binx whispers, glancing over her shoulder before moving deeper into the kitchen. "You need to grovel, brother. Get down on your knees and beg for a second chance. She's worth it and you two would be perfect together. I can't believe I didn't think of it before. I was trying to set her up with Maynard, but—"

"Maynard." My upper lip curls. "Cousin Maynard? With the hair all over his back?"

"Yes. He's fun. And nice."

"He looks like something a cat coughed up on a bad day," I shoot back, more irritated by this idea than I should be. "I've literally never seen a man that covered in hair. It stretches from his neck all the way down to his waist. And who knows how much farther it goes. I've only seen him in a swimsuit."

"So?" Binx shrugs. "Hair can be removed. Asshole is harder to fix. And since when did you get so superficial and judgy?"

"I'm not superficial and jugdy," I say. "I just think Tessa deserves someone better."

"Someone like you?" She arches a brow. "I happen to agree, but you fucked things up straight out of the gate. The only way out of a fuck up this big is sustained, persistent groveling. You have to prove you're seriously sorry and would never do anything like that again. Believe me, I know."

I frown. "How? No offense, little sister, but you haven't dated anyone in years."

She crosses her arms. "Sure, I have. I just keep things quiet. I get enough shit from Mom already. If she knew I was crushing on a guy sixteen years older than I am with a kid and a history of trouble with the law, she'd ship me off to a convent against my will."

My brows shoot up. "Woah. Yeah, she would. What kind of trouble with the law?"

She waves a hand. "Not bad trouble, just...trouble. And it was a long time ago, when he was young. He's different now."

I shoot her a dubious look.

"Seriously, he is," she insists. "He's an amazing father and a total badass in his new career. His business is about to blow up, he only goes out on Saturday nights, when his mom can babysit, and he loves working out, rock climbing, and tattoos as much as I do. He's a total catch." She sighs. "His only flaw is that he thinks I'm a child, when I am clearly a badass woman in control of my own destiny, who is perfectly capable of making mature decisions about who I want to date."

My eyes narrow as I try to connect the dots. But I don't know many single dads. I don't run in those circles. I spend most of my time with other lawyers or hanging out with my family.

I'm about to ask her for a name, figuring a background check from a concerned older brother could be a good thing to have, when my phone buzzes on the counter. Before I can reach for it, it buzzes again and again, as texts pop through one after another.

Frowning, I swipe up, my stomach cramping as I read the string of messages from my ex—

Camping trip last October, huh? Interesting. Because according to your social media timeline, you didn't go camping this past October.

But you did the OCTOBER BEFORE.

When you and I were still together, Wesley!

And you came back home the next morning acting all weird and saying you wanted to talk. But I never found out what you wanted to talk about because that was the morning, I told you I thought I was pregnant.

I guess that's why you didn't tell me that you CHEATED?

Is that why we didn't have sex again for the rest of our relationship?

Is that why you broke up with me, even though I was trying so hard to be what you wanted and even told my sister that she had to find somewhere else to live if we moved in together? (Even though Daria and I have always lived together, and you have FOUR bedrooms in your house and one of them is over the garage and you literally never would have had to see Daria if you hated her that much. But whatever. I guess it's not Daria you hated. I guess it was me.)

"Oh shit," Binx mutters from near my elbow, making me flinch. "Oh shit, Wes. This is bad. This is really, really bad."

No sooner are the words out of her mouth than a final text appears—*But that's fine. I hate you, too, now. Daria was right. You're an asshole and a liar and you never loved me the way I deserve to be loved. I should have let her handle you a long time ago. Guess now...I will.*

"Run," Binx says, squeezing my arm. "You have to run. Now."

"Don't be ridiculous," I mutter, my thoughts racing.

"I'm not," she says, squeezing harder. "She's going to kill you. And Tessa. And maybe me, just for being related to you and friends with Tessa."

"I'm not going to run from a woman half my size," I say. "I'll talk to Darcy again tomorrow. Once she's had time to cool down—"

"What part of 'let my sister handle you' are you missing here?" Binx screeches. "You have to get out of Dodge, bro. At least for a little while. Long enough for Daria to realize you aren't worth going to prison over."

"I think she's right," Tessa says from the doorway on the other side of the kitchen, making both Binx and I jump out of our skin, proving emotions are running ridiculously high. "You didn't see her, Wes. I've read about people having 'murder in their eyes' before, but I've never seen it myself until tonight. Daria is legitimately unhinged. And yes, we could call the police for help, but the police aren't going to take action until she does something sufficiently threatening to warrant their intervention. And by then—"

"By then it'll be too late," Binx cuts in.

I want to argue, but I've been up close and personal with too many unhinged people. I know from experience with my clients that restraining orders often don't work and the police aren't equipped to enforce them when dangerous people step over the line.

I also know Daria's history. Darcy confided in me early on that she's afraid to let her sister live alone. Daria's been violent since they were kids. Darcy's pulled her back from the edge of a big mistake more times than she can count. Without her sister's intervention, Daria would likely already be behind bars.

And now Darcy's decided to throw up her hands and let her attack dog off the leash...

"Maybe we should get out of town for a few days," I say.

Binx exhales a relieved rush of breath. "Thank God. Yes. Make it a week. I'll bust my ass while you're gone to calm things down. I have some friends of friends who run with Daria's crowd. With enough time and a delicate touch, hopefully I can negotiate a cease-fire."

"Sounds good, thank you," Tessa says. "I can go stay with family in Minneapolis for a while. My aunt hates ferrets and isn't overly fond of me, either, but—"

"No, you aren't going anywhere alone," I say. "Especially not anywhere Daria might be able to find you. We should stick together. Watch each other's backs."

Tessa pulls in a breath but pauses, her brow furrowing.

"He's right," Binx says. "I know you guys aren't getting along right now, but there's safety in numbers."

"I know," Tessa says. "I was going to say that there's no way Daria would go to the trouble of tracking down my relatives, but she did catch you in your lie about October in less than ten minutes."

"She's diabolical," Binx agrees, brightening as she adds, "But there's a silver lining here, you know. You both love camping and being in the great outdoors. You should road trip to a national park or something. I bet Matty would loan you his camper. He owes you one for all the times you loaned him your horses before you sold them." She lifts her phone into the air. "Should I call him? I'm sure he's asleep, but you know Matty, he can be awake and problem-solving in a hot second if someone's in trouble."

I glance Tessa's way, arching a brow. "Any interest in Arches National Park? I hear the weather's perfect in April. I can sleep in a tent and give you the camper bed. You don't even have to talk to me if you don't want to."

Tessa glances down as Freya appears at her feet, winding her way through her ankles.

"And Freya's invited, too," I add. "Of course."

Freya emits a sharp cluck that gives strong "damn straight, I'm invited" vibes. Tessa smiles, but by the time she lifts her gaze to mine, the grin is gone. "Okay. Arches it is. But once this is over, we do our best to avoid each other in the future. Clearly, this...whatever it is, is cursed. It's best if we pretend we never met."

"All right," I say, but I'm not capable of that level of pretend.

I am capable of taking good advice when it's offered, however.

Binx knows Tessa well and if she thinks groveling will work, well...I have a week to see if she's right.

One week to convince the woman of my dreams that we can put the ugliness of the past behind us and find something beautiful together.

And I intend to make the most of it.

Chapter 10

TESSA

By the time Binx fetches the camper from Matty, and Wes and I finish gathering his camping supplies from the garage and swing by my place to grab clothes and Freya's things, the horizon is smudged a rosy gray.

It's still mostly dark...but light enough to see the giant brown smear on my door all the way from the street.

"Stay in the camper," Wes says, putting a hand on mine when I reach for my seatbelt.

And yes, the brush of his fingers across my skin is enough to make my entire body tingle—even after a night like this one, even when I'm so tired I can barely see straight. Which means this road trip is an even worse idea than I thought it was when we concocted this hair-brained scheme.

But is that going to stop me from leaving town with him?

No.

No, it will not.

Partly because I'm legitimately terrified of what Daria

might do and think giving her time to cool down is a solid idea, but mostly because I just...want to. I *want* to run away with this man and leave all my problems behind.

Weakness, thy name is Tessa...

I *am* weak, but I'm also practical and adept at making the best of a bad situation. If I'm going to be stuck in a tightly enclosed camper with this man for a week, why shouldn't I enjoy it? As long as I remember the situation has an expiration date, a week of longer hikes and longer nights could be just what the doctor ordered.

I'll get all my lust for the wrong guy out of my system and return home ready to retire from romance and live peacefully ever after with my ferret.

Assuming, of course, that we make it out of town alive.

"No, I'm coming with you," I say, shifting my hand beneath his and pressing the release on my seatbelt. "You might need backup."

He exhales. "All right. But if she has anyone with her, run right back here and call the police."

My brows shoot up. "Who would she have with her?"

He shrugs. "She used to have a boyfriend. A very large, very dumb boyfriend. Chippy. Sweet guy, but not when Daria got him wound up. But he's on probation for breaking a guy's leg so he might be laying low."

"He broke someone's leg?" I squeak. "For Daria? What is she? A mob boss?"

"Not yet. But she's tight with Cassie Ann Sweetwater's granddaughters. Cassie Ann's the one who ran the mob around here before she skipped town and her grandsons ended up in prison. Now her granddaughters host a book club on their compound every other Sunday for women interested in 'badass reads and deeds.' Daria used to go. Said it was...interesting."

I hum beneath my breath. "It's interesting that Daria knows how to read."

Wes smiles. "I'm not sure she does. She only participated if the book had a movie version. And they spent most of the meetings talking about how badass it would be to rebuild the Sweetwater criminal empire from the ground up. Cassie Ann always favored the boys in the family, giving them the power and influence. Now that they're all in prison, the girls want to see what they can do."

I shake my head slowly back and forth. "Wow. And I thought my family was messed up."

"All families are messed up, I think. At least a little."

"Even the McGuires?"

"Even the McGuires," he says, his voice softer. "My mom's been so hard on Binx lately. For no reason, just because she marches to the beat of her own drum. My dad was the same way with Matty, when he was going through his...lost period." He shrugs and shifts his focus, gazing out through the windshield. "I don't know. I obviously don't have kids, but if I did, I like to think I'd take a gentler approach. Let my wild kids follow their bliss and offer the struggling a safe place to land when they fall down."

I study his profile, sadness tightening my ribs, even though I know we aren't meant to be. "Are you looking forward to having kids someday?"

"Yeah. If I'm lucky enough to meet someone great and start a family, that would be..." He turns, sending a prickle of electricity shivering across my skin as his gaze locks with mine. "Amazing."

I swallow past the lump in my throat and turn to peer out the window again. I wonder if I'll ever meet a man who doesn't care about having kids. Surely, there have to be at least a few out there in the world, though they certainly aren't hanging out in the rural Midwest.

But who cares? I'm going to be very busy with my ferret daughter, thank you very much. I wouldn't have time for a baby even if I could have one and wanted to start my motherhood journey this late in life.

Shaking off the moment of melancholy, I ask, "So, is the brown smear what I think it is? And if so, what should I do about it? Blast it with the garden hose? Hire someone to replace the door? Burn the house down and start fresh somewhere with no poop on it?"

"Don't worry about it. I'll hire someone to clean it up after we're on the road."

"You don't have to do that," I say.

"It's not a big deal. Christian has a few guys down at his old bike shop that don't mind a dirty job. And if they're busy, Chris will find someone. He has connections everywhere." He reaches for his door handle. "Just head in through the garage. I'll take pictures of the door, so you have a record of the property damage, and be right in to help out."

I glance over my shoulder, to where Freya is curled up on a bed of towels I made for her on the banquet table behind Matty's seat. "It's okay to leave her here, right? We won't be gone long."

"It's fine," Wes says. "Probably safer. If Daria's around, we don't want to give her another target."

The hair lifting at the back of my neck, I whisper, "Do you really think she's still here? We aren't walking distance from town and there aren't any strange cars around. All of the ones on the street belong to my neighbors and their kids. Where would she even be hiding?"

He leans past me, making my breath catch as his spicy, clean, Wes smell teases at my nose. Dammit, how does this man smell so good after being up all night loading a camper?

"Well," he says, lingering close, his cheek just inches away. "You do have an unusually...sprawling display of garden gnomes."

Ignoring the twist of awareness in my stomach and other places I refuse to think about, I ask, "An unusually *impressive* display, you mean?"

He shifts to face me, his breath warm on my chin. "Gnomes aren't my favorite. They're creepy."

I arch a brow, desperately trying to play it cool, but my voice is husky when I say, "I heard gnomes felt the same way about you."

His lips curve as his gaze slips down to my mouth, making every cell in my body ache to close the distance between us. "They think *I'm* creepy?"

"Super creepy," I breathe, my nipples tightening into tingling points that make me grateful for the sweatshirt Wes gave me to throw on over my bridesmaid dress. "It's the eyes, I think. Green like a snake belly."

His smile widens. "Should I get contacts?"

"To appease the gnomes?" I ask, deadpan. "Yes. As soon as possible. I would suggest a nice, flat brown. No gold flecks, no amber ring around the edge. Just basic brown. People would probably take you more seriously in court, too."

He nods, the playfulness leaving his gorgeous green eyes that should never be covered up by anything. Ever. "That reminds me, I have two meetings I need to reschedule for next week and a continuance to file with the court. Definitely need to send those messages when we pull over later to get some rest." He sits back in his seat, arching a brow. "Ready?"

"Ready," I say, checking to make sure Freya is still sleeping before slipping out the door and closing it as softly as possible behind me.

I start up the driveway, my head on a swivel, but the yard is empty. The only sign of trouble is the brown mess on my door and a couple of yellow dog waste bags on the front porch steps. Weirdly comforted that I've been attacked with dog poop instead of human poo, I punch the code into the panel on the garage door and duck under it as it rises, grabbing reusable bags from my stash in the laundry room on my way inside.

It only takes a few minutes to gather Freya's things. I toss a few extra toys in the bag with her food and treats, then move into the kitchen, quickly packing perishables in my small cooler and other snacks in a separate bag. Leaving those by the garage door, I head into my room, fetching my large camping pack from the closet.

I open it on the bed, tucking underwear and bras into the pocket at the top before selecting a matching black bra and panty set for the day. I glance toward the bathroom, wondering if I have time for a fast shower before meeting Wes outside. I mean, I *am* lightning fast in a pinch, a skill I picked up when I used to work an early shift at the local coffee shop before heading into the catering office at ten. I couldn't stand the smell of coffee grounds on my skin all day and had the three-minute shower down to a science.

Deciding it's way better to spend a few minutes showering now than wait until later, when I'm even more tired and forced to figure out the shower system in the camper, I grab a pair of leggings and a soft denim button-down and scurry into the bathroom.

Closing the door, I strip off Wes's sweatshirt and my dress, then tie my hair up with a scrunchie to keep it out of the spray. When I scoot the curtain to one side to start the water, I'm completely naked.

Which is perfectly normal and wouldn't have been a problem...if there weren't a dead body hanging from the shower faucet.

I scream bloody murder, my heart punching at my ribs as I scramble backward until my bottom collides with the cabinet by the sink. My hands flail out, searching for a weapon as my panicked gaze rakes up and down the form dangling from the spigot.

The armless, legless form, with large socket holes near the hips...

By the time I realize it's not a dead body and stop screaming, Wes is bursting through the bathroom door, a vintage garden gnome held over his head like a weapon.

Chapter 11

WESLEY

Naked.

Tessa is naked.

I'm not proud of it, but when I burst into her bathroom to help her fight off whatever made her scream, that's the first thing I notice.

I see bare curves, pale skin flushed with pink, and her thighs clenched together in fear, and all I can think about is when those thighs were wrapped around my hips. When her breasts were heavy in my hands and her nipples tight against my tongue and her pussy clenching around me as she came, calling my name.

"B-body," she stammers, jabbing a shaking finger toward the shower as she fumbles for the hand towel hanging by the sink with her other hand. "I thought it was a b-body."

She tugs the towel from the holder and clutches it to her chest. It's too small to cover more than her breasts, but that's apparently enough to help me get my shit together.

I jerk my gaze back to her face before following her

finger toward the spray, where the torso of what looks like a department store mannequin dangles from the shower faucet.

My stomach drops, and I tighten my grip on the gnome I grabbed on the way in. "Get dressed. Fast," I say, before glancing out into her bedroom.

The space is still quiet, and the house is as silent as it was before Tessa screamed, but that doesn't mean we're alone. Daria was clearly inside at some point, which means she could *still* be here.

"How did she get in?" Tessa asks, her voice shaking as she starts pulling on clothes from the puddle on the counter. "I always lock the front door. Always. There's no way I left it open."

"I don't know," I say, moving toward the thing in the shower. When I turn off the water and spin it around, my already churning stomach clenches. "But it was definitely Daria." I step back, motioning to the word scrawled in red across the mannequin's breasts.

"Slut?" Tessa reads with a soft *humph*. "Well, that's not very creative, is it?"

"No." I release the stump where the arm should be, sending it spinning back to face the other side of the shower. "But it's on brand. The same thing is on the porch steps. Written in feces."

Tessa tugs on her shirt, and I turn back to face her.

"Well," she says, pulling the scrunchie from her hair, sending it spilling back down around her shoulders. "At least she's consistent. And at least she didn't use poo in here. Though I'm pretty sure that's my favorite red lipstick." She shivers. "That bothers me more than the mannequin, honestly. That she was in here, going through my things, violating my privacy."

"I'm so sorry," I say.

"Stop it," she says, pumping something from a small bottle by the sink into her hands and running her fingers through her hair. "If you apologize again, I'm going to scream again, and we'll both keep wasting precious time. This isn't your fault. Men cheat all the time, and no one ends up with a mannequin in their shower and poop on their porch. This is a Daria problem." She sighs. "I guess we should call the police? I mean, she broke in. That's clearly against the law."

I nod. "Yes, but unless we have some way of proving it was her..." I motion toward the front of the house. "Do you have a front porch camera? Or any cameras in the house?"

Tessa nibbles her bottom lip as she pulls on her socks. "No, I don't trust cameras. I have an irrational fear that they'll record me when I don't want to be recorded and the footage will somehow end up on the internet. What about fingerprints?"

"That only works if her prints are on file, and to my knowledge, they aren't. And I'm not sure the police would dust for prints in a situation like this anyway, you know? When there's no sign of a break-in and nothing's been stolen. Nothing has been stolen, has it?"

She shakes her head. "Not to my knowledge. At least, I didn't notice that anything was disturbed until I pushed back the curtain." She turns, opening drawers beside the sink. "Doesn't look like anything's been moved here, either. Except for my lipstick. It's missing. She must have taken it with her." She glances at me over her shoulder. "Would that be enough do you think? If the police found my lipstick in her purse or something?"

"And how would they prove it's yours?" I ask. "She

could just say it was hers. Assuming it's a brand that's readily available to the public..."

Tessa curses.

I almost apologize again but stop myself. "I think the best thing to do is to document everything with photos and video and leave the mannequin hanging where it is. That way, if things escalate, the evidence will still be here when we get back in town. In the meantime, I'll get someone over to change the locks later today."

"Okay," she says, her shoulders hunching closer to her ears as she crosses her arms. "I definitely don't want to stay here alone until the locks are changed."

"And a security system?" I ask. "Can I have one installed? As long as the cameras are aimed at the outside, not the inside?"

She looks up, her gaze softening. "You don't have to take care of everything, Wes. I can have a security system installed myself. Like I said, this isn't your fault."

"But it kind of is," I say, deciding now is as good a time as any to attempt to explain myself. "I don't know why I didn't say something about Darcy that night in the woods. I should have. I usually *would* have, I just..." I sigh. "Like I told you that morning, we were already having problems. That's why I was out hiking alone, to get some space to think about what I wanted moving forward. I knew that wasn't Darcy. Truly. I was going to end things with her that morning anyway. I'd already made the decision, even before we were together." I drag a hand through my hair. "But when I got to her place, and she told me her period was late. Suddenly, there was a chance we might be having a baby together, and I just couldn't—"

"It's okay. It doesn't matter," Tessa says, cutting me

off with a sharp shake of her head. "It really doesn't. The past is the past and we have enough drama on our plates in the here and now." She pulls in a deep breath, letting it out with a flap of her arms. "If you want to grab the bags I put by the garage door, I'll finish packing and be out in a few minutes. The sooner we put space between us and your ex's sister, the sooner we can find somewhere to take a nap. I'm suddenly very, very tired."

"Got it, I'll meet you out front," I say, backing toward the door, feeling like shit.

Speaking of shit...

Might as well find someone to clean up the porch while I'm waiting.

Once I've deposited the cooler and grocery bags beside the camper, I pull my phone from my pocket. It's only five-thirty, probably too early for Christian to answer, but I can leave a message.

I put my cell to my ear, mentally composing what I want to say, but to my surprise, my brother answers on the first ring, bellowing, "Wesley! What's up, brother? Are you catching this sunrise? What the fuck, man? How is the sun so beautiful? How did we get so lucky? To be born on a planet with a sun like this one?"

"I love the sun so much," a feminine voice in the background—Starling, his fiancée, I'm betting— agrees.

"And I love you, woman," Chris says, his voice vibrating with emotion. "You're my fucking sun goddess, and I'm going to worship you until we're old and gray and your nipples drag the fuckin' ground."

Starling giggles. "Never going to happen, buddy. Sun goddesses keep it swag, we don't drag. Now stop talking about my nipples, you're going to make Wesley uncomfortable. I love you, Wesley. I can't wait for you to be my brother for real! We're *finally* setting a wedding date and you're going to be the best man because you'll dress up in a costume without complaining about it."

"Yeah, Barrett would be a whiny little bitch," Christian agrees. "And Drew is going to have too many kids to have time for fittings. They're pregnant again, did you hear? Mom figured it out last night when Tatum kept drinking virgin mimosas. Those two really love to raw dog."

Starling giggles. "Gross."

"Well, they do," Christian insists.

"So, how drunk are you?" I ask, pretty sure the answer is "very" based on the conversation so far. "I have something serious to ask you, but I don't want to waste my breath if you're not going to remember it in a few hours."

"Oh, we're not drunk," Christian says, dropping his voice dramatically before adding in a whisper nearly as loud as his normal tone, "We're on some kind of psychedelic herb thing Starling got from her friend who leads vision quests in Arizona. It was part of our sun goddess role-playing. I wasn't sure about it at first, but now...I love it, man. I am one with creation. I am a throbbing heart filled with love, connected to all the other throbbing hearts, and I'm psyched about it. My ego is dissolving in the warmth of the universal truth of our undeniable connection, and I couldn't be happier. Also, this breakfast sandwich is the best I've ever had."

"So good," Starling agrees with a euphoric sigh. "Best sausage ever. Best night ever. Best sunrise ever. Oh, and you're on speakerphone, Wes, just FYI. But we're alone at the lookout point so no one will hear us. We respect your privacy. Even when we're one with the sun and realize there is no privacy. Not in the deepest sense of the word. I am you and you are me and we are the everything and the nothing and all that lies between."

"That's exactly it. The perfect way to put it," Christian says, his voice reverent. "You're so fucking smart. When we decide to raw dog, our kids are going to be tiny geniuses."

Smiling despite my exhaustion, I say, "I'm glad you two had an amazing evening. Unfortunately, mine wasn't so great. It was pretty awful, in fact."

"Fuck, dude," Christian says. "I'm sorry. What happened?"

I briefly explain, prompting more cursing and scandalized sounds from Christian and Starling.

"That is so gross, I can't wrap my head around it," Starling says. "And I'm not talking about the poo. I mean, yes, the poo is super gross and repulsive, but the 'slut' thing? That's so messed up. When will people stop shaming women for our perfectly natural, healthy, species-continuing bodily urges?"

"I would never shame you for your urges, babe," Christian says. "I love your urges. Your urges are one of my favorite things about you."

"Aw, same, baby," Starling says, followed by some smacking sounds. I assume they are wasted-ly making out.

"Right," I say in a louder voice, fairly certain this has all been an exercise in futility, but figuring I might as well beg for the favor I called to ask. "Anyway, Christian, if you could hire someone to come clean up the porch for Tessa, maybe one of the guys at the bike shop, I'd really appreciate it. We're getting out of town for a while to give Daria time to cool off."

"Want me to take care of the mannequin, too?" he asks.

"No, we're going to leave that where it is, in case we need evidence of harassment down the line. But if you wouldn't mind calling Damon at Home Solutions to install new locks on the doors and a security system with exterior cameras, that would be amazing."

"Done," he says. "As soon as things open, I'll make some calls."

"Thanks," I say, hesitating a beat before I add, "Should I call you again in a few hours? Or text? How much of this do you think you're going to remember?"

"All of it," Christian says with a soft laugh. "My mind is laser sharp. I think it's actually working better than it usually does. For example, I just realized that Starling has a freckle on her shoulder that I've never noticed before. It's the cutest little freckle, and we've been naked together at least a thousand times, but I—"

"Probably two thousand," Starling cuts in. "We went through a really over-the-top lovemaking phase for a while. It was winter and we were pretending we were pirate smugglers stuck in an ice cave and the only way to survive was stripping naked and sharing the same sleeping bag. And well...turns out that really did it for us. We practically ran home from work every day to get naked and hang out in the shed without the space heater on."

"Good times," Christian says fondly.

"So good." Starling sighs. "You should try that one sometime, Wes. Pretending is really fun. So is sharing a sleeping bag."

"So, I've heard," I say, wondering if the universe is using my brother and future sister-in-law to punish me.

Sadly, my own shared sleeping bag situation didn't have such a happy ending.

As Tessa emerges from the garage, closing it behind her, she looks like she's headed to the guillotine. Her shoulders bow under her backpack, her chin droops toward her chest, and her hiking boots drag a little as she walks. Her body language is practically screaming, "I'd rather be anywhere else than here," and I can't say I blame her.

But maybe...

Maybe Starling's on to something with her "pretending" advice.

"Thanks for the help, guys," I say, my thoughts racing. "And for the ideas. Take care of yourselves and get home safe."

"You, too, man," Christian says. "I love you, Wes. You're made of stardust, brother. Don't forget it. You are literally stardust and there is nothing you can't do."

"Thanks again," I say before ending the call.

Nothing I can't do...

Well, I guess we'll see about that.

Chapter 12

TESSA

On the way out of town, Wesley is weirdly quiet, but that's fine with me. I wasn't lying about being exhausted.

Maybe it was the adrenaline rush after finding the mannequin in the shower that sapped the last of my energy. Or maybe it was Wes's "Darcy thought she was pregnant" speech that stomped my will to live into a soggy puddle on the bathroom floor.

I should be used to conversations like that by now. They happen all the time, especially in my current friend group.

Hanging out with people five to ten years younger than I am is great for keeping me out on the town and up to date on the most recent slang, but not so great when it comes to avoiding mentions of pregnancy. Someone is always getting knocked up. It feels like I'm bombarded by baby bellies on a daily basis. It doesn't help that my boss is pregnant, and we cater at least four or five baby showers a month.

But I've known I can't have children for a while,

since I was thirty-five and saved for months to freeze my eggs, only to learn that wasn't a viable option for me. I should be used to being on the outside looking in by now.

Usually, I am.

But everything feels so raw.

My body, my brain, my heart...

I can't have a week of no-strings-attached sexy times with Wesley. I don't know what I was thinking. The way he ran to my rescue and instantly took charge of ensuring the safety of my home was enough to make me long for more than a brief, friends-with-benefits situation. If I actually shared his bed for a week, if I gave in, let down my walls, and let our natural chemistry take over, I'd be head over heels in no time.

And that's the last thing I need.

I've already wasted too much of my life trying to make things work with the wrong man or pining for the one who got away. If Nate had tried to hump my leg at a wedding last spring, I might have gone running back to him. (I didn't know about the cheating with his art student part back then.)

Deep down in my lonely core, for the longest time, I would rather have been with a guy who'd ghosted me for months like an emotionally stunted jerk than keep tucking myself into bed alone.

But things are different now. I still don't love being alone, but I'm getting used to it. With Freya's help, I'm learning to divert my longing for romantic love into healthier outlets. I love my precious pet, my friends, my friends' kids, and my Saturday morning hiking group. I love cozy nights on my couch, good books in the sun in my backyard, and the freedom to spend my weekend baking in my hideous green onesie pajamas that make me look like Oscar the Grouch's little sister.

There's peace in letting go and freedom in accepting the present moment in all its beautiful imperfection.

"But not this much imperfection," I mutter with a yawn, rubbing at my itchy eyes as Wesley merges onto the highway headed south.

"What's that?" he asks, glancing my way.

I shake my head. "Nothing." I fight another yawn and lose the battle. "Sorry, I can't stop yawning. I don't think I've ever been this tired."

"Then go grab a nap in back," he says. "I don't mind."

"No, I'll help you stay awake until we find a place to park."

"It's fine, I'm not sleepy," he says. "And if I get tired, I can always pull over."

"Are you absolutely sure?" I press, old trauma raising its head. I've been in a situation like this before, with a man who wanted to keep driving when he was tired, and it ended about as horribly as that sort of thing can.

But Wesley isn't that man, a fact he proves when he says, "Absolutely. If my eyes get the slightest bit heavy, I'll pull over at a rest stop. I won't put you or Freya at risk, and I'm not keen on dying myself." He nods toward the back again. "Go ahead. Get some rest. Might as well take advantage of the fact that we have a rolling apartment on wheels."

I glance over my shoulder, where Freya is still snoozing away, resting up from our big night. "All right but wake me if you need moral support. I can sing 99 Bottles of Beer until we find somewhere to park."

He arches a brow. "That sounds horrible."

"I know. That's the point. Once you've reached a certain level of exhaustion, only horrible things can keep you awake. I could also slap you repeatedly across the face with a rubber chicken, but I forgot to pack mine in all the rush."

"Noted. I'll keep an eye out for rubber chickens when we stop for supplies." His gaze slides my way, making my heart beat faster as he adds in a softer voice, "Enjoy your nap."

"Thanks, I'll try." I unbuckle and make my way to the back of the camper, where a comfy-looking queen-size bed hides behind a privacy curtain.

For a moment, I consider crawling into the single lofted bunk bed above it so that Wesley can have the larger mattress, but being lower to the ground is probably safer if he has to slam on the brakes for some reason.

And the thought of climbing even the small ladder up to the bunk is suddenly too much. I haven't just been awake for twenty-four hours; I've been going hard almost that entire time. I spent the first half of yesterday running myself ragged helping Melissa get everything prepped for the wedding. I probably made ten-thousand, three hundred, and seventy-six trips from the catering van down to the barn and I'm feeling every one of them as I collapse onto the memory foam mattress, cover myself with a sinfully soft fleece blanket, and sink into something deeper than sleep.

❦

I'm literally out the second my cheek hits the pillow and wake who-knows-how-many hours later feeling disoriented and confused. It takes me a long beat to remember how I came to be asleep in a camper bed and another beat to realize the camper has stopped moving.

The familiar hum of the wheels on pavement and the soothing rocking from side to side is gone, leaving nothing but faint bird song and the fainter sound of...scratching.

Poking my head out from behind the privacy curtain, I look up to see one of Wesley's socked feet sticking out of the top bunk, but the scratching isn't coming from there. It's Freya, awake and making her typical mess in the litter box I set up by the door. She'll use the litter box when it's cold or I'm away at work, but she prefers to be set loose in the backyard to do her business, and makes her dissatisfaction with the litter situation known by flinging it absolutely everywhere.

From what I've learned on online forums, that isn't typical ferret behavior, but there's nothing typical about my fierce, but dainty little lady. She's equally offended by male humans and litter stink in the house, which feels meaningful.

"Okay, just a second," I whisper as she sends litter spraying across the floor with a paddle of her back feet. "I'll take you, just let me find your leash."

Tiptoeing across the camper to keep from waking Wesley, I locate her leash near my purse and hook it onto her harness. Stepping over the litter mess—I can sweep up later, after Wes is awake—I head outside, shocked to find the sun tracking toward the horizon.

Glancing around, I see that we're in a tidy parking lot with what looks like a trail marker on one side. After Freya does her business in the grass and gives a few nearby trees a thorough sniffing, I head toward the sign. Halfway to the marker, I hear rushing water, but I'm still bowled over by the view from the trailhead.

A wide waterfall spills over stones that glow a soft pink in the fading light, the lovely scene framed by the skyline of an unfamiliar city. A woman on a bike hops off as she nears the end of the paved trail. I flash her a smile and ask, "Excuse me, can you tell me what city this is? I'm on a road trip and was asleep when my friend pulled up."

"Sioux Falls," the woman says, returning my grin as she undoes the strap on her helmet. "Falls Park, specifically. It's a great place to pull over and stretch your legs." She glances down at Freya, her smile widening. "Even tiny legs. What's her name?"

I tell her and we exchange a few pleasantries before she rolls her bike away. On her way to the parking lot, she calls over her shoulder, "And if you're hungry, the café is still open for another hour, I think. It's in the old brick building closer to the water. They serve coffee, sandwiches, ice cream, that sort of thing."

I lift a hand, thank her, and start down the trail. A coffee probably isn't the best idea at nearly six o'clock, but it sounds amazing. And if I'm caffeinated, I'll be able to take over the driving while Wes rests. As nice as this place is, we can't stay here overnight. It's a day-use parking lot, not a place where campers would be welcome.

Over the next rise, Freya and I are treated to another gorgeous view of the falls and tempting smells from the café. At the door to the small structure, I gather Freya into my arms before pushing through the door, the better to keep her safe from customers not used to watching out for tiny pets.

But there aren't many customers lingering in the café

at this hour. It's just me, Freya, and a sleepy-looking teenager with red cheeks scrolling through his phone.

To his credit, he looks up as soon we walk in, tucking his cell into his back pocket with a friendly smile. "Hey. The chef left for the day and we're closing in half an hour, but we still have to-go sandwiches, a few baked goods, and coffee."

"Coffee, please," I say as I move to check out the offerings in the cold case. "Actually, make that two. Two coffees to go with room for cream and sugar." I'm not sure how Wesley takes his coffee, but I figure it's always better to err on the side of leaving room.

I collect two mozzarella, tomato, and basil sandwiches from the case that look fairly fresh, as well as a container of cheese, nuts, and a boiled egg for Freya. She prefers raw eggs, but she'll nibble on pieces of egg yolk or white as a treat between meals, and I don't know when I'll be lucky enough to find ferret-friendly food again on the road.

"She's so cute," the teen says, his pink cheeks plumping as he smiles. "Can I pet her?"

"We can try," I say, tapping my phone to pay as he bags up the sandwiches and gets a cardboard to-go carrier for the coffees. "But she kind of has a thing about men. She's not super fond of them for some reason."

"Maybe a man was mean to her when she was a baby," he says, sobering. "Animals are like people that way. If someone hurts them when they're little, the memories can stick around and mess them up later."

My heart aching for this earnest kid, who sounds like he knows too much about trauma, I nod. "You're right. I'm not sure what her babyhood was like. My cousin adopted her from a shelter when she was already grown." I glance down at Freya, who doesn't seem bothered by the boy, so far. "But you have friendly energy. Try extending your hand, palm up, fingers loose, and let's see how she does. Her name is Freya, and I'm Tessa."

"Hey. I'm Zack." He reaches out, slowly, carefully, a look of awe blooming on his face as Freya sniffs his hand for only a moment before licking the tips of his fingers. "Wow." He laughs. "That tickles."

"It means she likes you," I say, grinning. "Or that you have food on your hand. Maybe both."

Zack laughs again, relaxing as Freya lets him stroke her head. "She's amazing. I'm going to get a pet when I graduate and move into my own place. Pets are always happy to see you when you get home."

I wince in sympathy. Clearly, whatever parental situation he has at the moment is less than fulfilling. Poor guy. "Yeah, you're almost there. What are you...sixteen?"

"Seventeen," he says, still focused on petting Freya. "I have a baby face. It's the chubby cheeks."

"Wow, yeah. Seventeen. You'll be a pet-owning adult before you know it. It was nice meeting you, Zack."

He grins. "Nice meeting you guys, too. Have a great night and enjoy the sandwiches."

"Will do." I set Freya on the floor and grab the takeout, knowing I won't be able to juggle holding her as well as the food.

Back outside, the early evening sun is showing off, making the pink rocks beneath the water gleam like something from another realm, one better than this one, where no kid ever feels unwelcome in their own home.

Situations like Zack's confirm my belief that we're alone here on this spinning orb. If there were a higher power looking out for us, it wouldn't let assholes like Zack's parents have a child, while so many people who would make lovely parents—or at least not shitty ones—remain infertile.

I'm so busy thinking about Zack and juggling the food and carrier of hot coffee, that I'm not holding Freya's leash as tightly as I should be. When a man in jogging shorts charges around the corner, yelling something about profit margins into his ear piece, Freya easily tugs out of my grasp.

"Freya no, come back here right now!" I call out, crouching to set the food and drinks on the ground so I can chase after her.

Before I can stand back up—or Freya can reach the shouting guy's crotch—Wesley sprints up the trail behind the man. His hair is sticking up in all directions and he's sporting a five o'clock shadow that makes him look a little dangerous in the best way. As he cuts across the grass and leaps into the air, diving in front of the man to grab Freya before my fearless protector can reach her target, a zing rushes through my blood.

"What the fuck?" the man shouts as Wesley rolls across the grass on the other side of the trail, Freya cradled against his chest. "No, not you," the man barks into the phone before pressing his cell to his stomach and demanding in a none-too-friendly tone, "What the hell do you think you're doing? You almost knocked me down."

"I'm so sorry, he was just trying to grab our ferret before she jumped on you," I say, hurrying over, food and coffee in hand. "She's afraid of loud noises, and—"

"I don't give a shit," the man says. "If your animal doesn't know how to behave in a public space, it shouldn't be in one. Same goes for the two of you."

"She said she was sorry," Wesley says, rising to his feet,

a chittering Freya squirming in his hands, begging to be set free to handle this red-faced jerk on her own. "And we truly didn't mean any harm. It's a beautiful night, so why don't we just go our—"

"Shut the fuck up," the man says, his face flushing a deeper crimson. "Don't use that fucking 'calm down' tone with me, asshole. I have every right to be pissed."

"But she didn't hurt you," I say, inserting myself in between Wes and Mr. Roid Rage. "And neither did Wesley. Please, let's just go our separate ways and be done with it. We don't even live here, so you'll never see us again. I promise."

He grunts and his jaw clenches, but after a beat, he mutters, "Fine, whatever. I'm in the middle of a call anyway." He starts down the trail, but then turns, shouting back at us, "But keep your animal on a fucking leash. Or next time it attacks someone, it might end up with its head crushed under a boot."

I suck in a scandalized breath, while Freya lets forth a stream of ferret chatter so intense, there's no doubt in my mind that she's telling him just where he can stick his threat, his cell phone, and his bad attitude.

"Here, let me take the coffee and the bag," Wes says, gathering the supplies with one hand as he guides Freya into my arms with the other. "She needs her mom."

"Of course, she does," I say, cuddling Freya close and stroking her sweet little head, the one that I never want to imagine being smashed under a boot ever again. "I'm so sorry, baby. I should have held tighter to your leash. I know, I know," I add, lowering my voice to an even softer, more soothing murmur as I turn back toward the parking lot. "He was a dick. You're right." She clucks and whips her tail back and forth. "Yes. And probably on steroids. That's what I thought, too."

Wes snorts in soft laughter. "Me, too. I think his bicep was bigger than my head."

I shudder and stick out my tongue. "I know. So gross."

He arches a brow. "Not a fan of big, bulging muscles?"

"No, I like normal muscles. The kind that only strain a t-shirt a little bit." I fight the urge to glance down at his arms and lose. When he catches me, and his grin widens, I add, "Yes, like yours. They're nice. I can admit that your muscles are my favorite kind of muscles."

"Your favorite kind of muscles," he echoes thoughtfully. "That's nice to hear. Now I'm really glad I came running in just my undershirt when I heard you scream."

"You've been doing a lot of that lately," I say. "Hopefully tomorrow will be a less scream-y day."

"I've been thinking about tomorrow," he says. "About tomorrow and the next day, the whole week, in fact."

I frown, continuing to stroke Freya as she recovers from the excitement. "Okay."

"And I don't see any reason why we shouldn't take these lemons and make lemonade."

I arch a brow. "You mean enjoy the park? Hike and make s'mores, stuff like that?"

"Well, yes, but...more than that." He runs a hand over his wild hair. "How about we clean up in the camper, and I'll take you out to eat? We can have a nice dinner and discuss our options."

I nod, intrigued. "All right. I bought sandwiches at the

café, but they'll keep in the fridge until tomorrow. And Freya should be fine in the crate for a while after her walk. I wouldn't want to leave her loose in the camper while we eat, not after all the excitement with Mr. Roid Rage. She can get up to destructive mischief when she feels nervous."

"Me, too, Freya," Wes says, reaching out to run gentle fingers over her head. To my surprise, she leans into his touch, welcoming the show of affection.

Come to think of it, she didn't tear him limb from limb when he tackled her, either. After only a day, Wes has won over my savage little beastie.

You'd better watch out or he'll do the same with you, the inner voice warns. *You should probably skip that dinner. If he gets you somewhere with candlelight, you're done for, woman.*

But I don't tell Wes I've changed my mind about dinner. I simply slip into the tiny bathroom, wash up at the sink, and change into my dark brown sundress. I add a black cardigan as a nod to the chilly spring night and sweep on blush, lipstick, and mascara.

I want to look pretty for him.

That probably isn't a good sign either, but the way his eyes light up when I emerge from the bathroom feels good.

Way too good…

Chapter 13

WESLEY

Finding a nice restaurant close to the highway, with a parking lot big enough to accommodate a twenty-foot camper is a challenge, but my Secrets of the Wandering Wild app does me a solid.

By the time Tessa emerges from the bathroom, I have reservations at a mom-and-pop Italian place just a short jaunt down the road and only a mile from a campground with plenty of sites available.

"Sounds great," Tessa says, her gaze skimming up and down my frame, taking in my fresh jeans and a black button-down shirt. "You look nice."

"So do you," I say, taking the fact that she put on makeup as a good sign. She's beautiful with or without it, but the extra effort, when there's no one she knows around to see her, except me, feels significant. "Just give me a few minutes to shave and we can hit the road."

"Or you could...*not* shave," she says, with a breezy shrug. "I mean, if we don't have time." She shrugs again, her gaze lifting to the ceiling. "I don't mind a little scruff."

I arch a brow. "You don't mind it?"

Her lips turn down at the edges as she shrugs again. "Nah, a little scruff never hurt anyone. And it makes you look a little bit like Bruce Willis from his action star days, when he'd get all sweaty and scruffy..."

My smile widens. "Yeah? I think that can be arranged. I looked at the weather forecast for the park. The average high is eighty degrees this week and not a cloud in sight. I can deliver sweat and scruff."

She shrugs a third time—I think the lady doth shrug too much. "I mean, sure. If you want. That sounds nice. From a purely aesthetic perspective."

"Purely aesthetic." I reach over her head, closing the cabinet above the microwave, where I'm storing my toiletries until we have a chance to organize things. "Just a neutral appreciation of a man's face sort of thing."

"Right. It could be any man."

"Really?" I flatten my palm against the cabinet as I lean in, bringing my face closer to hers. "Any man at all?"

She looks up, her lips parting. "I mean, not *any* man. Scruff wouldn't improve Mr. Roid Rage. He'd still be an ugly meathead with a squashed nose."

"He did have a squashed nose," I agree. "With a weird texture, too. Like it had been run over by a dirt bike."

"Right." Her gaze slides down to my mouth with a sigh. "And I will admit, you do have very nice scruff. It's very...even," she says, her lips drifting closer to mine. "And dark, but not too dark."

"That's good to know," I murmur, bending down, so desperate to taste her again that I forget Freya's still loose until Tessa yips and pulls away.

A beat later, the ferret pokes her head through Tessa's hair near her shoulder, watching me with narrowed eyes.

"Oh my God, you scared me," Tessa says, laughing as she reaches for her pet. "She's never done that before. She just climbed right up the back of my dress."

Freya dooks and clings to Tessa's hand, shooting me a glance that lets me know I'm still on notice. But that's okay. I'll just add winning Freya's trust to my list, right under convincing her mom to get on board with my crazy plan.

Fuck...I'm going to need all the help I can get with that one.

"How do you feel about red wine?" I ask as Tessa sits Freya in her little stuffed bed and we settle into our seats.

"I feel like it's something we should have with dinner," Tessa says. "Preferably two glasses, maybe three. After the past twenty-four hours, I think we deserve a wine buzz and a good night's sleep with no alarm set for tomorrow morning."

"Agreed. The reviews said the restaurant has a decent selection, considering it's in the middle of nowhere in a two-room prison from the Wild West days."

Tessa glances my way, excitement flashing in her eyes. "Yeah? That sounds interesting. I hope they have one of those menus that gives the entire history of the place on the back. I love a menu that reads like a novel."

"I hope they have homemade gnocchi. And a killer charcuterie board."

Tessa rubs her hands together as the engine rumbles to life. "Yes, please. I love charcuterie boards. I make a pretty mean one, if I do say so myself."

"Oh yeah?" I pull out of our spot, guiding the camper toward the exit.

"Yeah. I know they're trendy now, but I've been charcuterie-ing for decades. I made my first one when I was only twenty-three. It was Valentine's Day, and my boyfriend did not appreciate my flower radishes and homemade pickles, but he did eat all the horseradish cheddar and leave me exactly zero slices."

"Monster," I say. "Horseradish cheddar must be shared."

"I know, right?" She shakes her head. "I should have known the relationship was doomed right then and there."

"But at least it wasn't Stilton with dried apricots."

She laughs as she shifts in her chair, facing me. "Oh my God, yes! Stilton is so good! But almost unanimously overlooked by charcuterie board makers everywhere. What's up with that?"

"I don't know. Maybe it sounds too British or something? It's sad, really."

"So sad." She chuckles. "We should start a campaign to raise Stilton awareness. Maybe then Marcy would stock it in the cheese section at The Farmer's Way. She eventually got on board with more than one kind of goat cheese, once I convinced her that there are actually several different kinds and they have wildly different flavors, textures, and cooking applications."

"Love goat cheese. Slap it on a pizza with some arugula and a little fig jam...heaven."

She moans. "Damn, that sounds good. In the summer I like to grill a little bit in a corn husk and then top it with a corn salsa and honey to make a dip."

I curse in appreciation.

"Amen," she agrees.

I shoot a glance her way. "I like it when you talk cheesy to me."

Her enthusiasm dims as I merge onto the highway.

She sits back in her chair, arms crossed over her chest. "Yeah, well, I do love cheese. It's a very honest food. Cheese is never going to trick you into thinking it's good when it's not, you know? Cheese will start to stink to high heaven or grow visible mold of some kind. It gives very clear warning signs that you should stay away from it if you want to avoid gastrointestinal distress."

Taking her meaning, I put my own twist on her metaphor, "But a little mold doesn't mean the cheese is all bad. Slice it off and there's still plenty of perfectly good cheese left to enjoy."

"But the cheese is past its prime by then," she counters.

"Past its prime cheese is still good cheese. And past its prime horseradish cheddar is still far superior to most other cheeses, even if they're brand new."

She arches a brow. "Now it sounds like we're talking about me. I'm the only past their prime cheese in this vehicle."

I shake my head but keep my eyes on the road as I say, "Not even close. You're clearly in your prime. And besides, you're not cheese, you're a fine wine, who's only going to get better with age."

She snorts. "Now who's talking cheesy?"

"Too much?"

"Nah. I'm a sucker for compliments, even cheesy ones. Especially after being called a wrinkled old prune last night."

"Daria is a liar and an asshole," I say. "That's been proven in multiple clinical studies."

Tessa laughs. "Can you imagine? She'd give the scientists heart failure."

"Nightmare. But maybe not our nightmare for much

longer. Christian texted earlier. Your door is all cleaned up, the security system went in this afternoon, and there's been no sign of Daria. Hopefully, she sobered up, realized she was a maniac last night, and came to her senses."

"Hopefully," Tessa says with a sigh, "but she doesn't seem like the kind of person who comes to her senses. She gave me more 'gator with its jaws locked in the middle of a death roll' vibes. And that mannequin…it gives me the willies just thinking about it."

I want to reach out and take her hand. Instead, I promise, "If a week away doesn't cool her down, I'll camp out in your yard and keep watch every night until this is over."

"You'd look pretty rough in court after a night in the front yard. And what about the gnomes? What if they come to life and attack you for calling them creepy?"

"I don't care. I'll brave a gnome uprising if I have to. I won't let her get anywhere close to you again, I promise."

Tessa's posture softens, her arms slipping away from her chest. "Well, thanks. I appreciate that. I confess, I am glad I'm not spending the night alone for a while. I'm probably at least four inches taller and quite a bit heavier than Daria, but she could still take me. I lack the killer instinct."

"One of the many things I like about you," I say, pushing on before she can start comparing me to bad cheese again. "Would you mind pulling the directions up on your phone? I still can't figure out how to pair my cell to the camper GPS. The name of the restaurant is Mama Maria's. Should be about twenty miles up the road."

"Oh, that's close," she says, quickly fetching her cell from the small black purse she pulled from her bag. Even with only ten minutes to pack, she did a much better job than I did. "I'm so glad. I'm starving." She reaches for her coffee cup from the holder on the dashboard and takes a sip. "I probably shouldn't drink this if we're aiming for an early bedtime, but it smells so good."

"We don't have to have an early bedtime," I say. "It's going to be a clear night. If we want to hang out around the campfire and watch the stars for a while after dinner, that's fine. Like you said, we can always sleep in late. We don't have anywhere pressing to be tomorrow. Our campground reservation at the park doesn't start until Monday night. They were full through the weekend."

"Sounds nice," she says. "It's been way too long since I sat around and stared at the stars."

Her words make me think about the night we spent in my tent, about opening the flap on top and gazing up at the dazzling sky with her in my arms.

It's a beautiful memory, one of my best. It makes me want to make more memories with Tessa, but the moment we pull up to Mama Maria's, I know tonight *isn't* going to be an evening I look back on with fondness.

It's going to be one I'll be lucky to survive...

Chapter 14

TESSA

"Are we high?" I lean forward, peering through the windshield, but the view doesn't change. "Maybe the kid at the coffee shop slipped some acid into our coffee or something?"

"Except that I didn't drink any coffee," Wes says, cocking his head sharply as one of the clowns outside the restaurant executes a sloppy front roll only to immediately bound into the air and scurry up a thick pole at the edge of the patio like a spider monkey.

"Wow." My jaw drops as the clown climbs higher and higher, his hands a blur on the small metal handholds. In under a minute, he reaches the top of the pole and rings a bell, summoning a round of cheers from the other clowns milling about. A few raise their wineglasses in his honor as the sound of a whoopie cushion being violently emptied echoes through the air, so loud I can hear it from inside the still-closed camper.

"Maybe we don't want to eat here," Wes murmurs, scowling at the unusual crowd.

"I think that was a whoopie cushion," I say, pointing

to a group of silently giggling clowns reinflating a giant pink balloon near the outdoor bar.

Wes's brow smooths. "Thank God. But still...clowns. I'm not a fan. They're worse than gnomes."

"I mean, clowns *are* creepy, yes, but they seem harmless." I glance back at the clown practically flying down the pole, his ruffled costume billowing in the breeze. "At least to other people. I'm not sure it's safe to be climbing poles after drinking wine. And it's going to be dark soon."

As if summoned by my words, the exterior lights flicker on, illuminating the patio and the front of the cozy-looking little restaurant. The golden bricks blend into the landscape and there isn't another building in sight, making it very easy to imagine what it must have been like to pull up to the prison in the 1800s.

"And I really want to look inside," I say, glancing back at Wes, who looks a little pale. But I chalk it up to hunger pains and nod toward the entrance. "Come on, let's at least take a peek. Maybe things are less crazy in there. I'll put Freya in her crate, and we can go."

He nods and swallows hard. "All right."

By the time Freya's tucked in with a little treat and we've exited the camper, sweat is breaking out on his upper lip.

I hesitate near the door, frowning up at him. "Are you okay?"

"Fine."

"You're sweating." I point at his increasingly dewy face.

He swipes at his lip with the back of his hand. "Sorry. Guess I got a little hot in the sun through the windshield." He reaches for the door, jerking it open before shooting a quick glance toward the patio. "Let's head inside. It's probably cooler in there."

But it isn't cooler in the restaurant. It's actually a little warmer than the breezy spring evening, probably because it's packed to the gills with more clowns.

All kinds of clowns. There are traditional white-faced clowns with their red noses resting beside their plates as they eat. There are edgy clowns with sad makeup and gritty steampunk-inspired outfits. There are cute little clown kids and sullen clown teenagers and terrifying horror clowns with razor-sharp prosthetic teeth I imagine make eating difficult, and everything in between. The small dining area has a surprising number of tables, and every one of them is filled with circus folk.

Well, except for an older couple in the far corner, who are slurping soup as fast as they can and watching their surroundings nervously.

I turn to Wes, intending to ask him what he thinks such a large gathering of clowns might be up to out in the middle of nowhere. But when I see his face, I start to wonder about more important things.

"Are you about to pass out?" I whisper, resting a gentle hand on his back. "Do you need to put your head between your knees? Or we can go if you want."

He shakes his head, forcing a tight smile for the hostess approaching from across the room. "No. It's fine. You're hungry. I'm hungry. And this is the only restaurant for another hundred miles."

I'm about to suggest that we could drive back to Sioux Falls or make do with the sandwiches and snacks in the camper, when the breathless hostess arrives in front of us.

Thankfully, the petite brunette isn't in clown gear

and her eyes wrinkle warmly as she says, "You must be McGuire, party of two. You're so lucky! We had a last-minute cancellation right before you booked." She collects two menus from the stand near the entrance to the dining area and nods for us to follow her. "We have you at a high-top table in the cell room. Right this way."

As I move forward, Wes reaches out, claiming my hand and holding on tight as we start after the woman. Instantly, I know this has nothing to do with flirting or romance. His palm is cold and clammy, and as we pass by one of the horror clown tables, where a woman with a blood-soaked ruffle is calculating the tip with the aid of her cell phone, he starts to tremble.

I squeeze his hand, giving him what I hope is a reassuring smile as we step through the narrow threshold into what was obviously once the holding area for prisoners detained here. There aren't any doors on the cells anymore, but the bars still stand, serving as separators for the three large booths on that side of the room.

Booths that are also filled with clowns...

As our hostess sets the menus on a high-top table in the corner, by an open window overlooking the grassland beyond—thank God, in case Wes needs to make an urgent escape—I ask, "So what's going on here tonight? With the..." I nod over my shoulder with a smile.

She laughs. "It's so fun, right?"

Wes murmurs something too wobbly to sound like an agreement and claims the seat closest to the window.

"My uncle runs the clown college in Sioux Falls. Pagliacci in Pink?" She waves a hand when my blank face apparently reveals I have no idea what she's talking about. "It's famous in clown circles. We've had clowns in our family all the way back to seventeenth century Italy. And we've hosted the clown college reunion every year since it opened in 1974." She glances around with a soft laugh. "Though we might have to look for another venue next year. It's getting so big! Thank goodness it's nice out tonight so we could seat some people on the patio."

As I slide into the seat across from Wes, the hostess reaches for a pitcher of water on the table by the window, filling our glasses as she says, "The specials tonight are a grilled octopus appetizer with toasted bread and an olive tapenade and a gorgeous filet mignon with truffle butter and a small serving of lobster ravioli on the side. That comes with your choice of green beans or grilled Broccolini, and your server will be right with you."

I thank her, turning back to Wes as soon as she's hustled into the other room. "Seriously, are you going to be okay to eat here? Is this like...a phobia for you?"

He nods ever so slightly and lifts his menu, brandishing it like a shield in front of his chest. "Yep."

My forehead wrinkling, I whisper, "Then let's go. Crawl out the window. I'll meet you back by the camper."

He shakes his head again. "No. I need to get the hell over it. It's ridiculous. These are just normal people, enjoying a celebration and a nice meal, nothing to be afraid of."

I cock my head. "Well, I don't know about the normal part but I agree that there's nothing to be afraid of. But fear isn't always logical, and that's okay."

He claims his cloth napkin, dabbing at his damp face. "Except that it's not. I'm thirty-three years old. I should be over getting trapped in the haunted funhouse at the county fair when I was six."

I wince sympathetically. "Who says? You were just a

baby. That must have been really scary. Why did your parents let you go into a place like that? Let alone all by yourself?"

"It wasn't my parents, and I wasn't alone. At least not at first," he says, his gaze darting around the room, like he's on the lookout for snipers. "It was Barrett. Hazard of having older brothers. Barrett was nine and determined to do the haunted funhouse for the first time. Drew was seven and too scared to go with him, so I volunteered, wanting to prove I was a big boy and Drew was a whiny baby." He exhales a shaky laugh. "But I was not, in fact, a big boy. Neither was Barrett, but he had a better sense of direction. When he ran, he found the way out pretty quickly. I got lost in the mirror room with a morbidly obese clown with food stains all over his costume. He kept laughing and popping out behind different mirrors, while I cried."

I reach across the table, giving his forearm a squeeze. "You poor thing. That's horrible, Wes. No wonder you were traumatized. That man deserves to have a hot poker shoved up his backside for torturing a kid like that."

His lips curve in a wobbly smile. "Thanks."

"And Barrett wasn't a very brave big brother." I shrug. "But he was only nine, so I guess I'll forgive him." I pet Wes's arm, racking my brain for something to say to help get his mind off those ugly memories. I find inspiration in the feel of his crisp arm hair beneath my fingers. "When I was little, I used to pet my grandpa's arm hair like this and pretend it was a cat named Fluffy. Gramps would play along, making meowing noises and pretending to drink milk out of my glass."

Wes's smile widens. "Sounds like a cool guy."

"He was. And the only one in the family as weird as me. I miss him."

"You're not weird," he says, his gaze locking on mine for the first time since we sat down. "You're fun. I'll never forget that time I walked into the catering office and you and Mel were on the prep tables, throwing potatoes at each other and using sheet pans as shields."

I laugh. "It had been a long week. And we had a lot of baby potatoes about to go bad, so..."

"It was great. I wanted to join in."

I smile. "You should have. You're allowed to be silly, too, you know. You don't always have to be the calm, sweet, levelheaded one who sees all sides of the issue."

His lips hitch up on one side. "Spoken by a woman who doesn't come from an enormous family. That's not how it works when you're one of eight. There are only so many ways to stand out in a pack of kids that large. Once you find something that gets you positive attention, you stick to it, even when you're grown." He stretches his neck to one side. "It's hard to break out of those patterns, especially when everyone you care about is still counting on you to be the same old Wes."

Nodding, I narrow my eyes, pondering the predicament, wondering if maybe we both need a break from our status quo. Maybe this last-minute trip is a blessing in disguise, a chance to connect with a side of ourselves we don't get to express in our everyday lives.

I love any excuse to let my hair down and play, whether it's running around the catering shop, pretending to be a witch with Chase, or putting on a goofy British accent with Mel while we make fish and chips. But I imagine a lawyer doesn't get as many chances to let his hair down.

And maybe that's just what Wes needs, a chance to be the man he is deep down inside, not the responsible guy everyone in his family counts on to be measured and reasonable all the time.

Our waiter arrives just as a plan begins to form. The tiny old woman with an apron full of pens takes our order for a bottle of the Cabernet Franc and the charcuterie board to start and departs.

Before Wes can start looking around the room and get freaked out again, I decide to apprise him of my brilliant idea. "You know what I think? I think we should do an experiment on this trip."

He sips his water. "What kind of experiment?"

"A 'be whoever you want to be' experiment. I'm the only person around who knows you, and I honestly don't know you that well. And to me, you aren't sweet, levelheaded Wesley McGuire. You're badass Wesley McGuire who saved my life in the woods and…" I trail off, blushing as I think of the other things he did to me in the woods, things that make me think of him as anything but "sweet." I clear my throat and add, "So, yeah. I don't have any preconceived notions. I'm a good travel buddy to have along if you want to feel free to be whoever you want to be."

A light flickers in his eyes. "It's so weird that you said that."

"I told you I was weird," I tease, and am rewarded by a smile.

"No, I mean…I was thinking the same thing. But I was thinking we could take it a step further. That we could pretend a little. Christian and Starling were in the middle of one of their role-playing things when I called him this morning and—"

"Role-playing?" My brows shoot up. "You mean...*role-playing* role-playing?"

"Well, yeah," he says, looking unsure of himself. "Sorry. I just assumed you'd heard about their leaked sex tape, the one where she was a princess and he was a serving boy or whatever? I obviously didn't watch it, but it was big news around town."

"Oh, I know. I heard about it. I just didn't realize it was an ongoing thing for them." I bite my lip, fighting a smile. "Are they always royalty or..."

Wes laughs and lifts his hands into the air, releasing his death grip on the menu for the first time since we sat down. "I don't know. We don't talk about the specifics. I just know it's something they really love. They were having a great time this morning, pretending Sterling was a sun goddess or something while they watched the sunrise."

I grin. "Sounds nice. They're a cute couple."

"They are," he agrees. "And I think they might be on to something. Sometimes it's nice to step outside the everyday and do something different, *be* someone different. Even if it's just for a little while. And I didn't mean anything...sexual. We could role-play as something purely platonic."

Our waiter returns at that moment, her perfect timing ensuring I have a few minutes to think about his suggestion as she pours the wine and assures us that the charcuterie board will be out in a few minutes. We place our entrée orders—the steak special for Wes and the sausage and pepper pasta for me—and she bustles off again.

When she's gone, I ask, "So who do you think we should be? Criminals on the run from the law? Two archeologists out in the field, hunting for fossils in the Utah desert?"

He grins, clearly pleased at my willingness to play along. "Interesting options. I honestly hadn't thought further than the suggestion. I just thought it might be a nice way for us to have a fresh start. Without any of the... regrettable stuff making the trip awkward. That way, we'd have the chance to see how we might have gotten along if—"

"If we hadn't had an illicit night in the woods and then things got really awkward for eighteen months?" I supply, seeing what he's up to now.

But I'm not angry about it.

In fact, I'm kind of...relieved.

I'm not good at holding grudges. Being angry with Wes and hurt by Wes, then awkward around him, once the anger and hurt faded, has sucked. And the whole Daria and Darcy thing has only made it suck more.

This is probably the only vacation I'll be able to take until late August, when I'm planning to tackle part of the Appalachian Trail on my solo trek. Do I really want to spend that being upset about Daria and angry at Wes all over again?

"Yeah," Wes says, his voice husky and low. "I'm sure that sounds selfish, and it is, I guess, a little. I just don't want to cause you any more pain and I thought, this might be a way to make the trip something you can truly enjoy."

I sip my wine, studying him over the rim of the glass. What do I have to lose? Just because Wes and I decide to let the past go for a week, doesn't mean I'm going to forget what happened. Once we're back home, all the history and drama and expectations from our family and friends will still be there. We'll have no choice but to deal with reality.

But until then...

I set my glass down. "All right."

His expression lifts. "Yeah? You want to give it a try?"

"I do," I confirm as a food runner delivers our charcuterie, a gorgeous spread that makes me at least ten percent happier just laying eyes on it. "Let's figure out who we want to pretend to be over meat and cheese."

He smiles like a kid set loose with a bag of potatoes and a sheet pan shield and I laugh.

"What?" he asks. "Am I too excited?"

I shake my head, still laughing, "No, you're funny. I like this silly side of you."

"And I love your dimple," he says fondly. "I've missed seeing it. You haven't smiled much around me lately."

I touch a finger to my right cheek. "You noticed that?"

"I did," he murmurs.

"I hated it when I was a kid. I thought it looked strange. Having a dimple on only one side and not the other."

"I think it's cute. Really cute," he says, reaching for a slice of salami. "So, we've established you're an extremely cute woman with an adorable dimple that I'm pretty obsessed with." He sighs dramatically. "It's a start, but we're going to need a lot more backstory."

Grinning, I agree, "So much more."

We spend the next hour and a half eating, drinking, and dreaming and it is, without a doubt, the best night I've had in ages. With our past set aside, Wes and I are free to be who we truly are, two people who get along really well. Who share similar senses of humor and taste in food and enjoy an impromptu juggling act when one breaks out at the table in the corner.

"I'm so glad the new me isn't afraid of clowns," Wes says when the show is over and the applause from the rest of the dining room has died down.

"Really?" I ask. "You don't feel sweaty and twitchy anymore?"

He laughs, leaning in as he whispers, "Maybe a little, but I'm going to fake it until I make it."

"Good for you," I say, hoping I can do the same.

Fake it until I've made it home and Wes and I can go back to politely avoiding each other.

But until then, I'm not going to think about the future. I'm going to be right here, right now, with my old friend, "Preston"—Wes's middle name—a treasure hunter who has a mission for us in the wilds of Southern Utah.

Chapter 15

WESLEY

It's an amazing night, the best I've had in ages.

The food is incredible, and the company is a hundred times better.

We finish our meal and head outside, to a sky dark and full of what feels like a million stars.

I stop beside the camper, tilting my head back. Beside me, Tessa does the same, sucking in a breath. "Wow," she whispers. "It's been way too long since I slowed down and looked up."

I hum in agreement. "Makes me feel small. In a good way."

She shifts to study my profile. "I say that all the time. About being outside. When I'm on a trail, I feel small in the best way. It's like suddenly I realize that all the things I've been worried about aren't such a big deal, after all."

I glance down at her, admiring the flush in her cheeks from the wine. She's even more beautiful like this, relaxed and well-fed and not worried about holding me at a distance. Reminding myself the only way to keep her that way is to keep this role-paying platonic—at least for now

—I refrain from telling her so, and simply add, "I get it. It makes me feel braver, too. When I think about how that tree in front of me is probably two hundred years old, and I only have half that time on earth, if I'm lucky... Makes you realize there's no time to waste playing it safe or holding back."

She smiles and leans in, nudging my arm with her shoulder. "I'd say you're doing a great job of being brave. Especially tonight. You walked out of there like you didn't have a clown care in the world. I was proud of you, Preston."

Grinning at my new name—I've always thought my middle name sounded more exciting than my given one—I tip my head in acknowledgement of the compliment. "Thank you, Lady Gray."

She giggles in response. "Is it wrong that I love our code names so much? They make me a little giddy." She bites her lip and rolls her eyes back toward the stars. "Either that or the wine." She sighs. "Should we take a walk around the park across the street before we head to the campsite? Or are you okay to drive?"

"I'm fine to drive," I say, reaching for the keys. "I'm bigger than you are. And I ate a lot more food. Besides, we need to get set up so we can start researching our treasure hunt. I don't want to leave Utah empty-handed."

She claps her hands. "Me, either. This is so exciting! Even better than a scavenger hunt. I loved those when I was a kid."

"Me, too," I say, never happier to be a nerd who follows treasure-hunting blogs. Like Tessa, I loved scavenger hunts as a kid and the idea that somewhere out there, mysterious treasures are waiting to be found. It isn't about the money for me, it's about the adventure.

"So, you really think we'll have several hunts to choose from?" she asks as I open the passenger door for her. We've decided to leave Freya in her crate until we're set up at the campsite, reducing the chances that she'll run off while we're hooking up water and electric and fetching wood for a campfire.

"Yeah, I think so. If we don't mind driving a little." Once I'm buckled in, I set off down the narrow road leading to the campsite, regaling her with tales of Montezuma's cursed treasure, an evil Spanish priest's ill-gotten gold, and Butch Cassidy's outlaw stash.

"Wow." She cracks the window, inhaling the sweet, grass-scented air. This area will be bone dry in a couple months, but for now, the grasslands are alive with smells and the sounds of insects humming in the cool night. "I think we're going to need a wardrobe adjustment."

I grin and tease, "Indiana Jones hat?"

She laughs. "I mean, yeah. Why not? I'd also enjoy a white linen shirt and some vintage khakis, but I can make do with my Gore-Tex hiking apparel, if needed. But the hat is non-negotiable. After we research treasure-hunting locations, I'll do some research on where to buy matching hats." She reaches out, her fingers lingering on my arm for a beat, even that brief contact making my blood pump faster. "You don't mind matching, do you?"

"Mind?" I scoff. "I insist on it. Every good team needs a uniform."

"We should get something for Freya, too. A brow ribbon or something. I doubt she'll tolerate a hat, even if we could find one small enough. She has very little patience for dressing up aside from ribbons and the occasional stretchy vest. The one time I put her in a dress, I thought she was going to have an aneurysm. She threw herself on the ground and thrashed until she was exhausted, then refused to move until I took it off."

"I think Christian did the same thing when our cousins dressed him up in their old pageant dresses when he was little," I say, shrugging as I add, "I didn't mind it, myself. Dresses are comfortable and good for airflow."

She giggles. "Tell me someone took pictures."

"For sure. Mom still has them in a family album somewhere. Me, Christian, Matty, and Melissa all dressed up in big floofy gowns. I don't know who was angrier, Christian or Mel. She hated girl clothes when she was a kid."

Tessa hums low in her throat. "I'm not surprised. She doesn't love them now. I can count the times I've seen her in a dress on one hand. Including last night." She runs a hand through her hair and leans forward as we near the gates. "Oh no, it looks like the check-in kiosk is closed."

"It's okay. I paid for our spot online and they sent directions for check-in and check-out. And there's a caretaker on site if we run into trouble. We're spot sixty-nine."

"You're kidding," she says with a soft snort. "Sorry. I have the sense of humor of a teenage boy sometimes."

I grin. "No, I'm not kidding. The website said it had one of the best views of..." I trail off with a chuckle. "Well, you'll see tomorrow morning."

"What will I see?"

I shrug. "The view. Unless the moonlight is bright enough to see it tonight."

She glances outside. "Maybe. It's pretty bright, but the moon won't be full for another four days."

"How do you know that?" I ask.

She shrugs. "I don't know. It's always just been something I keep track of. I don't like to miss a full moon if I can help it. It's a good day for tapping into cosmic energy." She lowers her voice before whispering, "I'm a little witchy, but in a nice way. I don't talk about it much, though. People in Bad Dog can still be kind of old-fashioned about stuff like that."

I slow as we near the end of a long row of mostly empty campsites. "Afraid you'll get burned at the stake?"

She laughs. "Um, yeah? A little? But that could just be PTSD from my mom finding all my crystals and spell book when I was a teenager. She threw everything away and made me have a meeting with Pastor Bob. Come to find out later, Pastor Bob was way more dangerous than my moon power spells. He was having an affair with one of the girls I went to school with, while she was still in high school."

"Gross," I say, my lip curling. "What's wrong with men like that? The thought of being involved with a girl that young literally turns my stomach."

"Well, we all know you prefer older women," Tessa says, making my focus jerk her way. She grins, adding, "I mean, Darcy is older than you are, right? Binx mentioned that Daria was thirty-four. Seeing as they're twins, I'm assuming Darcy is the same age."

"Yeah. She's about a year and a half older than I am." I swing into the empty spot across from ours so I can back into number sixty-nine. "But age doesn't really matter to me. As long as the woman isn't too much younger. I wouldn't trust that someone too much younger than I am is ready for a serious commitment."

"And you are?" Tessa asks as I angle the camper into our spot, stopping once the front of the vehicle is well out of the road.

I shift into park and shut off the engine before giving her my full attention. "Yeah, I am. With the right person." I nod outside. "I think I can see the view. Want to check it out before we hook up and set Freya free?"

"Yeah," she says, unbuckling her belt. "She's probably asleep, anyway. If she weren't, she'd be scratching at the door by now. She's had a big day."

"We all have," I agree. "We can still have an early night if you want. Save the treasure scouting research for tomorrow."

"Hell no," she says, making me smile. "I'm wide awake. Could be the coffee from earlier, but I think it's the excitement. If we find treasure, I'm using my half to buy a food truck. I used to think I wanted to open a restaurant, but a food truck is way better. Lower overhead, increased flexibility with location, and you can park it and take time off without paying rent. It's the perfect low-stress food service option."

"And what if we find enough to make us both billionaires?" I ask as we disembark, though I know the chances of that are slim to none. Even the largest of Utah's lost treasures wouldn't fetch that high a price. "Ever thought about what you'd do if you never had to work another day in your life?"

We start toward the back of the camper, side by side in the darkness, our eyes slowly adjusting to the dim light.

"I haven't," Tessa says. "But if I had all the money in the world, I think I'd still want to do something you know? And probably something with food. Life would be boring without a sense of purpose, and I love feeding people. It makes me feel useful, and important in a weird way. Food gives people comfort as well as fuel. I like being part of that comfort."

"Same," I say. "I know I do important work for my clients. I wouldn't want to give that up entirely, but I would love more time outside. In my ideal world, I'd work November to April and hike and adventure May to October."

"That sounds amazing," she says, "I—" She breaks off, laughing as she comes to a stop just a few feet from the back of the camper. "You've got to be kidding me."

"What?" I ask.

She points at the landscape ahead of us. "There. See it?"

I squint into the distance, but all I see are dark shadows on the horizon. The stars are still out, but a few clouds have rolled in, blocking the moonlight.

"Wait for it," Tessa says, looping her arm through mine. "The moon is about to come out from behind the clouds."

She's right. In a few moments, the clouds float away on the breeze, and I'm treated to my first glimpse of Buffalo Dick, silhouetted against the starry sky.

Tessa snorts. "It's a rock penis."

"It's Buffalo Dick," I say, earning another snort of laughter from my equally adolescent partner in crime. "That's what the Native Americans called it anyway. The white settlers tried to give it a more euphemistic name, but it didn't stick."

"White people." Tessa clucks her tongue. "Why do we have to be so uptight?"

"Puritanical origins, I guess? And it *was* the 1850s."

"Even in the 1850s, a dick by any other name is still a dick." She grins and lifts an imaginary glass. "Here's to you, Buffalo Dick. Long may you shadow the plains with your erect and noble bearing."

I laugh. "We can hike up there tomorrow, if you want. There's a trail. If you'd like a more up close and personal view of the...erection."

She snorts again, but shakes her head. "Nah, we have treasure to hunt. We should save our hiking legs for the mission, Preston." She glances up at me, the moonlight caressing her pale face. "Is it okay that we're still talking about our real lives, while pretending to be treasure hunters?"

"I think anything we say is okay," I tell her, struck all over again by how beautiful she is. With Tessa it's more than just her objectively attractive outsides, it's the way she's so completely herself, with no apologies. She has nothing to hide and nothing to prove and that's...sexy as fuck. "It's our game, after all."

She smiles. "It is." She goes quiet, studying the obscene plateau for another beat before she adds in a whisper, "And you'll really stop to buy Indiana Jones hats tomorrow? If I find a place? You aren't going to poo poo the fun when the sun's out and you're sober?"

"I told you, I'm already sober. And I'm no fun poo-pooer, Lady Gray. If being a family law attorney has taught me anything, it's that there's plenty of suffering in the world. Policing the fun is the last thing we need." I glance to our left, where our closest neighbors—a family of clowns, still in costume—are also out admiring the view. "Even if someone's idea of fun is putting on creepy white makeup and bringing nightmares to life."

Tessa chuckles as she takes my hand. "Don't worry, Preston. I'll protect you from clowns in the dark."

I curl my fingers tighter around her softer, smaller ones. "How did you know they're scarier in the dark?"

"Everything is scarier in the dark," she says. "Well,

almost everything. Come on, let's start a fire and I'll bring Freya outside on her leash. She said she wanted to look at the stars with you."

"Oh yeah?" I ask as we turn back toward the camper, moving through the short grass. "She said that?"

"Well, not in so many words. But when you tackled her at the park, she didn't bite your face off. That's a *really* good sign."

I smile. "Good. I like good signs. And my face."

"Me, too," she murmurs, her hand still in mine, which, for me, is the best sign of all.

Chapter 16

TESSA

Thanks to red wine, I sleep surprisingly well, especially considering Wes is in the bunk right above me, smelling like sexy man and campfire and making me ache to climb up and join him. But the wine works its magic and I'm out cold before I can find the courage to ask if he thinks Preston and Lady Gray should be lovers.

Of course, they shouldn't!

Things feel good between us for the first time in ages. Having hot, carnal, pull-my-hair-and-talk-dirty-to-me sex is what got us into trouble the first time. We're clearly better off as friends.

Last night was "just friends," and it was lovely.

Right... Because you always hold hands with your guy friends and think about how gorgeous they look in the moonlight. You should back out of this role-playing nonsense and rent a solo cabin as soon as you get to the park.

"Oh, hush," I mutter to the inner voice as Freya sniffs every square inch of the grass behind our camper, dooking urgent warnings about all the animals that were close to our home on wheels last night.

She glances over her shoulder as I speak with a look that asks "are you kidding me?"

"I wasn't talking to you, love," I assure her. "I was talking to myself. The voice of reason isn't going to ruin the fun this time. I'm too excited about hunting Butch Cassidy's treasure."

Saying his name aloud is enough to send a delicious shiver of anticipation down my spine. Our research around the campfire last night revealed the suspected resting place of Butch Cassidy's stash is only a little over an hour from the Arches National Park campground.

Another big bonus? It sounds like the treasure least likely to be cursed.

Butch Cassidy wasn't a good guy by any stretch of the imagination, but his sins were of the common criminal variety, and he was famous for doing his best to avoid killing people during his robberies. The other treasures were far more problematic. Montezuma was said to have cursed his treasure before he died and the Spanish priest who enslaved the Native Mexicans, forcing them to forge crosses from his stolen gold before he buried it in the desert, surely left an ugly psychic stain on everything he touched.

I'm all about the adventure, but my luck is bad enough without adding a curse on top of it.

Though, I don't feel unlucky this morning...

With the sun warm on my face, the breeze ruffling Freya's fur as she explores, and the proud shadow of Buffalo Dick stretching nearly a mile across the prairie in the early morning light, I feel like a million bucks.

And like I'm exactly where I'm supposed to be.

For some people, home is a place or a person. For me, it's this feeling, of being out under the endless sky, connected to nature in all its peace and beauty.

I pull in a deep breath, holding it in my lungs as I send out a silent thank you to the planet for being so fantastic. In times when the world feels dark and hopeless, I try to look back on moments like this. Moments when I feel the deep, steady pulse of Mother Nature and know she's going to be all right in the end, even if Homo sapiens end up destroying ourselves. Our planet will heal and foster new life, continuing to be glorious long after humans are fairy tales told around the campfire of whatever species rises to take our place.

"I'm voting for cockroaches," I tell Freya as she leads the way back to the camper, picking up the pace as she spots Wes putting shredded chicken into her bowl atop the picnic table.

His smile widens as we approach. "What a gorgeous morning."

"Perfect," I agree.

He pulls in a deep breath. "I wish I could spend every day like this. Out in nature, away from screens and all the problems humanity creates for itself."

"I was just thinking the same thing," I murmur, resisting the urge to lean into his strong chest and give him a hug.

Promising myself we can hug if we find Butch Cassidy's treasure—such a find would require a hug-level celebration—I ask, "Did you find a campsite for the night?"

"I did," he says as I loop Freya's leash around one leg of the table and set her on top to have her meal. "But we're going to need our fleece jackets if we go out to dinner. It's still cold near Aspen. The ski resorts are closed, but we're looking at a high of forty-eight today and a low near thirty tonight."

I clap my hands. "Yay! I love frosty evenings in the mountains. And I found an outdoor store just outside of Denver that has wide-brimmed fedoras in stock. It's only ten minutes out of our way."

Wes's eyes light up. "Awesome. Do they sell bikes? I was thinking mountain bikes might be a good thing to have. I'm not sure how deep into the desert we'll have to go on our hunt. Might be nice to have wheels."

Collecting a banana from the plate of snacks Wes brought out for breakfast, I nod. "It sure would…if we could both ride bikes."

His brows shoot up. "You can't ride a bike?"

"I don't think so. I haven't tried it since I was a tiny kid. My parents moved to a house on a gravel road when I was seven and there was nowhere to ride. I almost tried again when I was on vacation in my twenties, but my boyfriend complained about the price of renting beach cruisers in Santa Monica, we got into a big fight, and ended up throwing sand at each other instead."

"Jerk. A bike rental is always a worthwhile expense," he says. "And I've been wanting to buy a dirt bike for a couple years now. I'll get one for me and one for you. If you don't like it, we can always give it to Binx when we get home. She's a big bike rider."

I nod, frowning. "Right, but did you miss the part about me not being able to ride this bike?"

"You'll be fine," he says, biting into his apple and grinning as he chews. "That's why the phrase is 'just like riding a bike' not 'just like factoring a quadratic equation.' It'll come back to you like that." He snaps his fingers, earning a clucking sound from Freya that sounds way too much like a laugh.

"I think Freya's amused," I say dryly, as Wes chuckles along with my traitorous pet. "Or looking forward to how stupid I'm going to look before I go flying over the handlebars."

"Never. You're going to do great." He glances back my way, grinning. "But we'll get you a good helmet, just in case."

A little over nine hours later, after eating our sandwiches on the road to save time, and only stopping once for gas, we're pulling into Trout World, an outdoor store so enormous we might need mountain bikes to get all the way around it in the thirty minutes we've allotted for the stop.

I tell Wes as much and he laughs. "Nah, I know my way around a Trout World. If you've been to one, you've been to them all."

"No way," I say, sticking close as he sets off diagonally through the woman's fashion department, bound for signs that read "snow and ski" and "water sports." "There's more than one of these?"

"It's a chain," he says. "There's one not far from Minneapolis. Matty and I make a trip out there for fishing equipment before the big family party on the lake every summer."

"That party is so fun," I say, practically skipping past the snowboard display. "I get so sunburned every year, but it's worth it. The pool noodle game Binx invented is my favorite."

Wes grins at me over his shoulder. "I love that one, too. Hopefully, she'll still want to play this year. What with my mom and dad giving her such a hard time."

Some of my giddiness fading, I ask, "Can't you say something to them on her behalf? I mean, she shaved her hair off to raise money for a little girl's surgery. That's the sweetest. They would be so proud if they knew."

His grin fades. "Yeah, but..."

My brows shoot up. "What? You don't think it would make a difference? I mean, your mom is set in her ways, but she'd do anything for a kid in need. I would think she'd be proud that her daughter is doing the same."

Wes sighs, pausing at the intersection between life jackets and inflatable water toys before turning right. "I'm sure she would, but Binx will kill me if I tell them. She doesn't want them to accept that she shaved her head because she did it for a good cause. She just wants them to accept it, accept *her*, full stop."

"Yeah, I get that," I say. "Still, if it were me, I'd be tempted to tell them, just to smooth things over. Especially considering they're probably too old and set in their ways to change at this point."

He grunts. "Binx would say that kind of thinking is what allows assholes to keep being assholes and that age isn't an excuse for acting like a bag full of dicks."

I laugh. "She *would* say that. I love her. I wish I were that badass and firm in my beliefs, especially at her age."

"I think it's easier at her age," Wes says. "When I was twenty-six, I thought I had a good handle on what was right and wrong. Now..." He shrugs. "The older I get, the more I realize life is...complex. Occasionally things are black and white, but most of the time they're confusing shades of gray. Makes decision-making and standing firm in your convictions a lot harder."

I want to ask him if the situation with Darcy was a shade of gray and to tell him that I understand if it was. I've obviously never had a partner tell me he was pregnant, but if one of my exes had dropped an emotional bombshell on me right as I was planning to end things, I probably would have hesitated, too. Whether a relationship is going to work long term or not, I wouldn't want to hurt someone I cared about, or abandon them in a time of need.

Especially if their "time of need" was something I had contributed to creating, like a baby...

I was only weird about hearing his explanation because pregnancy is a triggering topic for me. Probably the most triggering. Being continuously rejected by potential partners for not being able to have babies, while also coming to terms with the fact that I can't have biological children, has been one of the most painful disappointments in my life.

Which is one of the many reasons it would be a good idea to come clean with Wes about my infertility. That way he can stop flirting with me, embrace our destiny as "just friends," and we can put that steamy night behind us, once and for all. There's no chance that Wes doesn't want children. He said he wanted them yesterday and having big, boisterous families is practically compulsory for the McGuires. It's as much a part of them as their dark hair, bright eyes, and killer senses of humor.

My lips part, the words on the tip of my tongue, but I swallow them down.

This isn't the time. We're on a mission for treasure-hunting supplies. We're Preston and Lady Gray, and

Preston and Lady Gray aren't concerned about things like infertility or incompatibility. They just want to find the gold and become part of a Wild West legend.

Ignoring the annoying voice in my head, assuring me I'm a coward living in a dream world, I point to the sign dangling from the ceiling not far ahead. "There! Hats!"

Dashing to the aisle, I breeze past the baseball caps, easily finding the Indiana Jones'-style fedoras and reverently plucking one from the shelf. I plop it on my head, turning to ask Wes, "How do I look?"

"Like a professional," he says with an approving nod. "Though you might want a larger size." He presses down on the top of the hat, only for it to pop right back up again. "Have to take the hair into account."

I take the hat from my head, handing it to him. "You're right. My brain is also very large, in addition to my hair. But this one will probably fit you."

He snorts. "With my much smaller brain?"

I shoot him a grin as I sift through the remaining hats, looking for a larger one. "It's okay. You probably use a lot more of it, percentagewise, than other small-brained people. I mean, you *are* a lawyer. That's not easy. You have to hold laws and precedents and all the facts of a case in your head. All I have in mine is an endless supply of recipes and acid and fat combinations."

He settles the hat low over his forehead, making me hum with appreciation. "Acid and fat?"

"It's the secret to leveling up any dish," I say as I finally find a size large. "Make sure you have a harmonious combination of acid and fat. They're like the yin and yang of cooking. You need a blend of hard and soft for a well-balanced meal."

"A well-balanced person, too," he says, tipping his

brim up, catching my gaze from underneath with a perfect Indiana Jones smirk. "I guess that's why I am the way I am."

"What way is that?" I murmur.

His eyes take on that piercing quality familiar from our first night in the woods. "You know."

I *know*...

His meaning hits and my cheeks flush. I *do* know. I know that Wesley is a sweetheart on the street and a filthy beast in the sheets. I also know it's probably one of my favorite things about him.

But it's not something I should be thinking about.

Not something we should be talking about.

And definitely not a reason to beg him to kiss me senseless against the hat shelf.

Thankfully, Wes turns away before I can do something I'll regret, announcing, "On to the bikes. We're burning daylight, Lady Gray. If we want to be settled in our campsite before dark, we have to stay focused."

Focused. It's good advice, but as we reach the bike section and Wes helps me try out several models, hovering behind me as I take increasingly confident rides down the wide aisles, it's easier said than done.

The feel of his hand on my back as he steadies me, the way he crouches beside my knee, his breath warm on my thigh as he adjusts my seat, all of it combines to leave me a tingling, aching mess by the time we've picked our bikes and rolled them toward the checkout.

I don't want to resist this man or be one of the many people who only know one side of him. I want to tackle him in the sleeping bag aisle and bite his gorgeous, muscled bicep while he fucks me like a freight train.

"Does that work for you?" he asks, turning from the checkout to arch a brow my way.

Blushing again, I stammer, "S-sorry, I was...wrestling with mind squirrels. What did you say?"

"The ten-year extended warranty. It's only thirty dollars extra per bike. Is that something you think you would use? It covers parts and labor and, like I said, there's a Trout World not far from Bad Dog."

I nod. "Sure, yeah, that sounds great. I can always borrow a friend's truck if I need to take it in. I don't think I'd be able to fit it in the back of the Jetta, even with the front wheel off and the seat down."

"I'll take it in for you," he says, slipping his credit card into the machine. "Anytime. All you have to do is ask."

All I have to do is ask...

I have a feeling the same could be said about the freight train fucking, but it would be such a bad idea. There's no future for Wes and me beyond this week. Things are too complicated back home. And even if Daria and Darcy both magically disappeared, his family is basically my surrogate family. I can't afford to lose them if Wes and I end badly.

Or just...end.

And we would end. All things end, especially romantic things. At least, for me. If my life thus far has taught me anything, it's that.

The thought helps tamp down the ache between my thighs. By the time we reach the camper, I've nearly convinced myself the ache is just tenderness from being on a bike for the first time in decades.

Still, who knows what might have happened if Wes and I had made it to Aspen on time. If we'd ridden our bikes to a gorgeous lookout, gotten drunk on snowy mountain views, and forgotten all the reasons it's best to keep our hands to ourselves.

But we don't make it to Aspen on time.

Instead, Wes opens the storage area in the back to reveal a small clown curled up in a nest made of our sleeping bags and extra blankets, my ferret napping on her wig, and we suddenly have much bigger problems.

Chapter 17

WESLEY

My first thought is that the little girl with the smeared white makeup, curled up in our sleeping bags, is dead.

My brain screams statistics about how long a small child can survive locked in a hot car, while my stomach bottoms out and my palms go cold and clammy on the handles of my new bike.

But then, the child shifts in her sleep, and I remember that it's spring in the Colorado mountains. It's too cool to worry about a vehicle overheating. We didn't crack a window for Freya for just that reason. It's chilly outside and with Freya loose in the camper, Tessa didn't want to risk her clawing a hole through a screen and getting out.

"Come here, Freya," Tessa whispers, making me flinch as the ferret suddenly materializes from the child's bright red wig.

"Shit," I curse beneath my breath. "I didn't see her there."

"She must have crawled in through the storage area

beneath the banquet," Tessa says, nodding toward the extra storage on the right side of the vehicle as she gathers Freya into her arms. "Hopefully she kept the little pumpkin company." She shakes her head with a sigh. "She must have been back here the entire time. Since we left the campground."

I drag a hand through my hair. "Why didn't we see her? I swear, there was no one back here when I loaded the chairs and camping supplies this morning. And why didn't she call out for help at some point? Especially when we stopped for gas. I was standing right there." I motion toward the gas tank. "Just a few feet away."

Tessa shakes her head. "I don't know. But we have to report this right away. Hopefully, the police will believe it was all an accident."

I gulp. "God, yeah. I didn't even think of that." I reach for my phone only to abandon the mission before I pull it out of my back pocket. "Should we wake her up first? Get her name? Her parents' names? Maybe she knows a phone number we can call?"

Tessa hums doubtfully. "She's awfully young, but we can try. Here, hold Freya." She passes the fretfully clucking ferret into my arms—Freya seems worried about our stowaway, too—before leaning down to touch a gentle hand to the girl's shoulder. "Sweetheart? Hello? Can you hear me, honey? My name is Tessa. I think you fell asleep in the wrong camper."

The little girl's lashes blink open. She reaches up, rubbing a small fist into her sleepy eyes, smearing her makeup more, before slowly sitting up. She glances around her before shifting her gaze back to Tessa, her bottom lip beginning to wobble.

Instantly, Tessa drops to a squat, bringing her face even with the child's as she reaches out to pat her small shoe. "Oh, honey, no, don't be scared. We're not going to hurt you, I promise. We just want to help you find your family and get you home safe."

The child sucks in a shaky breath and tears roll down her pudgy cheeks, breaking my heart in the process. Freya's dooking grows more concerned, as if she, too, is trying to comfort the little girl.

"She's right," I add in a gentle voice. "We just want to help. Can you tell us your name? Or your mom or dad's name? That would help us find a way to get in touch with them."

The girl gulps and shakes her head, pointing one trembling finger to her face.

"You can't talk?" Tessa asks.

The girl nods and her shoulders begin to shake.

"Oh, honey, it's okay," Tessa says, moving to sit beside her, resting a hand on her back. "Can I give you a hug? Would that be okay?"

The girl lunges into Tessa's side, wrapping her small arms tightly around her waist. Tessa hugs her back, stroking her wig as she murmurs soothing words I can't quite make out.

After a few moments, she shoots me a pleading look.

I bite my lip, trying to think of any other way to identify this poor kid. "I'm pretty sure there's pen and paper in one of the cabinets inside," I say, inspiration striking. "Can you write your name for us, buddy?"

The little girl looks up from Tessa's chest, where she's smeared white makeup all over her gray sweatshirt. She shakes her head again and pops her thumb into her mouth.

"I think she's too young," Tessa whispers. "Probably three or four. Still in preschool." She raises her voice a bit as she asks, "How old are you, honey?"

The girl sits up a little and holds out four tiny fingers.

Tessa nods. "Yeah, that's what I thought."

I sigh. "Okay. I'll just have to tell the police what we know. It isn't much, but..."

"I think so. Hopefully her family has reported her missing, and they'll know who we're talking about." She brushes a few strands of the girl's curly wig from her forehead before her hand drifts down to finger the ruffled collar of the clown costume. "Wait a second, Wes. Let me check something..."

"Okay," I say, my thumb hovering over the keypad on my cell.

"My mom used to write my name on the tags in all my school uniforms. And a clown costume is kind of a like a uniform." She cups the girl's cheek in her palm and leans down. "Can I peek at the back of your costume, honey? See if your mom might have written your name there?"

The girl's eyes widen, and she nods faster, hope blooming in her eyes.

"She did? Oh, that's great news!" Tessa smiles, exhaling a relieved laugh as she reaches beneath the rumpled wig and finds the tag. Her smile widening, she says, "Maddie Evans? And your phone number is 555-555-8989?"

The girl nods so hard that her wig flops off, revealing sweat-damp blond curls.

Tessa laughs. "Amazing." She glances at me. "Want me to read that again? I figure we should call the parents first, right? If I were a mom, I'd want to know my baby was safe as soon as possible."

"Absolutely," I agree. "I remember the number." I tap it in, my heart racing as I put the phone to my ear. "Fingers crossed they answer when they see an unknown—"

Before I can finish, the call connects and a panicked female voice asks, "Hello? Who is this?"

"Hello," I say, in my best "soothing a panicked client who was just served with unexpected papers" voice. "My name is Wesley McGuire. My friend Tessa and I were camping near Mama Maria's restaurant last night. We pulled out early this morning and just now stopped to load a few things into the back of our vehicle. When we opened the storage area, we found Maddie asleep in our sleeping bags."

The woman emits a strangled sound of relief. "Oh my God. Is she okay? Is she hurt? What happened?"

"She seems fine," I say. "But she indicated to us that she can't speak so we aren't sure how she got here or—"

"The makeup," the woman cuts in with what sounds like a cross between a laugh and a sob. "It's the makeup. She knows she's not supposed to talk when she's clowning, and we didn't take her makeup off last night. She fell asleep in the hammock before we could, so we just tucked her into bed. Then, this morning, she and the other kids were playing hide and seek, and she was the only one who wasn't found. We ran around the entire campground calling her name, telling her she was the winner and could come out and get her prize, but she never answered." She laugh-sobs again. "I was afraid she was stuck somewhere but wouldn't answer us because of the makeup. She's so young. I was afraid she might not understand that sometimes it's okay to break the rules." She sniffs. "Can you put her on the line? Let me tell her it's okay to talk to you guys?"

"Sure, I'll put you on speakerphone now." I do and lean down, holding my cell closer to Maddie as I add, "You're on speakerphone, and Maddie's listening. Maddie your mom wants to talk to you."

"Hey, baby," her mom says, her voice sending fresh tears springing into Maddie's eyes. "It's okay to talk with your makeup on. You're lost and when you're lost you have to do whatever it takes to be found. Even break the clowning rules. Okay? So can you tell me what happened? And if you're okay? Are you hurt?"

"No," Maddie whispers, her little voice wobbling. "But I want to come home. I'm sorry I did bad hide and seek, Mommy."

"Oh, you didn't do bad hide and seek, honey," her mother says, her voice shaky, too. "You didn't do anything wrong. Daddy and I should have been keeping a closer eye on you. You're still too little to play with the big kids without a grown-up around. That's my fault, and I'm so sorry."

"I want to be with you, Mommy. I don't like playing with the big kids," Maddie says, sniffling. "I want to go home."

"And we'll have you home in no time, I promise," her mom says. "Just let me talk to the nice man who found you and we'll figure this all out, okay? Just be brave for a little longer, and we can forget that this horrible day ever happened. Can you do that?"

Maddie nods and says, "Yes, Mommy."

"I'll take you off speakerphone while we figure things out," I tell Mrs. Evans.

Mrs. Shirley Evans, I find out, after we've spoken for

several minutes. She explains that while they're still at the campground—they've been helping volunteers search for Maddie in the grasslands surrounding the site all day—she has a sister who lives close to Denver, about two hours away. Maddie loves her aunt Frannie, and will be good to stay with her until they can get packed up and on their way.

"I'll explain everything to the police," Shirley finishes. "But they'll probably want to speak with you anyway. Can I give them this number?"

I assure her that she can, she thanks me again, and I put her back on speakerphone to tell Maddie goodbye and explain that Aunt Frannie will be on the way to get her very soon.

"And in the meantime, your mom said we could take you for an early dinner at The Burger Palace just over there," I say, pointing to the brightly colored restaurant across the complex from Trout World. "Does a cheeseburger sound good?"

For the first time, Maddie smiles. "I love cheeseburgers."

Her mom laughs. "You sound happier already. I knew a cheeseburger would make it all better. Just eat your burger and all your fries and relax with the nice people, okay? And then Aunt Frannie will be there to take you to her house and Daddy and I will be there as soon as we drive from the campground. We love you so much, Maddie, and we're so glad you're okay."

"Love you, too, Mommy," Maddie says.

I end the call only for my cell to ring a few minutes later, after we've tucked Freya into her crate and started across the parking lot. It's the Sioux Falls Sherriff's Department. I answer, remaining outside the restaurant to tell my story to law enforcement. The man takes down my statement and explains that Mrs. Evans has waived his offer to have a uniformed officer sent over to sit with Maddie until her aunt arrives.

"She trusts you," the man says, clearly not thinking it's the best idea.

"We won't give her any reason to regret that," I assure him. "Thanks for your time and feel free to call if I can clarify anything in the future."

I push inside, pausing as I see Maddie and Tessa giggling together at a table in the corner. They're bent over one of those coloring pages they give kids at restaurants, scribbling away with mischievous looks on their faces. Maddie looks like a completely different kid than the shattered girl we found in our storage area a half hour ago, and that's all because of Tessa. I know I wouldn't have been able to comfort her as well or as easily, no matter how hard I tried.

Tessa has a way with kids. My nephew Chase adores her. He runs to greet "Auntie Tessa" the second she arrives at one of our family gatherings, and that's not something he does for any of his other aunts, not even Binx, who lets him ride the quarter-operated merry-go-round at the bank where she works as many times as he wants. (And gives him extra lollipops to take home after Mel makes her deposits for the day.)

Tessa's special to Chase.

And to me.

I can't help thinking, as I cross the restaurant to join them, that I wouldn't mind this being my life someday. Solo adventures are fun, but not nearly as fun as an adventure with a gorgeous, fun, big-hearted woman. And if that woman were also the mother of my child?

It's a crazy thing to think, but I can't help it. After the pregnancy scare with Darcy, I convinced myself I wasn't ready to start a family.

But maybe I just wasn't ready to start a family with Darcy...

"Hey there, I ordered a burger for you with a side salad since you said you wanted something healthy, too," Tessa says, grinning up at me as I arrive at the table. "And now we're drawing clown noses and extra horns on all the animals. Would you care to join in?"

"I'd love to," I say, grabbing a crayon. "Can I give the turtle a mohawk?"

Maddie laughs. "That's silly."

"But we like silly?" I ask.

She nods. "I like silly. I make silly faces all the time in clown school."

I arch a brow. "Oh yeah? Can you show me one?"

Maddie's eyes fly open so wide she resembles an anime cartoon and her mouth rounds into a lopsided "oh!" that makes both Tessa and I laugh.

"Very good," Tessa says. "Clearly a girl who excels at her craft. I vote mohawks for all the animals."

By the time we add mohawks, clown noses, and a few heart-shaped tattoos to the coloring page's menagerie, our food has arrived. We eat slowly, but Maddie's aunt is still twenty minutes away when we finish, so we order a banana split to share.

When Aunt Frannie rushes in, her blue eyes the same hue as Maddie's and her hair a slightly darker shade of blond, Maddie's face is covered in chocolate ice cream and she's laughing like we've all been friends for ages.

The relief on her aunt's face as she crosses the dining room is palpable.

"Aunt Frannie!" Maddie jumps off her chair, dashing to her aunt, who swoops her up in a big hug.

"Maddie Bear," she says, cradling her close. "Man, we were scared. I'm so glad you're okay."

Maddie pulls back, gazing into her aunt's face. "I'm sorry. I already told mommy, I'm not going to play hide and seek ever again."

"Sounds good to me," Frannie says, glancing over her niece's head to us. "Thank you two so much. We're all so grateful that Maddie ended up with such kind people. What do I owe you for the dinner?"

I wave a hand, "Don't worry about it. It's our treat."

"We insist," Tessa cuts in. "It's no trouble at all. Maddie was so much fun to hang out with. I hope you have a safe ride to your aunt's house, Maddie. It was so nice meeting you."

"Nice meeting you, too," Maddie says, shier now that her aunt is here. She opens and closes her fingers to wave goodbye. "Thanks for the burger and fries and coloring and ice cream."

"You're so welcome," Tessa says, beaming at the little girl. "It was our pleasure. Take care and hug your mama tight tonight."

We say our goodbyes to Frannie and wave as she carries Maddie out to her car. When they're gone, I turn back to Tessa with a smile, "You did a great job with her. You've really got a way with kids. Have they always fallen in love with you at first sight?"

She pales as she glances down at her hands.

"I'm sorry," I say, sensing I've stepped in it somehow. "I just meant—"

"I need to tell you something," Tessa says as she glances up, her eyes shining, "But I need to get back to feed Freya first. She'll be upset if we don't let her out of her crate soon."

"Okay, of course," I say. "Whatever you need."

And I mean it. I want to give her whatever she needs.

I just need her to help me figure out what that is.

Chapter 18

TESSA

After our nearly three-hour delay—it took Frannie longer to reach us than Shirley expected—we decide against trying to make it all the way to Aspen. Wes cancels the campsite rental, and I look for a motel room nearby close to the highway.

But fifteen minutes later, I'm still searching and the sun is sinking low on the horizon.

"I guess we could camp in a Walmart parking lot," Wes says. "I hear they allow people to do that. But there wouldn't be any hookups for water, so no shower or flushing the toilet. Unless we bought a bucket and filled it with water, maybe?"

I shake my head, still scrolling. "No, I'll find something. I mean, this place just a few exits up has one cottage left, but..."

"But?" he prompts, his focus sliding my way.

I feel his gaze on my face but keep mine on my phone as I say, "It's a king-sized bed. Not two double beds. So..."

"Well, I don't mind sharing if you don't," he says.

"We can put a pillow barrier in the middle of the mattress if you want, and I promise I'll stay on my side."

"I'm not worried about that," I mumble.

"Then what are you worried about?"

"Nothing, I guess," I lie. "I'll book it."

I shouldn't be worried about anything. After all, there's no way forward for Wes and me in any version of the future. It won't matter that I can't have kids. He'll probably think I'm crazy for telling him—especially like this, like it's some kind of big deal and so upsetting I get teary when I think about it.

I don't usually get teary. It's just that Maddie was so sweet, and Wes was so good with her. He's clearly going to be an amazing father someday.

Someday in the future, when he finds a woman closer to his own age, one who can give him a family and the kind of life he wants. I might even get to be "Aunt Tessa" to his kids. Chase already calls me auntie and his cousin, Sara Beth, has started doing it, too. Pretty soon, I'll complete my metamorphosis into an honorary McGuire sibling.

Hell, maybe Wes will eventually come to think of me as a sister someday.

The thought makes me want to toss my cheeseburger.

"Everything okay?" he asks.

"Fine, why?" I say, finishing the booking.

"Your lip was all snarled up. Like you smelled something off."

I force a smile and reach for the GPS screen on the dashboard, typing in the motel address. "Sorry. My burger is talking back to me a little. I may take a walk when we get to the motel, just to help with digestion."

"All right," Wes says. "Is that going to be before or

after you tell me whatever you need to tell me? I don't want to pressure you, but I'd love to know what's on your mind. You can tell me anything, you know. I'll keep it to myself. I'm a vault. Ask any of my brothers and sisters. I'm the one they go to when they need to get something off their chest and don't want everyone else in the family to know about."

"It's nothing like that," I say, wishing I'd kept my mouth shut. "Not a big secret or anything. You'll probably wonder why I thought I should tell you in the first place, it's just..." I sigh, but I can't keep putting him off. It's best to get this out of the way now.

We'll be at the motel in ten minutes, and I can escape for a head-clearing walk, even if it's only around the parking lot a few dozen times.

Determined to keep things as light as possible, I keep my focus on the road ahead. "Sometimes I get a little emotional when people compliment my way with kids or tell me I'm going to be a great mom someday or...whatever." I swallow, my mouth suddenly dry. "Remember that old boyfriend I told you about? The one who didn't want to rent bikes in California?"

When I see Wes nod in my peripheral vision, I continue, "Yeah. Well, he wasn't good at having fun or driving. He insisted on trying to make it all the way home to Bad Dog on our second travel day. I begged him to pull over and get a room, but he insisted he could stay awake just fine. I tried to stay up with him, but eventually, I guess I passed out. When I woke up, the car was upside down and I had a piece of metal sticking out of my stomach."

Wes curses.

"Yeah, that's what I thought," I say, forcing a tight

smile. "Not a nice way to wake up from a nap, I'll tell you that. I was too scared to be mad at him at first, but once we were both out of surgery, and I knew we weren't going to die, I was so pissed." I clear my throat. "And that was before the doctor told me the shrapnel had destroyed my uterus. He'd hoped he would be able to repair it during surgery, but the damage was too extensive."

"I'm sorry, Tessa," Wes says, a sympathetic rumble vibrating his chest before he adds, "I had no idea."

I wave a hand. "Of course, you didn't. But yeah, so…I can't have biological children. It's something I've come to terms with, but sometimes I still get a little sad about it. I just can't help it, I guess."

He reaches out, resting a gentle hand on my knee. "You don't have to help it. Grief isn't a linear thing. It comes and goes. I still miss my grandpa all the time, and he died when I was a kid."

I nod. "Yeah, I know. I just hate pointless feelings. Feeling sad about what happened in the past isn't going to change the future. It just seems like a waste of time and energy."

His lips twitch. "Because human emotions are all about conserving time and energy. They're all so cooperative that way."

I laugh beneath my breath. "Good point."

He's quiet for a moment as he takes the exit and turns right on the two-lane highway that will lead us to Mother Meyer's Mountain Motor Lodge. "Can I ask kind of a personal question?"

"Sure. Shoot."

"Have you looked into egg harvesting at all? I mean, you can't carry a child, but if your ovaries weren't damaged, you might be able to retrieve eggs for a surrogate to carry down the line."

I sigh again, regretting taking a single step down this road. "I looked into having my eggs frozen when I was thirty-five. I probably should have done it sooner, when I was younger, and retrieving viable eggs might have been easier, but I didn't have the money until then. Freezing your eggs isn't cheap or covered by insurance, you know, and chefs don't make a ton of money unless they're working at a swanky place in the city." I stretch my neck to one side, rubbing at a knot that's suddenly formed there. "Anyway, it was too late. We tried one round of retrieval, but there was nothing viable. Either I was just born with fewer healthy eggs than other women or my ovaries were damaged in the crash, too. It doesn't really matter, I guess. The end result is the same. No biological children for me. Ever. Even if I met a wealthy Prince Charming willing to pay for expensive fertility treatments and started trying tomorrow."

"I'm sorry, I..." Wes trails off, his foot easing from the gas pedal. "Oh wow, is that..."

"Yeah, that's it." My eyes widening, I take in the small gingerbread-style house with a large red sign reading "Office Open" above the door. Behind it, a cracked and graying parking lot stretches toward the tree line, where several gloomy cottages crouch amidst the evergreen trees and melting snow. Brown grass pokes through the pavement, adding to the dilapidated vibe, but I can safely say I've never been so glad to see a seedy motel.

We're clearly going to be too busy dealing with the Mountain Motor Lodge crisis to keep talking about my gimpy lady parts, and I'm grateful.

"But the reviews said the rooms were super cute and very

clean," I add as Wes pulls into the lot and parks diagonally, taking up several spots. I frown, glancing around to see only two cars—a tiny red sedan parked behind the office and what looks like an abandoned gray van rotting in the shadows beside one of the larger cottages. "But why is there only one room available? It looks like we're the only ones here."

"Maybe everyone else is out getting dinner?" Wes asks, shifting the camper into park but keeping the engine running. "Or maybe they took one look at Mother Meyer's creepy fairy tale lair and kept driving?"

"It does look like a good place to get lured in by a candy shingle and end up in a witch's pot," I agree.

Wes grunts. "But we're a lot bigger than Hansel and Gretel. I guess we could head into the office and take a look around. If it seems sketchy or the room is awful, we can always leave."

"That's what every character who gets murdered in the first ten minutes of the horror movie says right before they walk into the killer's trap." I nibble my bottom lip. "But I'm up for it, if you are." I nod over my shoulder. "And we can bring Freya for backup. If anyone makes a move, you know she'll go straight for their crotch."

A wry smile stretches his lips. "I do know that. Firsthand." He shuts off the engine with a nod. "Okay then. Me, you, and Freya. And if they don't welcome ferrets, we take that as a sign to keep driving until we find a Walmart parking lot. I'll take point on bucket duty."

I snort and shake my head. "No, thank you. If a bucket is necessary, I'll handle it myself. I'm girly enough to want to maintain a certain air of mystery about my toileting activities."

He grins. "You're cute."

I roll my eyes. "I'm not. There's nothing cute about toilet stuff, I promise you."

"You're cute and nothing that comes out of you would change my mind about that."

"Ew, so gross. What's wrong with you?" I ask as I sneak through our seats to fetch Freya from her crate. But I'm secretly touched by his words and think he's pretty cute, too.

His smile widens. "I suspect many things are wrong with me. I may look like a mild-mannered lawyer, but I'm secretly kind of pumped at the thought of staying in this terrifying motel. Looks like a great place to run into Bigfoot after hours."

I strap Freya into her harness and stand with a shake of my head. "That sounds like Preston talking."

His green eyes light up. "Speaking of Preston, I hope they have Wi-Fi. Preston wants to do more research on Butch Cassidy's stash."

"Same," I agree, reaching for the door leading out of the main part of the camper. "I know it's probably crazy, but I really think we have a chance at finding it. I mean, someone has to stumble upon it, sooner or later, right? Why not us?"

"Why not us?" he echoes, his gaze caressing my face for a beat before he slides out of the driver's side.

I wait for him to circle around to meet Freya and me with a pleasant buzz flowing through my veins. I told him my secret and he's still looking at me like I'm someone precious and calling me "cute."

Maybe I was wrong about Wes. Maybe he isn't set on having children, or at least not biological children.

A part of me wants to ask how he feels about adoption. I mean, I thought I'd given up on the idea of having a family of my own, but...

I shake my head, reigning in my wild thoughts as we set off across the parking lot and keeping my lips zipped. My fertility confession can be explained away by the stress of our interaction with Maddie, but if I ask him about adoption, it's going to be clear why I'm curious.

Because I can't stop thinking about Wes as more than a friend.

I can't stop thinking about how much I'd like to kiss him again, yes, but it's more than physical attraction. I'm every bit as drawn to his curious mind, playful spirit, and good heart as I am to his lips and incomparable dick.

Though the dick *is* incomparable.

And if we decide to stay in the world's creepiest motel, I'll be sleeping in the same bed, just a few feet away from it and the tempting man it's attached to in just a few hours time...

Chapter 19

WESLEY

I want to talk more about kids and whether Tessa wants a family someday—whether that's through adoption or an egg donor or some other means I haven't thought of yet—but as usual, I'm getting way ahead of myself.

It's hard not to with Tessa.

Every minute we spend together only confirms my belief that I don't want to spend my minutes with anyone else. Not my romantic minutes, anyway. Before that first night in the woods, if you'd asked me if I believed in love at first sight, I would have rolled my eyes. I'd only been in love twice before and both times, the feelings came on slowly, gradually, a simmering pot that eventually came to a boil.

But the moment Tessa ran to me, her face streaked with tears, and I pulled her into my arms, I never wanted to let her go.

The past year and a half, being estranged from her and not knowing if she would ever even give me the chance to explain or apologize, has been pure hell. If I rush things, we might very well end up in the same place again. The fact that she trusted me with her private struggle is huge, but I still need to proceed with caution.

The last thing I want to do is scare her away.

Then you should probably get back on the road and find somewhere else to stay, the inner voice mutters as we step into the dimly lit office. *This place was clearly designed to scare people.*

"What's that smell?" Tessa whispers, her nose wrinkling, "It's like—"

"Vinegar and cloves!" a creaky feminine voice shouts from somewhere deeper in the cottage, behind the front desk and whatever room is concealed by the wall behind it. "Sorry! The smell is vinegar and cloves. I'm making pickles. Homemade sugar dills. They're going to be delicious when they're done, but you three won't be here for that. People never stick around for more than a night or two. There's just not enough to do around here. Though the trails are lovely in the summer. You should come back in the summer! And bring your ferret! Ferrets love a walk in the woods, though you can't push them too far. Thirty minutes is usually enough, but they're so small you can always carry them if you want to keep going. You could get a little sling, like the hippy moms put their babies in at the farmer's market."

"How is she seeing us?" I ask softly, glancing around the small office area, but unable to spot a camera.

Tessa shakes her head. "Or hearing us? I wasn't loud, was I?"

"Sorry! I have exceptional hearing. Just my silly superhuman skill. And I can see you in the mirror there by the deer heads. I'll be out to check you into your room in a minute."

Tessa and I exchange another baffled glance before inching forward to peer into the mirror. But the only thing looking back at us is our own reflection.

"Just need to get this last batch out of the hot water bath," the voice continues. "If you leave them in for more than twenty minutes, the cucumbers get mushy. My sister swears by twenty-five minutes, but she isn't the Meyer sister with three blue ribbons from the county fair for her sugar dills, now, is she?"

Tessa bites her lip, shooting me a "should we run now or later?" look.

I shrug, answering her with my best "I'm not sure, but this person doesn't seem dangerous, just strange" expression.

Before she can reply, a tiny woman with gray hair the same shade and texture as a used Brillo pad leaps out from the open doorway behind the desk. "You must be Tessa and Wesley!" she shouts, making us both flinch and Freya duck behind Tessa's leg. Cackling at our obvious surprise, she bounces over to her ancient computer, pushing her thick glasses up her nose before punching the keys with one gnarled finger. "I thought so. You look like a Tessa and Wesley." She glances up from her work, squinting. "Though I do think Wesleys are better when they're blond." She grins, baring large, white teeth, I'm guessing must be dentures. "But I've watched The Princess Bride too many times. Ever seen that movie?" She sighs, pushing on before either of us can answer, "As you wish... If I'd had a man say that to me, even once, I never would have let him out of my sight, even if he was just a farm boy."

She resumes tapping at her keyboard. "Okay, one night, two humans, one precious ferret that I'm assuming is potty trained." She looks up again, arching a thin white brow. "If she's not potty trained, you should take steps to make sure she doesn't make a mess in the room. I don't like to charge people's cards for damage, but I will if I have to. Gotta keep things tidy for the next guests. That's how I got my reputation as the nicest place to stay in town, and I don't intend to lose it."

Willing my face not to reveal my thoughts about this being "the nicest place in town" I assure her, "She's potty-trained and well-behaved."

"As long as you aren't threatening my welfare," Tessa adds. "She's very protective."

The woman nods, grinning. "Oh, they are. My little Diana was the same way. Never met a bad guy she wouldn't take on in my defense. One time a car full of addicts looking for drug money pulled in here with an eye to empty my cash register. Diana bit every last one of them right on the butt." She cackles. "They ran out of here so fast one of them fell over the porch railing and into the horse trough. I had a trough out there back then for the horse people. We don't get them around here anymore, though—too many cryptid encounters—so I took it out." She hoots again, slapping the counter. "But man, did they look funny dripping wet and clutching at their backsides as they piled into that old car."

"Cryptid encounters?" Tessa asks, her brows sliding up her forehead as she glances my way. She mouths, "Like Bigfoot?"

"Sure enough," Mrs. Meyer says. "Got a few different kinds, but the Tommyknockers are the ones who really put the horse people off. Your average Sasquatch is a shy creature. It sees someone coming and runs off into the woods to hide, unless it's a mama with a baby to protect, and she feels you're getting too close to her little one. But Tommyknockers?" She shakes her head as she taps a button, sending the printer behind her jolting to life. "Those little monsters love to dig holes on the trails, cover them up with leaves, and wait for a horse to come by and break an ankle. It's just cruel. My friend Zeke doesn't think they realize how much damage they're doing, but I've looked a Tommyknocker in the face more than once. Not a shred of empathy in their miserable little bodies."

She fetches the paper from the printer and slaps it down on the counter with a big grin. "Now, who's going to sign? Whoever it is, I'll need your driver's license and a credit card for the damage deposit. I saw you already paid for the room online, but gotta take a card just in case. Hope that's okay."

"That's...fine?" I glance Tessa's way.

"Yes, that's fine," she says, confirming she's up for a night in the forest with the cryptids. But I'm not really surprised. We both seem to have been bitten by the adventure bug.

Which reminds me as I pull out my ID and credit card...

"Do you have Wi-Fi, Mrs. Meyer?" I ask. "We wanted to do some research tonight on our next stop."

"Call me Merry," she says warmly, "everyone else does. And yes, I do. Network and password will be in your welcome brochure. It can get a little slow when everyone's on at once, streaming their TV shows before bed, though. So, if you have important things to do, I'd advise getting it done first thing, before everyone's back from dinner."

"So, there are other guests?" Tessa asks with a soft

laugh. "We were a little confused by the empty parking lot."

"Oh, my yes, booked solid now that you three are here," Merry says, her tone growing a touch more ominous as she adds, "Except bungalow seven. Don't go anywhere near bungalow seven."

"Why not?" I ask, as she passes over a brochure and an old-fashioned motel key attached to a carved wooden bird. "What happens in bungalow seven?"

She frowns. "Nothing happens, honey. It just has a hole in the roof I didn't catch until it was too late. Now there's mold in the walls. Gonna have to gut the entire thing and rebuild from scratch." Her frown morphs into another wide grin. "But I love renovating. Can't wait to give the Cinderella suite a whole new look. You're in the Beauty and the Beast bungalow. If I'd had my druthers, I'd put a sweet couple like you in the Sleeping Beauty suite with all the pretty flowers on the wall, but I already have an older guy in there. From Seattle." She lowers her voice to hiss, "He's not very friendly so stay away from bungalow five, too, if you don't want to get yelled at. Any questions?"

I glance back at Tessa, who shakes her head, before turning to Merry. "No, I don't think so. Thanks so much."

"You're welcome, but be sure to move that camper off to the side of the lot, will you, doll? That's the best way to be sure there's room for everyone else to park."

I nod. "Of course."

Tessa waves as we step toward the door. "Thank you. Have a good night and good luck with your pickles."

Merry cackles. "And good luck with yours!"

Outside, Tessa turns to me with a bemused grin,

whispering, "What do you think she meant by that? Surely not..." She glances down at my waist, her cheeks flushing as she laughs again.

"Oh, I wouldn't put it past her. She's a character." I hold up the key. "You want to go check out the room while I move the camper? Then, if the space seems safe, we can unload our things?"

"Good plan," she says, frowning.

"What's up?' I ask.

She shakes her head. "Nothing. I wanted to Google something but I'm not getting service. I'll log into the Wi-Fi once we get to the room." She nods to Freya. "Come on, cutie. Let's go see our room for the night."

I head back to the camper, the ominous feeling from when we first pulled into the lot returning as I load into the driver's seat and move the vehicle to the edge of the asphalt, as directed.

It's just so...quiet. And so dark.

The sun only set a few minutes ago, but it's already nearly black under the trees. I have to turn on the flashlight on my phone to follow the path to bungalow nine. The temperature drops beneath the fir branches, as well, making me wish I'd grabbed our winter coats. If Tessa decides she wants to stay, I'll run back and grab those and the camping flashlights before we go fetch the bags.

But that's a big "if" at this point. If the inside of our cabin is as faded and run-down as the outside, Tessa might prefer the relative luxury of the camper, even without running water.

I let myself in, calling out, "Hello?" as I swing through the door, stepping into...one of the cutest spaces I've ever seen.

I laugh as I turn in a slow circle, taking in the small

sitting room and large fireplace, decorated to look like an old French castle. There's also a small "dungeon" under the stairs, complete with bars and toys in bins—a great place for kids to play or...for ferrets to explore. Freya is already pawing through a bin of wooden blocks, chattering happily to herself.

"Looks like Freya approves of the new digs." I move through the sitting room to an equally cute and cozy kitchenette, complete with a breakfast nook beneath a window overlooking the murky forest. "This is nice, right?"

Tessa, perched on the edge of the bench beneath the window, looks up from her phone, her face pale.

"What?" I ask, my stomach tightening again. "What's wrong? Did you find a dead mouse in the bathroom?"

"No." She gulps as she turns her screen my way. "It's a Tommyknocker. That's what they look like."

I grunt, taking in a small, dwarf-like creature from a fantasy novel with green skin and a hint of a muzzle where its nose should be. "Creepy. But at least they're small. I think we could take a few of them in a fight."

"They look like leprechauns," she whispers.

I nod. "Yeah, a little, I guess."

"I hate leprechauns," she says, her eyes beginning to shine. "I hate them so much."

Before I can respond, something smacks hard against the roof—like a coconut falling from a tree—and Tessa dives under the table with a scream.

Chapter 20

TESSA

I remain under the table, trembling and muttering to myself until Wes returns from outside.

"It was a tree limb," he says, crouching down to peer at me beneath the pretty, strawberry-print tablecloth. "A big one, but it slid off the roof onto the ground out back. Hopefully, it didn't do any serious damage." He sighs, scanning my face. "Do you want to go? I can carry you to the camper and come back for Freya."

My lips twitch. "I don't need to be carried. I could run. If I needed to." I pull in a deeper breath, willing my racing heart to slow. "But if it was just a tree limb…"

"We can still go," Wes says gently. "You won't sleep well if you're scared."

And we might be murdered by blood-thirsty leprechauns before morning, I add silently.

Aloud, I insist, "No, it's okay. It's been a big day. I'm sure I'll sleep just fine…once I drink all the Sleepytime tea in the cupboard." I motion toward the play dungeon. "And Freya's having so much fun. Or she was. Did the limb scare her, too?"

Wes shakes his head. "It doesn't seem like it. She's still playing with the blocks. I think she might have a future in architectural design."

I force another weak smile. "Funny."

His brow furrows. "I think I know what we need to do."

"What's that?" I glance around my hiding place. "Get out from under the table? I may actually sleep under here. It's very clean. And if a leprechaun breaks in in the middle of the night, they're not going to look under the tablecloth."

"Don't you think it's a little strange?"

"Strange that there are leprechauns in Colorado? Yes, but I guess it's not all that crazy when you think about it. Ireland has mountains. Colorado has mountains. It's cold there, too. And green. They probably feel very at home here."

Wes settles onto the floor cross-legged. "No, I mean... Last night, we drove right into the middle of the biggest gathering of clowns I've ever seen. Tonight, it's cryptids that look like leprechauns. It's like we're both being confronted with our greatest irrational fears."

"It isn't irrational to be afraid of a creature who likes to drag humans underground and torture them for hundreds of years, just for fun," I say, knowing I sound crazy, but unable to stop myself.

"But that's only if you capture one and ask it for three wishes," Wes says. "They can't take you anywhere unless you strike a bargain with them or try to steal their treasure."

I frown. "Where did you hear that?"

"My great aunt and uncle. My grandmother knew a lot about the fair folk, too. The McGuires are about as

Irish as you can get without being born and raised in the old country."

I wet my lips. "My family, too. I know I'm being ridiculous, but I can't help it. I swear, I think I saw a leprechaun once, when I was playing by the spring with my cousin when we were little. I was by the rope swing, getting ready to jump. Nancy was already in the water, telling me to hurry. I looked down to tell her that I was working up to a big swing and right there, under the water, I saw this evil, bearded face rising beneath her. The spring was so clear, I could see every detail, from his terrible sharp teeth to the horrible grin on his little face."

Wes curses.

I exhale a rush of breath. "It was terrifying. And then it pulled Nancy under. I'll never forget how wide her eyes got or the way her hands clawed at the water as she sank." I shiver. "I started screaming and ran back toward the house to get her dad. But by the time I got back, Nancy was sitting by the rope swing, wringing the water out of her hair and laughing. She said I was crazy. That there hadn't been anything else in the water. It was just her playing a prank on me because I was a baby who was too chicken to jump."

"Mean prank," Wes says.

"It would have been, but...I don't think it was. I know what I saw, Wes." I glance up at him, grateful that he isn't looking at me like I need antipsychotic medication. "And Nancy was never quite the same after that. She was meaner, more impulsive. She just didn't seem to care about anyone the way she did before. Even her mom and dad."

"You think the leprechaun kidnapped your cousin

and replaced her with a fairy changeling?" Wes asks, proving his Irish elders taught him all the old stories.

Embarrassed, I nod. "I mean, not really, but...maybe? I mean, you've met Nancy. She's awful. No way she's fully human. She was going to give Freya away just because some dumb guy didn't like her. Who does that?"

Freya appears beside Wes, dooking inquisitively as she climbs over his legs, clearly wondering what game we're playing here. He strokes her back with a shake of his head, "I don't know. Personally, I would assume the person I loved and the animal they loved were a package deal. And Freya's not an unreasonable creature. Look how much she's warmed up to me in a few days. I think if Nancy's man had put in a little effort with her, they could have been friends."

I scratch Freya's scruff as she sniffs the floor around me. "No, they couldn't have been. Freya isn't friends with assholes. She only likes nice people." I shoot him a wobbly smile. "Like you, Preston."

He grins. "Exactly what I was thinking, Lady Gray. Lady Gray doesn't strike me as the type of woman who's afraid of leprechauns."

I shake my head, my grin stretching wider. "No way. Lady Gray eats leprechauns for breakfast." I raise my voice, calling out to the rest of the quiet room and the forest beyond, "I mean that. Literally. I fry up leprechaun patties to eat with my scrambled eggs and toast, so you'd better stay far away from bungalow nine."

"Damn straight," Wes booms, making Freya flinch and leap into my arms. We laugh and he apologizes, "Sorry, Freya. Just wanted them to know we mean business." Shifting his focus my way, he asks, "Want me to go get your coat before we unload? Or I can get whatever you and Freya need from the camper if you don't want to go outside. Just give me a list."

I shake my head. "No. I can come. But I'm going to need my hat. Feeling like brave, adventurous Lady Gray is easier with my fedora."

He smiles. "Understandable. I'll wear mine, too."

He starts to stand, but I reach out, taking his hand. "Thanks," I whisper. "For not thinking I'm crazy."

"Never," he promises. "I've got your back, Lady Gray. For as long as you'll let me."

I release his hand and crawl out from under the table, feeling even more mixed up than I did before. Yes, I'm still spooked by going out into the dark with the evil leprechauns, but a part of me is more spooked by the look in Wes's eyes, the look that assures me he wasn't kidding. He's here for me, for Tessa, every bit as much as my adventurous alter ego.

Even after the things I told him today, even after watching me freak out and hide under a table like a kid who watched too many scary movies at a sleepover. Even after the way I've pushed him away for the past year and a half...

Suddenly, it seems so clear.

This man isn't here with me, on the run from his ex and her volatile sister because he feels obligated to clean up a mess he helped create. He's here because he cares about me, because that night in the woods meant something to him, too. *I* mean something to him.

On impulse, I reach out, catching his hand before he gets to the door.

He turns back, the curiosity in his eyes quickly turning to something more intense when his gaze locks with mine.

"We should probably check the bedroom before we grab our things," I say, my pulse throbbing in my throat. "Just to make sure it's going to be okay for us to sleep up there."

"Good idea," he says, his voice a deep rumble that sends electricity prickling across my skin. "Lead the way."

"I think it's up here," I say, holding onto his hand as I start up the stairs and Freya darts back into the dungeon to play with her blocks. Anticipation building with every step, I'm practically hyperventilating by the time we reach the small bedroom tucked beneath the sharply slanted roof.

Wes has to duck down until we're in the center of the space, but he seems as charmed by the bedroom as I am.

"Very cute," he says, gazing down at the large bed festooned with wispy cream-colored curtains hanging from the ceiling on both sides. The comforter showcases a single red rose, like the one in Beauty and the Beast, and the wall behind us is all bookcases, displaying hundreds of hardcover books in various colors.

"It's more than cute," I say, squeezing his fingers. "It's perfect. I mean, Beauty and the Beast is all about leaving home. About finding out who you are and what really matters to you, while in exile from everything you've ever known, right? About realizing that things that look perfect on the outside aren't always what's best for you and...vice versa?"

Wes pulls me closer, looping one arm around my waist as he cups my cheek. "Lady Gray are you saying what I think you're saying?"

"Call me Tessa," I say, my pulse spiking as I add, "Or good girl. I really liked that, too."

His arm tightens on my waist, making my breath rush

out as he crushes me against him. The hand at my cheek dives into my hair, fisting there, holding me captive as he whispers, "I don't want just a night, Tessa. I don't want this to be a lapse in judgment or a vacation fling. I want to be yours. And I really want you to be mine. The thought of another man fucking you makes me crazy. Just seeing Nate's hands on you on the dance floor was enough to make me lose it."

"I know." I loop my arms around his neck, my entire body humming as he backs me toward the bed. "It was sexy."

"I thought it pissed you off."

"It did," I say, my pulse spiking again as the backs of my knees hit the mattress. "But that doesn't mean it wasn't sexy. Or that I didn't want to drag you into the hayloft and do filthy things to your body."

"Once I get you in that bed, I'm not letting you out," he says, his hand shifting to squeeze my ass through my soft travel pants. "You're going to have to stay there, naked and well-fucked, while I get our things, feed Freya, and take her out to pee."

My lips curve in a wicked grin. "I think I can get on board with that. Will you deliver snacks to my naked and well-fucked self, if needed?"

"Snacks, gold, your phone charger, the heads of your enemies," he says. "Your wish is my command, beautiful. Now lift your arms. I need your tits in my mouth ten minutes ago."

Holding his gaze, I obey, my blood singing in my veins as he rips my light sweatshirt up and over my head and tackles me onto the mattress. And then I'm under him, this man who drives me wild, the one whose touch has haunted me every day that we've been apart.

And even though we might be surrounded by evil leprechauns closing in on our cabin as we roll across the covers, devouring each other, there's nowhere else I want to be.

Just here.

With him.

Chapter 21

WESLEY

This is it. I don't need to go to the desert and hunt for gold. The only treasure I need is right here.

The taste of her, her smell, the sounds she makes as I pull her nipple into my mouth, sucking deep...this is all I've wanted, what I've been craving like an addict since the last time she was under me.

But the last time we were in a tiny tent, in a sleeping bag only lightly cushioned from the hard ground underneath.

Now, I have her in a giant soft bed, and I mean to make the most of it.

"Roll over," I say, already gripping her hips and flipping her beneath me.

"Yes," she moans, moving to shift onto her knees.

I stop her with a palm at the small of her back. "No. Stay like this."

"I've never done it from behind like this before," she says, glancing at me over her shoulder.

I smile as I dig my palm in gentle circles at the base of

her spine, summoning a happy sound from low in her throat. "We can do that in a little while if you want, but first, I'm going to give you a massage."

Her brow furrows. "That's sweet, but...I don't think I want a massage."

"You'll want this one," I assure her.

"No, I want your cock," she says. "It's been a long time, Wes. Your cock was my last cock. That's almost two years without sex. That's way too long."

"Tell me about it. Fucking torture," I agree, my hands moving down to knead into the perfect swells of her ass.

Her lips part. "You too?"

"Me, too," I confirm, thumbs caressing the base of her bottom, right above her sit bones, fighting a grin as her lids flutter and linger at half-mast.

"Wow, that's..."

"Turning you on?" I ask, fingers probing lower, but still deliberately avoiding the obvious places. I don't intend to touch her pussy until I'm gliding inside her.

"I was going to say amazing. And special. About the 'not having sex with anyone else' part, but y-yes." She pulls in a deeper breath, letting it out with a soft sigh. "But the rubbing is good, too. I feel it...deep inside. Not just where you're touching."

"The clitoris isn't just the part that shows on the outside. It has roots that stretch down around your pussy and...deep inside."

"Are you mansplaining my clitoris to me?" she asks, making me laugh.

"Maybe a little bit. Sorry."

She grins, biting her lip as I knee her thighs farther apart, giving me better access to every soft inch of skin between her legs. "It's okay. I actually didn't know that.

But I could feel it when you were rubbing me before. You could rub me there again...if you want."

"I will," I promise, digging my thumbs into her hip flexors, summoning a deeper, slightly pained moan from her this time. "Just trying to spread the love around."

"Damn, that hurts, but I like it. I had no idea I was so tight right there." Her eyes close as she breathes through the release. As her muscles relax, letting me in, I rock my thumbs a little deeper. "How did you learn so much about women's bodies, Mr. McGuire?"

"I'm a research nerd about all my favorite subjects, Ms. Martin. And I had an older lover in college. One of my professors, actually."

Tessa's eyes open. "Really?"

"Really."

"How much older?"

I sigh, my lips curving as I confess, "Fifteen years."

Tessa's brows shoot up. "Fifteen? Are you sure you weren't molested?"

I snort. "No. Not at all. She was thirty-five. I was twenty. It was fine. Great actually. She was a good person. Taught me a lot of valuable things." I skim my palm up her back until I reach the nape of her neck. Curling my fingers around the slender column, I add in a huskier voice, "Like the value of foreplay."

Tessa's breath rushes out. "Yes, please. I love your fist in my hair. I've been thinking about it ever since that first night."

"When do you think about it?" I ask, slowly threading my fingers into the thick strands, letting my fingers skim along the sensitive skin on her scalp.

She swallows, her lips parting again as her breath comes faster. "When I'm in bed."

"In bed with your hand between your legs?" I ask, tightening my grip, until I have a solid handful of her silky hair firmly in my grasp. Pulling her head gently back, I lean down to whisper near her ear, "Do you think of me fucking you when you touch yourself, Tessa?"

"Yes," she says, arching her pretty ass higher in the air. "I think about you fucking me and telling me how perfect my wet pussy feels around your cock."

"We shouldn't have fucked without a condom," I say, so turned on pre-come is beginning to leak from the tip of my cock. "That was irresponsible."

"I want to be irresponsible again," she says, her hips squirming against the mattress. "I love feeling you come inside me."

Muttering a curse beneath my breath, I knee her thighs even farther apart and lengthen myself on top of her. "You're doing your best to hurry the foreplay along, aren't you?"

"Foreplay next time" she murmurs, reaching back, dragging her fingers over my hip and down until her fingers brush my erection. Her breath rushes out. "God, Wes. You don't know how many times I've thought about us like this. I promise, I'm ready. Past ready. I need you so much. I need to know you're mine."

"For as long as you'll have me." I shift lower, until my cock is cradled between her thighs. The feel of her slick pussy on my fevered skin is all it takes to bring me fully on board the "foreplay later" train. "I'm yours," I promise as I push forward, bliss and gratitude making my breath catch as her body welcomes me in. "And you're mine," I rasp, burying myself to the hilt with one long, steady thrust as I pull her hair back again.

She groans and shudders beneath me, the rush of

fresh slickness over my cock assuring me she loves the thought of that as much as I do.

And then my mouth is on her neck, kissing and biting as I take her with a barely contained ferocity, the kind that used to upset Darcy. With my ex, I always had to reign myself in, pull back, watch my mouth, and temper my instincts. With Tessa, I'm free to give her everything in me, to show her just how much I want her.

More than I've ever wanted a woman before...

"You fucking destroy me," I murmur into her ear. "After that night in the tent, I couldn't be with anyone else. I tried, but all I could think about was you and this sweet pussy and your gorgeous ass in my hands and the sounds you made when you come. Are you going to come for me again, baby? Are you going to drench my cock like a good girl?"

She whimpers, a sound that becomes a gasp as I drag my teeth over the delicate skin of her earlobe. "Yes, Wes. God, yes. Pull my hair harder. Fuck me harder. Please. Harder."

"You never have to say please," I say, giving her exactly what she's asked for. "All you have to do is tell me how you want me, baby. All I want to do is please you, beautiful girl. Fuck, yes. God, Tessa." My thrusts grow wild, erratic as she wiggles her hips back against my thrusts, slickness leaking down her thighs as she moans and curses and calls my name like a prayer.

I'm seconds away from losing control when she arches beneath me, going still for an achingly perfect moment as her inner walls lock and pulse around me.

I come with a groan a beat later, gasping, "Good girl. Fuck, so good, Tessa. I love your pussy, baby. Your body. Your smell. Everything about you." As I collapse on top of her, my cock jerking, I grip a handful of her perfect bottom, squeezing it as my orgasm continues to rock through me. "And this ass. This perfect fucking ass. I love this ass. I've wanted my hands on you like this so many times since we left town. You have no idea."

"I do," she says, still breathless. "Same here. I've been fantasizing about biting your bicep, right beneath the edge of your sleeve, almost constantly. Preferably while you're inside me. I'm a terrible friend."

Grinning, I pull out, kissing away her moan of protest as I roll her over onto her back beneath me. She wraps her legs around my hips, returning the kiss.

"I adore you," I whisper against her mouth, fighting another smile as I add, "But you're right, you're a terrible friend."

She huffs out a soft laugh and swats my ass.

I grin and double down, "Sorry, but you are. Friends don't fantasize about biting friends in a sexual way, Tessa. Or a non-sexual way. Biting isn't a friendly thing to do."

She glares up at me, but her eyes are glittering with amusement. "Says the man who just bit my neck and my ear and got sassy with my nipples the last time we were together."

"Sassy in what way?" I cup her breast, teasing my thumb under her perfect peach areola.

"Don't play dumb," she whispers, her amusement tinged with desire.

"If you don't like my teeth on you, just let me know," I say, capturing her nipple between my fingers and thumb and giving it a light squeeze. "I can stop at any time. Like I said, all I want to do is please you."

Her lashes flutter. "You know I like it. I love it. And you like it when I return the favor."

"I do," I say. "Just thinking about your teeth on me is enough to make me feel a certain kind of way." I lower my hips, pressing against her slickness, letting her feel how quickly my cock is rallying for round two. "I guess we'll just have to agree to be more than friends."

"Yes, please," she says, wrapping her legs more firmly around me. "Now bring that bicep over here and let me see if it's still as fun to nibble as it was before."

And because her wish is my command, I do, and in just a few minutes, I'm inside her again, taking her slower this time. We grind together, languid and deep, kissing and biting and teasing until the last few moments, when all I can do is stare into her eyes.

Those gorgeous blue eyes that show me all her secrets…

In the seconds before she comes again, I see all the way to the heart of her. I see her bravery, her sweetness, her fear, and her pain. I see all the love she has inside, desperate for a home, and the dreams she's started to think might never come true.

As I lose myself inside her a second time, I silently promise to make them come true. I want to be her home, her refuge from the shit show of the world, the man she can trust never to let her down.

After we catch our breath, I pull back, gazing down at her, searching for the perfect words to tell her that I'm all in without scaring her away. I know it's too soon to tell her I love her, even though it's true.

Before I can find any words, let alone the perfect ones, a sharp chuffing sound comes from behind us.

I turn over my shoulder to see Freya standing at the top of the stairs with her eyes narrowed. She's on her back feet, giving her a clear view of the bed...and my very exposed, very vulnerable parts.

"Should I be worried about my crotch?" I ask, the words ending in a rush of breath as Freya charges the mattress.

My heart leaps into my throat, but before I can even think about moving to protect myself, the avenging ferret scampers past my ass. She stops by the head of the bed, sticking her tiny snout in between us, sniffing Tessa's cheek.

"Stop," she says, laughing as Freya's nose probes into her hair. "I'm fine. I promise."

Clearly unconvinced, Freya climbs onto Tessa's chest, crouching between us.

Tessa laughs harder. "No, buddy. No furry friends in the bedroom. We need boundaries."

"We need a bedroom door," I say, reaching for my clothes.

"Or her crate," Tessa says, sitting up and shooing Freya onto the covers beside her.

"On it," I say, already off the bed and halfway into my jeans. "Don't go anywhere. You stay naked and in bed, that's the deal."

Tessa shakes her head, her dimple popping. "I need water. And so does Freya. We'll get back in bed later. I promise." She makes shooing motions at me this time. "Go, fetch things. The sooner we give this hungry, nosy girl her dinner, the sooner we can tuck her into her crate for the night."

"All right," I grumble, playing up my annoyance to make Tessa laugh again.

I love her laugh.

I love knowing I don't have to hide how much I want her even more.

I'm so high on good feelings, I don't remember to be creeped out by the spooky forest until I've already gathered our things from the camper and am almost back to the cottage. I hurry the last three steps to the door, ignoring the "watched" sensation prickling up the back of my spine.

Back inside, the uneasiness fades quickly, but I don't protest when Tessa insists on putting a bowl of cream on the back porch as a goodwill offering to the fair folk and cryptids.

Afterwards, we feed Freya and snuggle with her on the couch for a bit, while Tessa reads from a book of fairy tales on the coffee table. When the ferret's eyes slide closed, we tuck her into her crate and head back upstairs.

Sometime around midnight, when we're finally too tired to go again, Tessa rests her head on my chest. I hug her close, drifting off to sleep with only one thought in my head—*This is it*.

This is what I didn't realize I was looking for until I met her.

This is all I'll ever need.

This is worth fighting for, no matter what happens when we get back home.

I kiss her forehead, chest tightening when she hums happily and snuggles closer to my side.

Maybe I'll be able to tell her I love her sooner than I thought.

Chapter 22

TESSA

The next morning, I slip quietly out of bed, the better not to awaken the sexy beast sleeping beside me. After his performance last night, he definitely deserves his rest.

Body humming with happy memories, I tiptoe downstairs and take Freya out to roam the front of the cottage for a few minutes.

After she's used the bathroom and is devouring her breakfast on the kitchen table, I put the kettle on for coffee. Then, I peek out the back door to check on our dish of cream, not really surprised to see it empty.

It's been licked clean by...something.

But whether that something was a wild animal or a cryptid or a fairy, the forest doesn't feel nearly as threatening this morning. The sun is shining through the thick foliage, the birds are singing, and the crisp air holds a hint of spring warmth that has me even more excited to reach the desert later today.

I pull in a breath, holding the clean air in my lungs for a beat before collecting the cream dish and closing the door behind me. When I turn back, Wesley's in the kitchen, pouring coffee grounds into the top of the pour-over carafe I found in the cabinets.

With his morning scruff, rumpled hair, and soft pajama pants riding low on his hips, doing nothing to conceal the thickness behind the fabric, he looks good enough to have for breakfast.

Biting my lip, I cast a meaningful glance to his thighs before slowly dragging my gaze back to his face. "Is that all for me?"

"Every inch," he says, setting aside the coffee grounds as he crosses toward me. "I was dreaming about you riding my cock, but when I woke up and reached for you, you weren't there."

I tut sympathetically, fighting a grin as he pulls me into his arms. "That's a sad story," I say, moaning as he grips my hips and pins my ass to his erection. "And that sounds like the kind of dream that needs to come true."

"You. Me. The bathroom," he says, murmuring the words in between kisses.

"Why the bathroom?" I ask, smiling against his lips.

"Because it has a door we can close to keep the little gremlin from spying on us, without having to wrangle her back into her crate. And shower sex with you is on my bucket list."

"Clever man," I say, letting him pull me into the bathroom, where he proves just how clever he is.

Our shower is the sexiest in recent memory, leaving me drunk on orgasms all over again. At this point, I don't really need coffee to wake me up, but the grounds still smell delicious.

Leaving Wes to finish up in the bathroom, I head back out to the kitchen to reheat the water. I dry my hair with a towel and roll a ball for Freya with my foot, deciding to give Binx a call and check in while I wait for the water to boil.

She answers on the first ring with a flat, "Are you two still somewhere far away from here?"

Laughing, I say, "Yes. Why? Was Daria caught on camera smearing poop on my door again?"

"No, but she's still being a giant pain in the ass. She bought a billboard by Bubba Jump's and pasted a picture of Wes up there with the word 'Cheater' across his face in giant green letters."

I wince. "That's...not great."

"No, it's not. She also photoshopped devil horns on his head and scribbled in a dead tooth. It's a very high-school yearbook breed of psycho."

"Well, at least it's on the way out of town. Not many people are going to see it."

"And the people who do, will think it's hilarious," Binx agrees. "It's just fucking annoying. Just leave my brother alone, woman. I mean, technically, yes, he cheated, I guess, but he's faced consequences for it. I mean, you two would be perfect together, and you won't even consider dating him. That's a serious price to pay."

Nibbling my bottom lip, I roll the ball for Freya again, smiling as she bounces across the room to fetch it.

"Right?" Binx presses when my silence goes on a beat too long. "Or is there something I should know about, Tessa? Are you finally going to give my lovesick brother a chance at your heart? Or at least your pussy?"

Choking on my next breath, I'm still laughing when Wes emerges from the bathroom with a quizzical expression on his face. His damp hair hangs over his forehead in a way that makes me want to drag him upstairs for one last quickie before we leave.

Instead, I wave a hand his way, silently assuring him I'm fine, before answering Binx, "I don't kiss and tell, but...there might be something to that theory."

"There might be?" She exhales an exasperated breath. "Come on, don't leave me in suspense! I need all the details so I can brag to Mel about my superior matchmaking skills. I was the one who suggested you two get out of town together. Remember that when you're picking a maid of honor."

My cheeks flush, but the thought of walking down an aisle to Wes isn't as absurd as it probably should be. Still, I'm not ready to share too much with Binx or anyone else. I don't want to do anything to jinx this.

"We're headed out the door," I say. "I'll text you when we get to the park tonight. Let you know we arrived safely."

"I don't care about you arriving safely," she says, amending quickly, "I mean, I do. Of course, I do. But I want details way more. At the very least, don't tell any other McGuire the hot gossip before you tell me. Nothing. Not a single word."

Grabbing Freya's harness from the entry table, I ask, "Why's that?"

"You know me, I would never tell everyone in the family about your and Wes's personal business. But Anya is not nearly as closed-mouthed."

I frown. "What? Who's Anya?"

"The new server at The Dirty Taco? The cute redhead Mom adopted as her new surrogate child because she has a soft spot for orphan redheads?" She emits a dubious hum.

"I mean, as long as they're not Tatum when she first moved to town and was trying to hook up with her favorite son. Drew is totally the favorite. Don't believe anyone who tells you different. Yes, Matty is the genius and they're proud of him for that, and Christian is objectively pretty enough to be a male model and they like that, too, but Drew is the golden boy. Even Barrett can't compete. Sure, he's a doctor, but Drew is squeezing out grandbabies left and right and always knows when to keep his mouth shut."

"I would agree," I say, sufficiently familiar with the McGuire family dynamics to feel qualified to weigh in on the subject. "But what does that have to do with Anya? Or me and Wes?"

"Nothing," Binx says. "That last part was a tangent because I was up all night helping my friend keep a fox out of his chicken coop. His daughter has three pet chickens she's obsessed with, but we couldn't get to the hardware store to buy more chicken wire to fix the hole in the pen before it closed, so we had to stand watch over Hilda, Henna, and Hermione all fucking night. I'm exhausted. And I think my hair smells like chicken poop, even though I shampooed it twice." She sighs. "Yeah, so my brain is garbage, but that doesn't mean I won't eventually get to the point. Anyway, Anya waited on Daria and Darcy the day after you left, when Darcy was still upset and crying. She heard all the gory details and, much like my mother, she can't keep gossip to herself for more than five minutes. So, she told Mom, who told Mel, who told Matty, who told Nora, who told Starling, who told Wren, who told Tatum, and now everyone knows, and Christian is running a pool so the family can gamble on whether you guys are going to come back a couple, mortal enemies, or something in between. It's a whole thing."

I sag onto the couch. "Oh God."

"What?" Wes whispers, pausing on his way up the stairs.

I wave a hand again, but this time it's an "I'll explain later" hand. To Binx, I say, "Okay. Well, that's embarrassing, but fair enough, I guess. That's what we get for doing something worthy of gossiping about. But aside from the family speculation and associated gambling, things are okay? No one's seen anything on the cameras around my house?"

"Not a thing," Binx says. "Aside from a family of raccoons that comes to steal cat food from your neighbor's house and stops to play in your backyard on their way back to wherever they're shacking up. They're super cute."

I nod. "Good. Hopefully, things will continue to calm down and the worst will have blown over by the time we get back."

"Fingers crossed," Binx agrees, before continuing in a wheedling tone, "I mean, that would be for the best since the two of you are developing a serious thing for each other...right?"

I smile. "Goodbye, Binx."

"Oh, come on! I've literally had one, maybe two hours of sleep. I need some exciting news to keep me going through my shift. Being a loan officer is boring enough without being tired and gossip-deprived on top of it. At least tell me if you're having a good time."

"I'm having a fantastic time," I murmur as Wes comes back down the stairs with our bags in hand. I catch his gaze and we both grin. "Absolutely fantastic."

I end the call just as Binx is launching into another monologue, knowing she'll forgive me for hanging up on her. Especially if I'm able to give her some juicy gossip to help her win the latest McGuire family pot...

"If we decide to keep dating, are you okay if I tell Binx first? Before we head home?" I ask as Wes crouches in front of me. "Since we put her life in danger before we left, and she's been such a great help with everything?"

He arches a brow. "Why?"

"Everyone in your family knows what happened between us and they're placing bets on whether we'll be an item by the time we get back."

He rolls his eyes. "Of course, they are. Wouldn't be my family if they weren't up in my business before there's even any business to be up in."

I smile, brushing his damp hair from his forehead. "I don't know about that. I'm pretty sure last night was some pretty serious business. The shower, too."

His eyes flash. "Damned straight." His hands curl around the backs of my knees, guiding my thighs apart as he comes to kneel between them. "And what do you mean by 'if we're still dating,' woman? Do I need to remind you how good this is? I thought I did a decent job in the shower, but..."

Grinning, I loop my arms around his neck, welcoming his slow, sensual kiss. "You did an amazing job in the shower," I whisper against his lips. "But I have a terrible memory."

"Is that right?"

I hum in agreement, arching my back to make it easier for him to cup my ass. "It is. Just horrible. I might need vitamins or something. Maybe some Gingko Biloba."

"I'll be your Gingko Biloba, baby."

Giggling, I fall back onto the couch, and soon Wes and I are putting on another show for Freya, who thankfully seems to lose interest shortly after my top comes off and scurries away in search of more wholesome entertainment.

Though, honestly, even wild, primal sex with Wes still feels kind of wholesome. Maybe it's the warmth in his eyes or the care in his touch. Maybe it's the way he's so attuned to my body, sensing the exact moment to pull back or go harder.

Or maybe it's the way he pulls me in for a hug afterward and kisses my forehead, murmuring, "You're the best. The very best," in a way that makes me believe it.

Whatever it is, by the time we leave our creepy, but enchanted fairy tale cabin in the woods, I suspect I've caught something far more serious than a crush.

Chapter 23

WESLEY

I'm no stranger to remote work. I work from home most Fridays during the summer and the entire office went remote during the pandemic. I learned to catch up on emails, while taking a meeting on Zoom and researching precedents for my cases, all at the same time.

I should be able to tackle emails and delegate essential tasks to my team in the back of the camper while Tessa drives with no problem.

But the problem is: I can still see Tessa.

Smell Tessa's perfume drifting through the air...

Remember exactly how Tessa's pussy feels locked around my cock when I'm coming buried deep inside her...

Clearing my throat, I turn back to my screen. Must not think of Tessa's pussy. Must not think of Tessa at all until my work is done and I'm free to play.

That's what it feels like, being with her—play. Shopping at Trout World felt like play, devouring a nice meal surrounded by clowns felt like play, and last night was the steamiest, sexiest play of all. I just have such a good time with her. It feels like I've known her so much longer than a few years and like I've been wanting to know her even longer than that.

I'm pretty sure she's my person, my partner in crime, the Lady Gray to my Preston, the Beauty to my Beast, and a friend I'd be lucky to have by my side for the rest of my life.

Yeah, and telling her that anytime soon is a good way to end up as unhappy as Mr. and Mrs. Yackoff. You need to slow your roll, dude, or you'll scare her away all over again.

Admitting the voice of caution has a point, I force myself to focus on Yackoff vs. Yackoff until I have all my research completed and my recommendations sent to my client.

Thankfully, by the time Tessa pulls over for gas around lunchtime, I'm finished with everything that can't wait until next week. After slipping Freya into her harness, I emerge from the camper.

"Hey," Tessa says, smiling as I join her at the gas tank. "How's the donut making going?"

"The donuts are all made," I say, passing Freya into her arms and leaning in for a kiss, my chest filling with more warm bubbles when she hums happily against my lips. "Everything has been delegated, and I'm free until next week," I say as I pull back and nod toward the grassy area beside the convenience store. "Go ahead and take Freya for her potty break. I can finish up here."

"Okay." She snuggles Freya closer, scratching her neck. "But then we have to have a serious discussion about whether to do sandwiches for lunch or stop for barbeque at Wild Bill's Barbeque Rodeo Palace."

My brows lift. "Barbeque Rodeo Palace? That sounds exciting. A little confusing, but exciting."

"Right?" She laughs, her dimple popping in that way that makes me want to kiss it, to kiss *her*.

Fuck, I'm so glad I'm done with work and get to sit up front with her for the rest of the drive to the park. That's all it takes to make me feel like I've won the lottery, just the chance to be close to her.

"We *are* about thirty minutes ahead of schedule," she adds, batting her lashes at me. "Since I'm such a fantastic driver and all. We should have time to stop and still make it to the park in plenty of time to set up camp and get a short hike in before dinner."

"Let's do it," I say, tapping my credit card to the sensor. "But fair warning, I'm a filthy animal with a plate of ribs. I'll have to wear a bib."

She winks as she backs away. "Hot. I can't wait to see that."

I waggle my brows, mouthing, "Bibs make you horny?"

Laughing, she nods, before turning and jogging toward the grass, Freya in her arms. Making a mental note to procure an extra bib to take with us to the park, one I can use to surprise Tessa with a "bib only" strip tease later tonight, I start filling the tank, scrolling through my texts while I wait.

I always turn off my notifications while I'm working, so I'm not surprised to have a few messages waiting. I am, however, surprised to see that one is from Darcy.

Stomach tightening, I scroll past the text from my mother asking if I remembered to pack sunscreen, opening the message from my ex that reads—*Hey, Wes.*

I've been doing a lot of thinking. And I've decided I don't want to be mad anymore.

The tension in my jaw releases with an audible pop as I continue to read.

Yes, what you did was shitty, but...what I did was shitty, too. I knew you were going to break up with me when you got back from your camping trip. I just knew it. And I knew I should have kept the pregnancy scare news to myself until I had time to find out if I really was pregnant.

The text is followed by a gif of a stuffed bear looking ashamed of itself, which doesn't really feel appropriate considering the seriousness of the topic, but is very Darcy.

In her next message, she continues, *But I didn't keep it to myself. I told you, partly to shame you into staying with me. And I held off telling you that I'd started my period for about six weeks after I knew we were in the clear.*

My head rears back. That's the first I'm hearing about *that*. As far as I knew, she didn't start her period again until a couple weeks before we broke up. We weren't sleeping together anymore at that point, so I had to take her word for it.

So, I guess I lied, too, she adds in the next text.

"You guess?" I mutter to myself, scowling at the screen.

I'm sorry about that. And I'm sorry for letting my ego and hurt feelings take control this past weekend. I'll make sure Daria leaves you and Tessa alone from now on. I've already hired someone to take down the billboard with your face on it. Though the devil horns and dead tooth did kind of make me laugh. *smiling emoji* Hope you're okay and... sorry again. I don't think we'll ever be friends, but I do wish you well. I hope whoever you end up with makes you happy.

"Everything okay?" Tessa asks.

I glance up, considering sharing the message with her, but deciding the less said about my ex, the better. Tessa and I are finally moving on from all the Darcy drama, and I don't want to do anything to derail that.

Tucking my cell back in my pocket, I nod and smile, "Yeah, everything's great. I'm excited about barbeque and hikes and hunting treasure tomorrow."

She bounces up and down with a soft squeal, echoed by Freya who clucks in excitement and runs back and forth at our feet. "I can't wait. I'm ridiculously excited about this treasure hunt, Wes. Even if we don't find anything, it'll be a real adventure. I haven't had enough of those in my life."

"Then we'll have to keep adventure high on our priority list," I say as I slide the gas nozzle back into its holder. "Make up for lost time."

She smiles up at me. "That sounds good. I like making up for lost time with you."

"Same," I assure her, sealing the words with a kiss.

An hour later, I'm kissing her again, this time while wearing a Wild Bill's Barbeque Rodeo Palace bib and a plastic crown with the words "King of the Rib Plate" emblazoned across the front.

"So proud," Tessa murmurs, laughing as she wipes a bit of rib sauce from my chin.

I return the favor on hers. "Thank you, but I couldn't have finished the entire thing without the help of the woman who wore me out last night."

"And this morning," she says, her eyes dancing. "Don't worry, we'll burn even more calories during our hike this afternoon."

I nod seriously. "Right. The hike. That's probably the

only exercise we'll be getting today. After all the driving you've done, I'm sure you'll be too tired for anything else."

She mimics my earnest tone, "Right. And you've been working. And neither of us slept much last night. We should definitely call it an early night."

Spoiler alert—we *don't* call it an early night.

Not even close.

Chapter 24

TESSA

I should be tired. Exhausted, even.

Wes and I stayed up until ten, watching the stars put on a show in the desert sky, then putting on our own show between the sheets until after midnight. But when I wake up at six a.m., I'm practically vibrating with energy.

I bounce out of bed, donning my fedora before I even start the water for coffee.

Because today is a day for Lady Gray, a sunny, clear, gorgeous day, perfect for treasure hunting.

As soon as the coffee's ready and the toast is browning in the toaster oven, I throw back the privacy curtain on the bed and announce in my best British accent, "Up we go, darling. Time and tide wait for no man. Or woman. Carpe diem and all that!"

Wes blinks up at me from his pillow, smiling. "Nice hat."

Tipping the brim lower over one eye, I bat my lashes, continuing in my "Lady Gray" voice, "Thank you, darling. But compliments will get you nowhere this morning, I'm afraid. I'm after a different sort of treasure than the one between your legs."

Wes's snort becomes a cough and then a laugh. When he can finally draw a clear breath, he says, "Thank you? I think? I mean, at least you called it a treasure. Even if you don't have time for it in your busy schedule at the moment."

Clucking my tongue, I shoot him a thumbs-up. "Absolutely. A treasure indeed."

His gaze darkens. "Nice accent. Any chance you might talk dirty to me like that later? If I'm a good boy?"

Crawling over the rumpled covers on my side of the bed, I come to hover over him on my hands and knees. "Dirty talk isn't for good boys. Dirty talk is for boys who are deliciously naughty."

"I think I can manage that," he says, his fingers curling around my wrist, sending a sizzle across my skin. But sizzling will have to wait until later. We should get going before the sun gets higher and besides...delaying satisfaction can be fun.

"Oh, I bet you can. Later." I bend, teasing the tip of my nose against his as I add, "Now, stop flirting, get up, and get dressed before I feed your toast to the ferret."

He grunts. "I'm up, cruel temptress." He swats at my ass, but I easily dodge his hand, laughing as I bounce off the bed. I fetch Freya's chicken chunks and mealworms from the fridge, filling her bowl and setting it on the floor beside the door.

Wes pops into the bathroom. After a few moments, I hear the water turn on in the sink and call out in my normal voice, so he knows I mean business, "Don't shave. We don't have time and I like you scruffy."

He opens the door, shaving cream already on his cheeks. "You're bossy this morning."

I smile. "I'm bossy every morning. You just don't know me that well yet."

"I know you," he says, in a low, lovely voice that makes me feel warm all over. "Just let me wash this off, then, and I'll be ready for breakfast."

"Almond butter or peanut butter?" I ask.

"Surprise me," he says, bending to splash water on his face.

Twenty minutes later, we've eaten, double-checked our gear bags, set up an obstacle course and toy area for Freya to keep her entertained while we're gone, and Wes is pulling our bikes from the storage area in back.

"Do you think she'll be cool enough inside?" I ask, fretting as I glance up at the cloudless sky. It's beautiful, but once the sun gets a little higher, it will be baking the top of the camper for most of the day. The trees on the right side of our spot won't provide shade until the sun starts to set.

"I have the air conditioning set to seventy-five," he says, collecting our helmets before shutting the storage door. "If it gets any hotter than that, it'll kick on and keep her cool."

I lean into him, looping my arms around his neck. "So prepared. I love it."

"I also packed extra protein bars and iodine pellets in case we need more water and can't find a safe source out in the wild." He draws me closer, his hands settling above the curve of my ass in a way that feels just right. "How sexy am I now?"

"Really fucking sexy," I purr, teasing my nails up the back of his neck into his hair. "I mean, if we weren't already outside with the camper all locked up..."

"It can be unlocked in five seconds," he says, making me grin.

"You're a sex fiend."

"Only for you, Lady Gray," he says, kissing me slow and deep, his tongue stroking against mine. His hands drag up from my hips, molding to my ribs, his thumbs brushing back and forth beneath my breasts as the kiss deepens. By the time he finally pulls back, my panties are soaked, and I'm thinking maybe a ten-minute delay wouldn't be so awful, after all.

"Nope, off we go, intrepid explorer," he says when I suggest it, grinning as he plucks my fedora from my head and sets the helmet down in its place.

I narrow my eyes. "You did that on purpose. To torture me a little."

His smile widens. "But just a little. Now, for a serious question. Where to put our fedoras while we're cycling?"

In the end, we decide on strapping our hats gently under the top flaps on our backpacks and set out from the campground just as the morning sun clears the top of the bluffs in the distance. We could have cut at least an hour off our biking if we'd driven to another nearby park before setting out, but we already had our campsite set up and agreed that leaving straight from the camper felt like more of an adventure.

By the time we've been cycling for nearly two hours, however, my nether regions are demanding to know what the hell I was thinking, and my trembling quadriceps aren't too thrilled either.

"Ow," I mutter, wincing as I swing off my bike in the shade of a small rock formation. We're not far from our final turn, the one that will lead us the last mile up into the foothills, where Butch Cassidy's treasure is alleged to be hidden in the sprawling cave systems beneath.

But honestly, the thought of getting back on my bike anytime soon isn't appealing. I waddle, slightly bowlegged, back and forth in the shade, sipping from my water bottle. The movement eases the ache, but I know I'll be right back where I started as soon as I reboard my torture device.

Wes makes a considering sound low in his throat. "Saddle sore?"

"Very," I say, grimacing as I turn back to him. "I'm sorry. I didn't realize my crotch needed to be in shape to bike long distances."

"Your crotch is in incredible shape," he says, pushing on when I arch a wry brow. "But I know what you're saying. This is my fault, too. I forgot how sore you can get the first time back on a bike after a long break." He glances around. "Want to lock up here and walk the rest of the way?"

My shoulders relax a little. "You wouldn't mind?"

He shakes his head. "Not at all." He grins. "My crotch could use a break, too."

I hum, playing up the worry in my voice as I say, "Oh, no. What if both our crotches are in such bad shape by the time we get back to the camper that we have to abstain from our usual festival of carnal delights?"

He laughs as he shakes his head. "Festival of carnal delights. I like that."

"I do, too, but sometimes the mind is willing but the flesh is weak."

He steps in, gripping my hip in that possessive way that drives me wild. "Ice packs. I put them in the freezer last night in case one of us was sore after the ride today."

My lips hook up on one side. "Oh, yeah? So, we're going to put ice packs on our nether regions? Sounds…unpleasant."

"Not as unpleasant as going a night without fucking you," he says, sending a different sort of ache tingling in to mix with the bruised feeling between my legs.

I tip my face closer to his, murmuring, "How do you do that?"

"Do what?"

"Make me want you without even trying?"

"I'm always trying," he says, kissing me slow and sweet this time.

When he pulls back, I sigh and whisper, "Yep, that's just what I needed. Now, I'm ready to hike."

We find a rock thin enough to wrap our locks around its base, but tall and heavy enough that no one will be able to move it and leave our bikes behind, setting off up the trail into the mountains in the mid-morning sun. Thankfully, we reach the top of the first rise just as the heat is starting to build and step into the entrance to one of the more well-known caves to cool off in the shade as we eat our lunch.

Then, it's just a matter of deciding where to explore first.

Reinvigorated by our meal and the excitement of being so close to our prize, I bounce on my toes. Wes spreads out the paper map we were given at the ranger's station last night when we checked in and bought our caving permits.

He points to the largest black dot on the mountain. "We're here, at the entrance to Smugglers Notch. If we have time later, we might want to come back to this one. There are supposed to be handrails on the path leading down to the main cavern and motion-activated lights so you can look around at the rock formations."

"Totally," I say, "sounds like fun. But we should probably head farther afield first. It sounds like all the caves on this side of the mountain have a good amount of foot traffic. Surely, if there were treasure to find here, someone would have found it by now."

"True, but..." Wes points to the entrance of another fairly well-known cave about a half mile from our current location. "I was thinking about Devil's Roost last night. I know we want to try a system that hasn't been explored as much, but the Roost is the only cave mentioned by name by any of Butch Cassidy's gang when they were interrogated by the police. And it opens up on the other side of the mountain, not far from the lesser-known systems."

I nod. "So, if we don't find anything in there, we can move on to poking around somewhere else. Sounds good." I glance up at him, bobbing my brows. "And probably less of a chance of running into a colony of cranky bats in a place people frequent more often."

"But if the brochure warnings are to be believed, we're going to run into some sooner or later." His eyes flash. "I can't wait."

"Me, either," I say, smiling. "I'm glad we're logical people who are scared of credible threats like clowns and leprechauns instead of silly things like bats and rabies."

He nods and winks. "Thank God. But the bats won't

bother us if we don't bother them, and we both have headlamps. If we see anything sketchy, we can always turn around and head back the way we came."

Sobering, I agree, "Totally, and I think we should plan on playing it safe. Yes, I have a lust for adventure, but I'm more excited about living to see another day. And to eat the yummy stir-fry I'm going to make you tonight."

"And Freya's depending on us to come home," he says.

Touched by the fact that my pet is on his mind, I lean in, pressing a kiss to his cheek.

He smiles as I pull away, his voice soft, "What was that for?"

"For worrying about my little girl."

"She's a cutie," he says. "And we've come a long way since she tried to bite my dick off."

Laughing, I agree, "You have."

But not nearly as far as Wes and I have come.

Just a few days ago, we were barely speaking. Now…

Now, he feels like a member of my team, a person I can trust with my life, and the only man I want making me tingle for the foreseeable future.

I lift a hand, cupping his scruffy cheek for a beat, on the verge of saying things I shouldn't. *Feeling* things I shouldn't. It's only been a few days. It's too soon to tell him that I'm falling in love with him. But maybe by the next time we head off on an epic adventure…

We've already started talking about reworking our summer plans to go hiking together. The fact that he isn't the slightest bit apprehensive about heading out into the wilderness alone with me for two weeks speaks volumes.

So does the warmth in his gaze as he leans into my touch. "I have so much fun with you," he says softly.

"Me, too," I say, the back of my nose stinging a little. "With you."

But what higher compliment is there in the world than to be told that you bring someone joy? What are we here for if not to lighten the load for each other with jokes, fun, and affection?

I lean in, kissing the tip of his nose before pulling back with a laugh. "Okay! Let's do this. I told Freya I'd buy her a jewel-studded collar if we find treasure."

He chuckles. "She'd look swanky in a jewel-studded collar. But I'd prefer you in one. And nothing else."

Cocking my head as I pull on my pack, I murmur, "If that's what you want to spend your treasure money on, I wouldn't complain."

Laughing and teasing, we step into the sun, the strongest I've felt on my skin since last summer, making me grateful we're headed back into the shade soon. There's only so much sunscreen can do when you're bone white from being indoors all winter.

We reach Devil's Roost in about twenty minutes and pause for a beat in its ominous shadow.

"Well, I guess we know why it's called *Devil's* Roost," I say, scanning the large, horn-like formations framing the entrance.

"Scared?" he asks.

I shake my head. "No, but there's a vibe here, right? Do you feel it? Something a little...off? Kind of like the forest last night?"

He pauses, lifting his nose as if scenting the air. "It definitely feels wilder out here. Like no humans have been this way in a while."

I shiver as a cold breeze brushes across my skin and frown. Where is a breeze like that coming from on an eighty-five-degree day? When I realize it's wafting from inside the cave, I shiver again. "I think we should put on another layer."

Wes nods. "Our waterproof jackets, I think. It could be damp in there, too. And we can always stop and add a sweatshirt underneath later if it gets colder as we descend."

"Descend?" I squeak, wondering if maybe I'm a little afraid of tightly enclosed spaces, after all.

"The cave drops about two hundred feet before leveling out as you start toward the other side of the mountain." Wes pulls his zip-up jacket from his pack and slips it over his head, tugging it down around his hips. "The forum I was reading last night after you went to sleep said the ground is pretty uneven, so it's good we wore hiking boots."

I frown as I slip on my own jacket. "You did more research last night? You should have woken me up. I would have helped."

He smiles as he pulls out our headlamps, stored in the front pocket of his larger pack. "You were already snoring. I didn't want to interrupt your rest."

I prop my hands on my hips with a huff. "I don't snore."

"Except when you do," he says, his grin widening.

I huff again. "No, I don't! If I did, someone would have told me by now. I have slept with other men, you know. All night long, sometimes for years and years at a time."

His eyes narrowing and his smile falling away, he nods. "I know. And I'm jealous of every single one."

My lips twitch, my irritation at being falsely accused of a crime fading. "You are?"

"Very, very jealous," he says, bending to kiss me before whispering against my lips, "And it was a cute snore. Nothing to be embarrassed about."

I glare up at him, fighting a smile. "I'm not embarrassed. Because I don't snore, a fact I will prove by recording myself sleeping every night for a week once I get home. And when I prove to you that I am snore-free, I'm going to expect an apology."

His lips curve. "And when you realize I'm right, I promise I won't say 'I told you so.' At least not more than once or twice."

I wrinkle my nose, cursing beneath my breath. "I snore? I really do?"

"Come on, woman. We find enough treasure and we can afford to buy you and Freya both jeweled collars and a CPAP machine for your cute little snoring habit."

Groaning and laughing, I follow him up to the cave entrance. "Ugh, no. I don't want a CPAP machine. I dated a guy who had one of those when I was younger. It's like sleeping next to Darth Vader."

"I think they're quieter now. Technology advances pretty quickly with things like that. Speaking of technology..." Wes passes my headlamp over and slips his on. "Looks like the path dips down and things get dark right away. We're going to want these."

"Right." I ease the lamp on, tightening the strap until it feels snug but not too snug. Then I pull in a deeper breath and ask, "Ready?"

"Ready." Wes flicks his lamp on.

I do the same and start across the rocky terrain behind him, doing my best to ignore the anxiety prickling at the back of my neck. It's just human instinct to feel anxious in tight, dark places. This is my ancient lizard brain trying to keep me safe from saber-toothed cats and dire wolves, nothing to logically be afraid of.

"Did you know that dire wolves were real?" I ask as we start down a steeper section of the path, bracing ourselves on the cool, but thankfully dry cave wall.

"Like from Game of Thrones?" Wes asks.

"Yeah. They were real. Lived in prehistoric times. In caves. They had a bite force like…thirty times more intense than a modern wolf's. They could snap horses in half with one bite."

Wes grunts. "Be careful. That flat rock there is loose."

"Got it."

"Well, that's terrifying, but weren't horses smaller in prehistoric times?"

I frown, racking my memory. "I'm not sure. Maybe?"

"I think they were. Horses were tiny, but sloths were enormous. As big as an elephant with long claws and the kind of teeth that make scientists think they could have been carnivores. Or at least omnivores open to eating a tasty human if they came across one taking a nap in the forest."

"Aw, no, I hate that," I say, my grip tightening on a sturdy rock sticking out of the wall as I follow Wes down a nearly three-foot drop. "Sloths are so cute. I don't want to think of them murdering my ancestors."

"It wouldn't have been murder, just survival. The circle of life."

"Speaking of the circle of life, Chase just realized where pork chops come from," I say. "He was devastated. He loves his cousin Theo's pig, Pippa Jane, so much, Mel's afraid he's going to make their entire family swear off meat of all kinds."

Wes makes a sympathetic sound. "Poor kid. I

remember figuring that out when I was little. I didn't connect the dots until I was a lot older than four, though."

"He's a genius," I say, smiling. "And the sweetest little man. I've never met a kid that young with so much empathy. He can't stand to see anything hurting, whether it's human, animal, or that poor Monstera plant I keep nearly killing in the front of the shop. I just love that kid."

"Me, too," Wes says. "I'm a lucky uncle. My niece and nephew are amazing little people. It gives me hope that humanity is getting better. Kinder."

"Me, too," I say, wishing again that I could be part of raising the next generation of kinder humans. But I guess...I am. I may not be raising Chase or Sara Beth or any of the McGuire littles, but I'm a part of their lives. I'm a grown-up they can trust to love and look out for them and that's special.

I'm about to mention that to Wes—how it's nice to have trusted adults in your life who aren't your parents—when he grinds to a sudden halt. The path is narrow here, with the cave walls so close that, if I held out my arms, I could touch both sides.

It's so tight, I can't see what's made him stop.

Before I can ask, Wes slips on something underfoot, sending several large rocks rolling into the darkness ahead.

A beat later, the air explodes in a flurry of dark leathery wings.

Chapter 25

WESLEY

I try to shift backward, to ask Tessa if she's up for crawling under a colony of sleeping bats, or if she'd rather retrace our steps and find another way over the mountain to the other cave systems. But the ground is wet here, and I slip on something slick underfoot, sending loose rocks rolling loudly into the cave ahead, gaining momentum as they barrel downhill.

Before I can tell Tessa to run, the bats burst into startled flight, a dense cloud of strongly-scented fur and wings barreling straight toward us.

"Get down!" I reach for her as I drop into a crouched position, pulling her to the cave floor beside me, but I'm too late.

"Hair! Hair! They're in my hair," she screams, her eyes squeezed shut as her hands flap frantically around her head.

I reach out, lifting a heavy section of hair on her right side, setting two small, panicked-looking bats free. Their eyes are round and terrified in the glare of my headlamp before they race to join the rest of the fleeing colony. The rational part of my brain understands that the bats are every bit as terrified as we are and only want to fly away to safety.

The irrational part of me can't think of anything except how damned creepy they look with their fangs, squashed faces, and horror-movie wings.

"Another one," Tessa shouts, her voice trembling with terror. "Oh my God, it's on my neck, Wes. I can feel it!"

I shift forward, hoping to gather her abundant hair in my right hand and shoo any bats still underneath away with my left, but my feet slip again.

I fall flat on my belly with an "oof," and start sliding, gaining momentum fast on the smooth stones. My hands scrabble on the cave floor, but the slick mess beneath me makes it impossible to find purchase.

Only, it's not a mess.

It's shit. Bat shit.

The realization hits and I lift my hands with a gagging sound, but that only speeds my fall. Worse, it turns out to be pointless. My palms are already coated with the stuff, frustrating my attempts to grab onto the cave wall. My fingers slide off one stone, then another and another.

By the time I hit open air and start to fall, I've gathered an impressive amount of momentum.

I have a split second to see the roof of the cave illuminated in my headlamp before I hit the ground again—hard—knocking the lamp from my head and plunging me into darkness.

I try to suck in a breath, but the wind has been knocked from my chest. I hear Tessa screaming my name, but I can't call back to tell her I'm okay. All I can do is writhe on the ground, my bruised body aching as I wait for my lungs to remember how to pull in air.

Finally, I'm able to cough, gasp, and call out, "I'm here! Down here. Be careful, the cave floor is crazy slick."

"Oh my God, oh my God. Thank God," I hear Tessa sob from what sounds like a great distance, way farther than I could have fallen in just a few seconds.

Or, at least, I hope that's true. I suppose that last drop could have been longer than I thought. I can't see anything right now. Without my headlamp, the cave is pitch black, like the bottom of the sea.

I shiver, feeling like an idiot for getting myself—and Tessa—into this mess. I'm a lawyer, for fuck's sake, not a professional spelunker.

Swiping my filthy hands on my hiking pants, I sit up, wincing as pain flashes through my hip and up the left side of my back, but nothing's broken. I'm just a little bruised. The only thing truly wounded is my pride.

But I'm not sure about Tessa...

"Were you bitten?" I call out, heart racing in the darkness as I fumble around on the thankfully clean rocks beneath me, searching for my headlamp.

"No, I don't think so," Tessa says, her voice closer now. "But my adrenaline is pumping so hard, I'm not sure I'd feel it if I had been. I'm pretty sure we're both going to need rabies shots, though. Just in case. I'm seeing an emergency room trip in our future."

I wince. "I'm sorry, Tessa. So fucking sorry."

"Don't apologize. This is as much my fault as yours. I'm almost forty years old, I should know better than to go climbing around in caves pretending I'm Indiana Jones." Suddenly, a beam of light appears above me, slanting across the top of the pit. Before I can call out to warn her again, Tessa says, "Are you down there?"

"Yes," I reply. "Be careful. It's deeper than I realized."

"Okay." Her light tips down. I wince, shielding my eyes for a beat before she shifts the beam to my right. "Sorry. Are you sure you're not hurt?"

I do another quick body scan, then shake my head. "No. Just a little bruised."

She sighs. "Well, that's good at least. Think you can crawl out? If I keep the light on the side of the wall so you can see the rocks? It looks like there are some decent footholds and..." She trails off with a soft gasp. "Wes, look!"

I glance down, scanning the circle of illumination around me. "Do you see my headlamp?"

"No, look! There!"

I turn again. "I can't see where you're pointing. All I can see is the glow of the light."

"About four feet behind you and a little to your left," she says, the excitement in her voice making my stomach tighten. "There, can you see it now?"

She shifts the beam slightly, until it centers on a small pile of rocks. The stones are arranged in a pyramid shape that reaches nearly to my knees, and clearly aren't something that occurred naturally. Someone stacked them that way.

And why would someone do that here, at the bottom of a pit, halfway through a cave unless...

"Should I see what's under there?" I ask.

The words are barely out of my mouth before Tessa hisses, "Yes, but be careful. If you feel any cursed vibes, stop right away."

My lips twitching, I ask, "What do cursed vibes feel like?"

"You'll know them when you feel them," she says. "Just take it slow. And maybe say a Hail Mary or something before you start."

I glance up at her, squinting into the light.

"I don't know," she says. "That's supposed to help in times of need, right? Sorry, I was a really bad Catholic. My mom only made me go until I was eight. Then she got into a fight with the priest about birth control and we never went back. He apparently didn't think I should be an only child, but she very much did. I did, too, honestly. My mom's a good person, but she shouldn't have been a mom. It was obvious to me, even as a kid, that she didn't enjoy children."

My brow furrows. "I'm sorry. That sucks."

"It's okay. We get along much better now that I'm a grown-up and give her space. And I don't take it personally. At least, not anymore. Some people just aren't maternal." She exhales. "Now, are you going to see what's under there or not? The suspense is killing me."

Pulling in a bracing breath, I nod. "Yeah. On it. Let's see if we can find my headlamp first, though. I'll be able to see what's going on under there better if I have more light. Can you scan the floor for me?"

"Sure thing," she says, slowly guiding the light around the rest of the small depression until it lands on my headlamp. "There. See it?"

"Yeah, thanks." Wiping my hands on my pants again, I reach for it, positioning it on my head, almost gagging again at the smell lingering on my fingers.

As far as shit goes, it isn't awful—more of a musty, ammonia-tinged scent—but I've never wanted a wet wipe as much as I want one now. I have hand sanitizer in my pack, but it won't do anything to clean the actual filth from my skin and there wasn't a single body of water between here and the campsite. I'll just have to deal with my stink until we get back to the camper.

Holding my breath to ease my gag reflex, I move back toward the stones, pausing to study them in the brighter light of my own lamp. There's no dust or anything down here in the cave, nothing to hint at how long ago these stones might have been gathered.

They don't look like something that's been lying in wait for over a hundred years, but I can't know for sure. Time passes in strange ways inside caves and underground. It's why so many archeological finds are discovered in places like this, places protected from the elements that damage artifacts left in the open air.

"Any bad vibes?" Tessa asks.

I shake my head. "I don't think so." I reach for the stone on top, letting my fingers linger on the rough edges for a beat before I shift it gently to one side.

"Still good?" she asks again, making me laugh. "Sorry, I'm excited. If we actually find something, we only have to feel half as embarrassed about getting scared by bats and covered in poop."

I glance up at her over my shoulder. "Shit? Did you fall in the shit, too?"

"Oh yeah. Covered in the stuff," she says. "But on the upside, I caught myself before I came sliding into the hole after you. And I found your phone when I fell."

My brows shoot up as I touch my pants, realizing my cell isn't tucked into my back pocket where it usually is.

"Don't worry, it's fine," she says. "I mean, it's filthy, but not broken."

My shoulders relax. "Good. Thanks."

"No problem." She makes a disgusted sound I feel at the back of my throat. "I think we're going to need showers before the emergency room. Surely, as long as we get the shots sometime tonight, we'll be fine, right? Do they still make you get a circle of rabies shots in your stomach? Or is that an urban legend?"

"I'm not sure," I say, turning back to the stones. "But I can look it up on my phone once we have cell service. I had two bars for most of our ride."

"Good idea," she says as I begin to dismantle the pile in earnest, shifting larger and larger rocks to one side. "I should have brought my phone, but it wouldn't have done us much good. Since Freya unplugged the charger last night." She makes a worried sound. "I hope she's okay. And won't be too mad at us for showing up stinking of bat poop and then leaving again. But I can't take a ferret to the emergency room, not even on a leash. Sorry, I know I'm babbling. I'm just nervous. Logically, I know this isn't the part of the movie where the intrepid adventurers make the mistake of continuing to pursue the treasure, even after they should have run away—we're not in a movie; this is real life—but my gut is screaming that we're about to be attacked by hungry outlaw ghosts."

I grunt, not wanting to admit out loud that I'm feeling the same way. Instead, I ask, "What would outlaw ghosts be hungry for?"

"I don't know," she says. "But it wouldn't be something we'd be keen on giving them. Probably our blood or our souls. Maybe the skin on our faces. I have an irrational fear of losing the skin on my face."

"I think that's a perfectly rational fear. It would be really unpleasant to live without skin on any part of your body, especially your face," I say, my pulse picking up as I near the bottom of the pile, and something dark gray and smoother than the stones comes into view.

I move faster, depositing the rest of the rocks in the new pile as Tessa asks, "What is it? Is there something there?"

I take a beat, catching my breath before I shift to one side, letting her headlamp beam fall on what we've discovered.

She sucks in a breath. "Am I crazy or is that an antique lockbox?"

I smile. "You're not crazy. I think we might have just found Butch Cassidy's long-lost treasure."

Tessa emits a soft squeal that makes me laugh. "Should we open it? Or take it outside first? I'm putting on a brave face, but honestly, I'm ready to get back out into the sun, where me and the bats have more room to stay away from each other than we do down here."

I try pushing the buttons on the front of the box, but they're rusty with age and the lid remains firmly closed. "I can't open it. It's either stuck or we need some kind of combination. I'll put it in my pack and we can work on it later."

"Sounds good," she says, squealing softly again as I slide my backpack off my shoulders and angle the large rectangular box inside. It's made of some kind of iron and isn't light by any means, but I think the nylon fabric will hold long enough for us to get back to camp. "Could be slipping in poop was the best thing that happened to us today!"

I zip my bag and slide the straps back on, grinning up at her as I start to climb. "As long as we don't die of some kind of exotic poop-borne illness."

She makes a gagging sound. "Oh God, I didn't think of that. We should research that first. First, bat poop illnesses. Then the protocol for rabies shots."

"Sounds good," I grunt, pulling myself up the wall, wincing as my bruised hip twinges in protest.

"Actually, you have bars down here," Tessa says from above me. "Crazy. What's your passcode? I'll start googling while you climb."

"Five, four, three, two, one," I tell her, earning a judgmental huff I deserve.

"Yeah, you're going to have to change that," she mutters. "A passcode like that is a good way to..." She trails off, going so silent that I call out after a moment, "You okay up there?"

"I'm fine," she says, but her voice is tighter than it was before, all the fun, and even the anxiety, gone out of it.

I want to tell her that she doesn't sound fine, but I'm currently using all my strength to cling to one rock while finding a foothold higher up the wall. The next few minutes pass in almost eerie silence, building the anxiety swelling in my chest. By the time I pull myself over the edge, I half expect Tessa to be gone, stolen away by those hungry ghosts she was worried about.

But she's crouched a few feet back from the edge of the pit, my phone in hand.

As I emerge, she looks up, her wounded features illuminated by the blue light as she asks, "So, were you going to tell me that Darcy texted you and we were fine to go home? Or were you going to lie about that, too?"

Chapter 26

TESSA

We barely speak on the way back to the campsite.

Wes tries to talk, but I shut him down.

A part of me insists I'm overreacting—it wasn't a lie, so much as a failure to share information—but the rest of me is already in lockdown. Finding out Wes is keeping things from me shouldn't be scarier than having bats in my hair, but it is.

I was falling *so hard* for him, so hard that I'd let myself forget how much it hurt the first time he let secrets get between us.

Now, it all comes rushing back, making my head spin.

How much it hurt to learn the man I'd been making love to all night was in a relationship with another woman. How my heart shriveled in my chest when that break-up he'd promised didn't come. How I wanted to jump through a wormhole to another dimension when I spotted Wes and Darcy at a table in my favorite café a few days after our night in the woods.

They didn't look happy—not even close—but that didn't matter. He'd still chosen her, not me.

It's the story of my life.

For one reason or another, I am always the unchosen one.

If I were a character in a fantasy novel, I wouldn't be the princess who learns she has magical powers or the slayer who has to save the world from zombies. I wouldn't even be the spunky sidekick who assists the heroine with my encyclopedic knowledge of healing plants or weapons expertise. I'd be the mayor's daughter who's killed by bad guys in chapter three, a plot device to show how bad the bad guys are.

Back at the camper, I quickly clean up and change clothes, but when I cuddle Freya, she can obviously still smell that I've been getting up close and personal with other furry things. I endure her frantic sniffing of my hair patiently, wishing I had a similar skill set. If I could smell other women on my man, maybe lies wouldn't feel like such a big deal.

But even as the thought drifts through my head, I know that's not the real problem.

I'm not worried about Wes cheating. Maybe I should be, but I'm not. I believe that he's falling for me as hard and fast as I'm falling for him, and that he clearly feels terrible about keeping Darcy's texts from me—regret is etched in every tense line of his face as he emerges from his own clean-up in the bathroom.

I just want to be able to trust my person. I *need* that.

And I need to know that he trusts *me*. I can't live with this kind of uncertainty, always wondering if I'm being told the whole truth, always waiting for the other shoe to drop. Over time, even little white lies can come between two people, and Wes's lies aren't white. They're an "I like to manipulate things behind the scenes without telling people" shade of gray.

At the Emergency Room, we learn we do indeed need to start the rabies vaccine protocol. Apparently, bat teeth are so tiny and sharp that we could have been bitten and not even know it. We'll need to get one round of shots now, and then another shot at the three, seven, and fourteen days post exposure. The day three shots, we can get here at the hospital in Utah, the nurse says. Afterwards, she can send the vaccination records to our primary care providers in Bad Dog, so that we can finish the protocol when we're home from our trip.

If we decide to stay the rest of the week.

Right now, that's a big "if."

I just want to go home. I want to crawl into bed with Freya, watch reruns of Gilmore Girls, and remember that even Lorelei Gilmore, a gorgeous, spunky, intelligent, hardworking woman, with a fantastic sense of humor and a heart as big as the burgers at Luke's diner didn't find her happily ever after until late in life.

I don't have to commit to a future of ferret-nurturing spinsterhood. There's still time for me to find my person. With time, I'll forget the dazzling, magical, perfect way Wes made me feel. I'll forget that he's the only man who's ever appreciated my goofy side as much as my sexy one, the only man who's looked at me like I'm the answer to every question, the only man who's ever felt like home.

"Can we talk? Please?" Wes asks from the door to the camper.

He ate the burger and fries we picked up on the way back to our campsite inside at the banquet. I ate out here by the fire, Freya cavorting on her leash beside my chair, gratefully snatching at the tiny pieces of meat I tossed her way.

Even after the exhausting day, I just wasn't that hungry, and I still don't want to talk. But I owe Wes that much.

I nod toward the other camp chair.

He settles into the seat, leaning forward with his elbows braced on his knees, his expression still drawn. "I have something to tell you."

My brows lift.

After a beat, he continues, "I don't want lies between us anymore, not even lies of omission. I understand why you're upset, but honestly, Tessa, the last thing I'd ever want to do is hurt you. I just didn't want to ruin the fun by bringing up Darcy's texts. I was going to tell you, I swear. And now that I know how much things like this upset you, in the future, I would know to tell you right away."

I sigh and cross my arms tighter over my chest.

"I'd be fine with you going through my phone if you wanted," Wes adds, making me frown. "Whenever you wanted to."

"I don't want to go through your phone," I say. "I just want to know I can trust you, Wes."

He leans closer, his fingers threading together into a single fist. "And you can. I swear. I have nothing to hide." He pauses, his teeth dragging over his full bottom lip. "Or...I won't. Once I tell you one last thing."

My stomach knots around what little food I managed to force down. "Okay," I say, even though I'm not sure I want to hear his "one last thing." I'm already struggling. I don't know if I'll be able to let my walls down and trust him again.

One more lie might be all it takes to put the nail in the coffin of this relationship.

"It's about Carl," he says, surprising me.

I sit back, blinking faster. "Carl? The man in the woods?"

Wes nods tightly. "A few days after he attacked you, I mentioned what happened to an old high school friend of mine who's a cop. I was just wondering if I needed to come in and give a statement or something. But she said no one had reported anything like that. When I realized you hadn't told the police about what happened, I thought about coming to talk to you, to try to convince you to come to the station with me." He sighs, dragging a hand through his hair. "But then I started thinking about all the women I've represented in court, all those restraining orders that did jack shit to keep their abusive partners away from them. One of my clients ended up in the hospital with a broken jaw. Another...didn't make it out of the relationship. She ended up going back to her abuser. He'd made it too scary for her to keep fighting for her freedom. Every time I see her in town, she looks smaller, more...hollow inside."

He trails off, misery clear on his face.

I want to reach out to him, to pull him in for a hug and tell him how sorry I am that he has a front row seat to the worst aspects of humanity. But the hugging part of me is still locked away with the rest of the vulnerable emotions that ran for shelter when I read that text.

Instead, I hold out my fast-food bag. "My churro chunks are still in here. I couldn't eat them."

His lips twitch. "Thanks, I'm good."

"Are you sure? Sugar makes everything better."

"Maybe later. I have to get this out first. My stomach is in knots."

"I get it." I tuck the bag back in the side pocket of my camp chair and close the Velcro flap, keeping it safe from Freya, who is still prowling around the fire, looking for microscopic pieces of meat she might have missed.

Wes sighs. "So, yeah, I thought about all that and understood why you'd decided against reporting."

"He didn't really hurt me, Wes," I say. "I mean, he did, obviously. I was terrified, and I have no doubt that he would have done very bad things to me if you hadn't shown up. But he didn't get to follow through on those things. In the eyes of the law, he was only guilty of roughing me up a little. That's not enough to land him in prison or get him off the streets for any length of time. It's only enough to make him even more angry and myself more of a target."

He nods, his jaw tight. "I thought about that, too. Our system is so messed up. The fact that we have to wait until clearly violent people step over the line drives me crazy. So..." He clears his throat and blows out a long breath. "This is hard," he mutters. "You're going to think I'm crazy."

"Just tell me," I say, my own stomach churning. "The suspense is worse than whatever you did."

He glances up, arching a thick brow. "You want to bet?"

I let out a nervous laugh. "Jesus, you're scaring me. What did you do? Kill him?"

He pauses just long enough to make the blood drain from my extremities before he says, "No, but I stalked him. Or, paid a private detective to stalk him for me, since I didn't really have the time."

My eyes bulge. "What?"

"He wasn't an accountant, like he told you. He wasn't from Redwood Falls, either. He was a janitor at a high school in Chicago."

My jaw drops. "Chicago? But his location tracking said—"

"He must have been using a VPN or something to make it look like he was local," Wes cuts in. "In reality, he lived with his mother in a bad neighborhood in South Shore and had a reputation for being a creep. The police knew he wasn't quite right, but they were busy dealing with gangs and drug dealers. Carl had never done anything bad enough to get more than a ticket for trespassing and a strongly worded warning to quit lurking outside the girls' locker room at the YMCA."

"Gross," I say, my nose wrinkling.

"Yeah." Wes pauses, unlacing and relacing his fingers, his gaze shifting to the fire as he adds, "He was gross, but he wasn't doing anything criminal. Not anything we could use to get him locked up, anyway. Not until my guy realized he hadn't brought groceries home in close to three weeks."

I frown. "Is that a crime? If so, I might be guilty. Sometimes I go weeks without hitting the store. I live on leftovers from catering events, frozen soup, and fancy oatmeal."

"He wasn't bringing home leftovers, either. And his house didn't look like the kind of place where people were freezing soup or whipping up batches of oatmeal, if you know what I mean," he says, his gaze still locked on the fire. "It was a hunch, really. The PI and I both felt in our gut that something was wrong in there. We suspected his mother, a shut-in who'd had several strokes, was probably being abused."

"Oh no," I say, feeling terrible for the woman. Monsters like Carl usually aren't raised by sweet little homemakers, but no one deserves to be trapped or forced to go hungry.

Wes gives a short nod. "Yeah. But...it was worse than we thought."

My hand comes to cover my mouth, my sinking gut already knowing where this is headed.

"She'd been dead for a while," he adds. "And not from natural causes. Apparently, he'd choked her and left the body in the back room so he could keep collecting her social security and disability payments. The cop who did the welfare check said the smell was horrific."

"Oh God." I suck in a breath that catches halfway down my throat. "Oh my God, Wes. Why haven't I heard about this? Was it on the news?"

He shrugs and tosses a few more sticks on the fire. "Chicago's far away. And a lot of bad things happen in big cities. The news can't report on everything."

I sit back in my chair, stunned. "Wow. So, is he..."

"He's in jail awaiting trial. But it'll be a slam dunk. He's going away for a long time. You won't have to worry about him showing up in your life again." Wes looks up from the flames, his gaze uncertain. "I hope that didn't make you hate me more. I was only trying to keep you safe."

My chest aching, I shake my head. "I don't hate you. I could never hate you."

"But you don't trust me," he says, his gaze still sad. "And why should you? You're right. I'm a liar." He rubs a hand at the back of his neck. "I've always thought of it as sharing information on a need-to-know basis or keeping my private business private, but...withholding is a form of lying. Even if you have someone's best interests at heart."

Biting my lip, I think over everything's he's said, everything he's done. When I take a step back to look at the big picture, it's suddenly clear what they all have in common. "It's part of being the 'nice one' in your family, isn't it? You keep secrets to keep the peace."

His brows lift, but after a moment, he nods. "I guess so. But I promise, I mean well. I honestly do."

"But you also want to be able to do what you want without facing the consequences. Or hearing everyone else's opinions about your choices."

His lips press together. "That, too."

"It's hard to change lifelong habits," I say softly.

His gaze locks with mine. "It would be way fucking harder to lose you." Uncertainty creeps into his expression. "But I guess in order to do that, I would have had to have had you in the first place."

The backs of my eyes sting as I whisper, "You had me. You *have* me. You stalked the man who hurt me until you got him thrown in jail, Wes. Is that crazy? Yes. Super crazy." I swallow past the lump in my throat. "But it's also the most wonderful thing anyone has ever done for me."

"I would do it again in a heartbeat," he promises. "But next time, I'd tell you first. I swear to you, Tessa. No more secrets between us, no more withholding information, no more trying to control the narrative. From now on, I'm committed to transparency. Even when it's hard."

I nod, my stomach sinking again as I remember all the other roadblocks in our way. "I believe you, but...are you sure about this, Wes? Are you sure you want to hitch your wagon to a woman six years older than you are for the long haul? I mean, even if things work out perfectly, I can't give you children."

"I don't know if I can have biological children, either. I've never tried." He shifts his chair closer to mine, until our knees touch and relief prickles across my skin. I wasn't sure I would ever touch him again. Even this small contact feels like being pulled back from the edge of a terrible fall. "That doesn't mean we can't be a family," he continues, curling his hands around the backs of my knees. "The two of us. Together. With Freya. That's a family. And if we decide someday that we have a baby-shaped hole in our hearts, we can adopt." He shrugs. "Or maybe we'll be happy being the cool aunt and uncle and spending our free time out in the woods doing things people with kids don't have time to do."

"Like having kinky sex in our tent and eating marshmallows for breakfast?" I ask, the tension between us taking on a different quality as he leans in.

"You haven't seen kinky yet, Lady Gray," he whispers. "There are still so many things I want to do to you. *With* you. Will you still be my girl?"

Biting my bottom lip, I nod, my smile stretching wide at the happiness that blooms on his face. "Yes, I will," I say, laughing as Freya pops up between us, her face poking through our knees. "I think Freya wants to be your girl, too."

"I think she wants the food in the pocket of your chair," he says, as she crawls over my thigh and up to my hip, reaching over to paw at the Velcro.

I smile. "I think she wants both. A girl can have her churro bites and true love, too. I mean, unless you're a ferret and can't eat things like that without getting sick."

His expression sobers. "True love, huh?"

"I'm getting there," I whisper, hopeful wings fluttering in my chest.

His grip tightens on the backs of my knees, sending electrical pulses flowing up my thighs. "Me, too. Can I take you inside and show you how close I am?"

I nod, my every cell flooded with longing as his fingers thread through mine.

After tucking Freya into her crate—the better to keep her from ripping my chair apart for forbidden treats or sneaking in to watch things she shouldn't—we come together in the dark, his lips on mine and his hands everywhere.

And it's even better than before, because there's nothing between us but the truth of how much we both want this to work.

"Ouch," I hiss, wincing as I toss my shirt to the floor, sending pain flashing through my injection site.

"Should we take it easy?" Wes asks, pausing on his path toward the bed.

"Never." I thread my fingers in his hair, pulling him down for another hard kiss that he returns with an intensity that banishes the hint of discomfort.

It banishes everything but the need to have him inside me.

On the bed, I push him back on the mattress and tear at his clothes, freeing his cock and stroking him up and down, loving the groan my touch wrenches from the back of his throat. Shifting to one side, I quickly pull off my leggings and underwear, before straddling him again.

"Yes," Wes says, cupping my breasts in his hands as I lean over him, bracing myself on the pillows beneath his head. "I like you like this, on top of me with your breasts in my face." He lifts his head, dragging his tongue back and forth across my nipples, teasing them both before he settles in to suck my right nipple deep into his mouth.

Breath already coming fast, I grind against his erection, coating him with my arousal before nudging him into place with a wiggle of my hips. There's a hint of resistance as I sink down, but that feels good, too, the way he stretches me, filling every empty inch.

"Fuck, Tessa," he breathes, lifting his hips, forcing his cock just a few centimeters deeper. "You feel so good, but you really suck at foreplay."

"*You* suck at foreplay," I say, moaning as he pinches my nipples, sending a fresh shock of arousal straight to my core.

"No, I don't," he says.

"No, you don't," I agree, beginning to ride him in earnest. "But I don't need foreplay all the time. Sometimes I just need you, inside me, showing me that you feel it, too."

"I feel it, too," he assures me. "It's perfect. You're perfect."

"*We're* perfect." I rock my hips, taking him deep again, shifting the angle until the head of his erection brushes against that electric spot inside. "Yes, oh, yes. Right there."

"Yes," he says, still rubbing and squeezing my breasts with one hand as he reaches down to grip my ass hard with the other. "Just like that. Ride your cock, baby. Ride me until you come all over me. I love how wet you are, how you take what you need from me. Fuck, yes, Tessa, I can feel you going. Fuck, baby."

I come with a wild cry, losing control—and my rhythm—as fierce waves of pleasure pulse through me. But that's okay. Wes takes over, gripping my bottom with both hands and moving me up and down on his hard, hot length.

He isn't gentle and half the words spilling from his lips are too foul for polite company, but I love every second of it. By the time he comes with a deep groan, lifting me off the mattress as he thrusts up and into me one last time, I'm at the edge again.

I come again, cursing and whimpering and telling him how much I love him and his dirty mouth.

"Love it," I pant again. "Love what a filthy talker you are."

"And I love feeling your come all over my thighs."

I lift my head and arch a brow. "That isn't all mine, buddy."

He grins. "I also love not using condoms. You've ruined me for all other women, Lady Gray."

"Good," I say, giggling when he gently swats my ass. I sink back onto his chest with a sigh. "Let's always fuck like filthy bunnies, okay? Even when we're old and tired and I have arthritis in my hips and you have trouble getting it up?"

"Never going to have that problem," he says. "Not with you."

And then he proves it by nailing me against the wall in the tiny bathroom before we shower, and it is...the happiest ending to the craziest day ever.

Bar none.

Chapter 27

WESLEY

I'm nearly asleep, lulled into a deep sense of peace by the warm weight of my favorite person resting on my chest, all clean from our shower and well-fucked and smelling of her floral shampoo, when I remember—

"The lockbox," I murmur into the darkness, sending Tessa's head shooting up so fast, I chuckle.

"Oh my God, how could we forget?" she asks, slapping my side with her hand. "Some treasure hunters we turned out to be, Preston."

"My apologies, Lady Gray," I say, scooting off the mattress behind her. "I was distracted."

"By what?" she asks, pulling on my t-shirt before flicking on the small light above the stove.

With her legs bare beneath the white fabric and her hair long and damp, hanging all the way to her round ass, she's so beautiful, it takes my breath away.

I swallow and give a slight shake of my head.

Her gaze softens. "You like me," she murmurs. "And you think I'm pretty."

"The prettiest," I say. "And if we're millionaires, I

need you to promise that you'll still sleep in my old t-shirts."

"And you have to promise to sleep in nothing at all so I always have easy access to your fabulous dick," she says, her eyes glittering as she nods toward the lockbox, still snug in my pack by the door. "Ready to crack this sucker open?"

"I'll get the bolt cutters," I say, pulling on my jeans with nothing underneath.

Tessa's brows shoot up. "Bolt cutters? You brought bolt cutters? What do you usually do when you're camping? Breaking and entering?"

I chuckle. "No, I hit the hardware store across the street from the hospital while you were getting your shot. Figured I might as well make myself useful."

"You're always useful," she says, her gaze dragging down to the top of my jeans. "And sexy. Have I told you how much I love your hips? Specifically, the chiseled parts on the sides..."

My lips curve. "You mean my V cut?"

"Is that what it's called?" she murmurs, her eyes still glued to my body in a way that makes my cock perk up behind my fly.

"It is." I tug my jeans lower, teasing her, and am rewarded with a sexy giggle from the woman I love.

I do love her. So much. Thank God I get to keep loving her.

Hopefully, for the rest of our lives.

"Stop," she says as she sways closer. "If you keep that up, we're never going to learn what's in that lockbox."

"The lockbox will still be there when I've made your box come on my mouth."

She shakes her head. "You're a bad, bad man." She

stops inches away, lifting her chin with a sexy smile. "But you have a very talented mouth, so..."

An hour later, after we've done more very good bad things to each other and let a fussing Freya out of her crate to roam the camper, we settle at the banquet with the lockbox and my new bolt cutters.

Within just a few minutes, our treasure is unveiled.

And it isn't what either one of us expected...

Not even close.

Epilogue

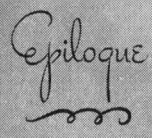

Tessa

Five months later...

It's another McGuire family end-of-summer lake party and Mother Nature has pulled out all the stops. Early September has never looked so good.

The sun is shining, the water is refreshing, and all the people—and animals—we love are enjoying a well-deserved Friday off. The older cousins ride jet skis, while the younger cousins jump off the diving board in the middle of the lake in their life jackets, with Kyle the turkey and his growing family right behind them.

On our pontoon, Pippa Jane the pig, Keanu Reeves the dog, and our own furry bundle of trouble splash in a kiddie pool amidst a cacophony of oinks, dooks, and rusty barks. They're making such a racket, I don't hear Binx shouting for me to join the next bout of Pool Noodle Peril until she throws a beach ball at me from the next boat over.

"Hey, watch it," Wes says, grabbing the ball and turning to hurl it back at his little sister.

Binx laughs and ducks the projectile, before standing with her hands lifted at her sides. "Tessa said she wanted to play against Mel. I didn't want her to miss her turn just because Keanu Reeves has volume control problems."

"He does not," Wren says from behind her, where she's busy setting up snack time for the toddler set, including her own precious boy, Reed, while wearing his new baby sister, Riley, strapped to her chest. "He's just not afraid to speak his truth. Loudly."

Keanu Reeves throws back his head, making a sound somewhere between a howl and a bunch of silverware tossed into a woodchipper. In response, Freya climbs on his back, reaching around to wrap both paws around his lips, making Wes and I laugh.

"Are you okay on critter duty alone for a little while?" I ask, standing to toss my straw hat onto the bench beside me.

"You bet," he says, his gaze raking up and down my torso as I strip off my cover-up, revealing my gold one-piece bathing suit. He makes a rumbling sound low in his throat, and I roll my eyes.

"It's a one-piece," I hiss.

"It's hot. You're hot," he murmurs, still devouring me with his eyes.

"And you're incorrigible," I say, aiming my cover-up at his face.

He catches it easily in one hand and smiles. "Yep. I

have no interest in mending my wicked ways. In fact, I think I might need to take you out on the Sea-Doo later. To a little secluded cove, I happen to know about, where no one will hear you scream my name."

My cheeks heat and butterflies fill my stomach. Even after five months of getting naked with this man every chance we get; I still can't get enough of him. If anything, I want him more with every passing day.

But not enough to risk getting caught by one of the teenagers out riding their own Sea-Doos.

"Tonight," I promise. "I have a surprise for you."

His brows lift. "Yeah? A sex surprise?"

"Let's just say my treasure chest order finally came in," I murmur vaguely.

The lockbox we found in Utah didn't contain Butch Cassidy's loot, after all. Which turned out to be a good thing, Wes and I realized later. Butch's treasure would have been protected under a 1979 law that gives the government ownership of all archeological finds. Our treasure—a time capsule buried by a group of high society Ivy Leaguers on a summer adventure in the 1950s—was exempt from the mandate, allowing us to do with the contents what we wished.

We kept the earrings, photographs, and delicate champagne glasses as mementos of our first find. We sold the vintage baseball cards and first edition of The Catcher in the Rye for a startling amount of cash.

And when I say startling, I mean enough to fund our Appalachian Trail adventure three weeks ago and buy the food truck I plan to turn into my full-time gig by next summer. And we still had enough left over for each of us to have five hundred dollars to spend on something nice for the house.

Wes moved in with me just a few weeks after our camping trip, and we couldn't be happier. Especially since he spent his five hundred dollars constructing a gorgeous brick pizza oven on my back patio. We made wood-grilled pizza all summer, experimenting with new toppings and dough recipes while Freya played in the yard.

Soon, we'll be able to end magical autumn nights by our brick oven with a visit to the sex swing in our bedroom...

Christian was nice enough to install it for me on the down-low this morning, while Wes and I were out buying drinks for the party before heading to the lake. Christian isn't the most discreet McGuire brother, but he's great with tools, and Wes has enough dirt on him that we can trust him to keep his mouth shut about our swing.

After all, we've kept *our* mouths shut about his sun goddess thing with Starling and the time Wes had to go let a naked Christian and Starling out of their shed after a tree fell across the entrance while they were playing "Love in a Zombie-Apocalypse Fallout Shelter." (Weird, but whatever floats their boat. After all the hair-pulling and spanking Wes and I get up to on a regular basis, I'm certainly in no position to judge. And the handcuffs and blindfold... And the thing he did with ice cubes on a particularly steamy evening last week...)

I shiver as I blow him a kiss and leap off the end of the boat, grateful for the cool water closing over my head. I need something to cool me off or I'm never going to make it the next four hours until we head for home.

Over at the Pool Noodle Peril obstacle course and battle station, I pull myself up on the floating dock beside Melissa, who is wearing a nearly identical one-piece to mine, though hers is blue and allegedly still maternity wear. She's only four weeks postpartum, but looks incredible. Aside from her much larger than normal breasts, I would never guess that she'd just had a baby.

But little Jonah James Boudreaux is currently napping in the shade with his grandmother on the largest pontoon, oblivious to the fact that his mother is about to defend her Pool Noodle Peril title just a dozen yards away.

"Don't be scared," she says, grinning like the shark she is as we pick our noodles from the garbage bin full of long foam floaties. "I'm not in peak condition. Jonah still isn't sleeping through the night, and I was up feeding him at four this morning. There's a chance you might actually move on to the semi-finals this year."

I laugh and nudge her hip with mine. "Right. And pigs are going to fly out of my ass."

"Pippa Jane is way too big to fly out of anyone's ass. And she doesn't have wings," she says, her eyes dancing. "Just know I love you and kicking your sweet bottom is going to hurt me as much as it hurts you."

"Right," I say, laughing as Binx blows the airhorn to start the next bout and Melissa and I jump into the water, swimming hard toward the first obstacle while batting at each other with our noodles.

I hold my own across the water trampoline—even managing to bounce Mel off her feet once—but by the time we reach the rope swing and the floating foam lily pads on the other side, Mel is pulling ahead. When she bats me off the second lily pad with her noodle, sending me crashing into the water, I know it's over, but I don't give up. I pull myself up onto the diving board dock and hurry after her, crossing the finish line a mere fifteen seconds after the reigning champion.

Once we've both swum back to Binx's boat and wrapped up in towels, Mel pulls me in for a damp hug. "Sorry, pumpkin. You know I love you."

I return the hug. "Love you, too. Even though you're filled with pool noodle blood lust."

She giggles maniacally. "I really am."

"Good job, Mommy!" Chase shouts from where he's waiting in line for the shorter diving board on the other side of the boat with his stepdad, Aaron. "You kicked booty!"

Mel waves at him, but instead of moving to rejoin her family, she turns to me, catching my elbow. She lowers her voice, her smile fading as she whispers, "Hey, can we chat for a second?"

Frowning, I nod. "Of course. What's up?"

She reaches down, taking my hands in hers, sending a shiver of apprehension up my spine. I hope she isn't upset about the food truck thing. I told her I didn't intend to leave the catering business until next spring, giving her plenty of time to find my replacement.

But she might still feel I'm being disloyal, abandoning her when she has a little one and a newborn and needs to lean on me more than she has before.

She pulls in a breath, her eyes shining as she says, "I just want you to know how happy I am for you, for all the good things happening in your life, both personal and professional. And if you decide you want to launch your business earlier than planned, I'm on board, okay? You've waited long enough for your dreams to come true. You shouldn't have to wait any longer. Not because of me, anyway."

I squeeze her hands. "Thank you, babes. That's so sweet, but I can't afford the renovations I'll need to make to the truck until next year. I need time to save up."

"Small business loan," Binx says, suddenly appearing beside us, a sweating beer in hand. "You'll be approved. I have no doubt. I mean, as long as you get your butt in and apply before I quit in October."

My brows shoot up. "What? You're quitting the bank?"

"I am," she says, "but that's not the important part. The important part is that you don't have to wait to start Easy Breezy Cheesy. Which, as far as I'm concerned, is good news for everyone. I need gourmet grilled cheese in my life like, yesterday."

"Same," Mel says, beaming up at me, her eyes still misty. "It's time to fly the nest, Tessa Marley Gray McGuire."

I bite my lip as emotion swells in my chest. "Don't jinx it," I say with a soft laugh. "He hasn't asked me yet."

Binx and Mel exchange a look I don't understand until Binx nods over my shoulder. "I think you should turn around."

Pulse picking up, I turn to see Wes standing on the deck of our boat and Freya picking her way expertly across the small rope ladder stretching between the two anchored pontoons. She's wearing her fancy blue bow from the wedding, the one Wes removed earlier so that she could swim without getting it wet.

But it isn't just the bow. There's something else tied to the satin. I see it even before she reaches the edge of the ladder.

I reach for her with shaking hands. "Wesley McGuire," I say, my voice trembling nearly as hard as my fingers as I untie the bow, freeing the gorgeous diamond ring dangling from Freya's neck. "Did you seriously just trust a ferret on a rope ladder wearing a slippery satin bow with our future?"

He grins, his eyes crinkling at the edges as Freya climbs up to perch on my shoulder. "She promised she wouldn't drop it. Besides, she's part of our future, too. She told me she thinks you should say yes, by the way."

Holding his gaze across the few feet of water separating us, I say, "Maybe I will. Once you ask me."

Without missing a beat, he sinks down onto one knee, triggering murmurs of surprise from the surrounding boats. Someone shuts off the music and even Keanu Reeves and Pippa Jane fall silent in their baby pool as Wes says, "Tessa Marley Gray Martin, you make me happier than I ever thought I could be. Even on my hardest days, when I'm reminded of all the shittiness in the world, it doesn't drag me down. Not anymore. Because I know I'm coming home to you."

I press my lips together, fighting tears as he continues, "You make me a better man, a braver one, and every time I look into your eyes, I know I'm where I'm supposed to be, with my person. I love you more than anything, and I promise I'll spend the rest of my life proving it. All you have to do is say yes."

"Yes," I say, the word bursting from my chest as I nod so fast it sends the tears in my eyes streaming down my cheeks.

"What'd she say?" one of the elderly members of the McGuire clan shouts from a nearby boat, making us all laugh.

"Yes!" I shout. "I said yes!"

More laughter and cheers erupt from the party at large as Freya begins grooming my hair and ears, doing her part to make me presentable for my shiny new fiancé. After sliding the gorgeous ring on my finger, I hug her to my chest, watching as Wes strips off his shirt—yes, please—and jumps into the water.

A few moments later, he's on the boat beside me, gathering Freya and me into his damp arms. I shiver and press closer, looping my wrists around his neck.

"Want to elope?" he asks, kissing my cheek. "So we can spend the autumn being obnoxious newlyweds?"

I beam up at him. "Yes. Immediately. Weekend in Vegas? I hear you can get married in less than twelve hours."

"That would leave another whole day for hunting treasure in the desert," he says, proving he's my man.

Mine...

It's for real now. For keeps.

"It would," I agree, brushing his wet hair from his forehead. "But I think I already hit the jackpot."

"Aw, so cheesy," Binx says, drawing our attention to the group of McGuire adults and toddlers currently watching us from the shade beneath the pontoon's awning. "But so sweet. You two are the real deal. Can I please throw you a big party when you get home from eloping? We could do it in early October at the vineyard. Before it gets too cold. My friend Trixie said she could get me a discount on the venue as long as we do the catering ourselves."

"I'll cater," Mel says, without missing a beat. "I know all the foods you two like best. You won't have to do a thing except show up." She lifts her arms, swaying from side to side as the music kicks back on and *Uptown Girl* by Billie Joel floats across the lake. "And dance all night. Getting married reminded me how much I love dancing."

Wes pulls me close, swaying to the song as Freya climbs onto his shoulders, licking the water from his skin. He frowns and shoots her a sideways glance, but doesn't stop dancing. "I guess this means she approves?"

I grin. "It means she loves you and wants to keep you warm, safe, and dry."

"I love her," he says, his gaze softening as he wraps his arms tighter around my waist. "And you. I can't wait to make you my wife."

Joy bubbles up inside me, so fierce that it makes me tear up and laugh at the same time. "Sorry," I say, sniffing and giggling. "I'm just so happy, I don't know what to do with myself."

"How about we swim over to our boat and start looking for plane flights on my phone? I don't have to be back in the office until Wednesday. If we fly out early tomorrow, we can stay three nights."

"Except that I have a banquet to cater on Monday," I say, my lips turning down.

"I bet your boss would give you a day off," Wes says, raising his voice as he glances Mel's way, "Wouldn't you, Mel?"

"Wouldn't I what?" she asks.

"Give Tessa an extra day off, so she doesn't have to come in until Wednesday?"

"I told her," Mel says. "She can quit and start working on her food truck tomorrow if she wants." She spins, slapping a hand to her forehead before she continues dancing, bumping hips with Binx, who's also getting into the groove. "Actually no, you can't quit until November 1st. We have that huge fish banquet for the Bad Dog Anglers Club the last weekend in October, and you know I don't do fish. At least not without wanting to vomit the entire time. But yes, take the extra day, and I'll see you on Wednesday."

"November 1st sounds perfect," I say, my blood fizzing with excitement. "And Vegas sounds even better."

Thirty minutes later, Wes and I have booked the last two seats on the seven a.m. flight to Vegas, Freya has a sleepover date with Binx for the next few nights, and we're loading up our bowls for ice cream sundaes amidst an abundance of well-wishing family members.

Family...

This is my family. Mel, Chase, Binx, and all the other sweet and crazy McGuires, they're mine now, too. I'm not just getting the husband of my dreams, but dozens upon dozens of incredible people to love.

"I'll never be lonely again," I whisper to Wes on our way home, tears pricking at my eyes.

He reaches across the car, threading his fingers through mine. "Me, either."

I'm so happy, so in love and busy thinking of all the things I need to pack for our last-minute wedding/treasure-hunting trip, that I totally forget about my surprise. It isn't until Wes shouts—"I thought I couldn't love you more. I was wrong"—from the bedroom while I'm feeding Freya that I remember.

Giddy and grinning, I dash down the hall, laughing as I spot him by the swing, his eyes glittering like he just got all his Christmas presents early. "You like?" I ask.

"I *love*," he corrects, moving toward me. "The things I'm going to do to you on this swing, Mrs. McGuire."

I sigh. "I can't wait, Mr. McGuire."

"You don't have to," he says, shutting the door behind me with a shove of his palm and pulling me into his arms.

My clothes vanish as we kiss like we're starved for each other, like we're never going to get enough. I know I won't. I could make out with this man every day and never get tired of his taste, his touch, the way he makes me feel like I'm the only woman in the world.

By the time he lifts me into the swing, adjusting the straps so my shoulders are lifted high enough for me to watch as he fits us together, there's nothing but him. He's my focus, my center, the rock I know I can depend on today and every day, for the rest of our lives.

He grips my hips, letting the momentum of the swing send me gliding forward, until he's buried deep, filling me the way only he can.

And *wow*, the swing is fun, but it's the connection between us that makes our love life so explosive. It's knowing I can trust him with every part of me and he can do the same.

Later, after we've showered, packed, and made sure all our bags are by the door, ready to go for the early flight, we snuggle with Freya on the couch, watching trashy reality television about hot people trying not to have sex with each other in order to win money. Just a few minutes in, Wes and I decide we would definitely be kicked off the island the first week.

"I can't keep my hands off you," he says, proving it as he curls his fingers around the thigh I've stretched across his lap. "No amount of money is worth a week away from this pussy."

I grin. "Agreed. And I'm pretty sure treasure hunting is more lucrative than reality television. At least so far. I'm excited for our next adventure, Preston."

"Me, too, Lady Gray," he says, his hand creeping up

my thigh. "Especially now that we've had our rabies shots. Bats don't scare me anymore."

Humming beneath my breath, I murmur, "They still scare me. A little bit. But I'll wear my hair in a braid, give them fewer places to get trapped when they fly for freedom." The words make me wonder... "Speaking of freedom..." I trail my fingers up his muscled forearm. "Are you worried about that at all? Are you sure you're ready to be a one-woman man?"

He smiles, a relaxed grin that leaves no doubt he means it when he says, "I've never been more certain of anything. As long as the woman is you."

Freya chuffs and stretches across our laps, wiggling as if to say, *Less cheesy love talk; more petting the ferret, please.*

So, we do, spoiling our little girl with affection to make up for leaving her with her auntie Binx for the next three nights.

And then, bright and early the next morning, we load our things into Wes's car and embark on our biggest adventure yet.

The one that's going to last the rest of our lives...

Not ready to say goodbye to the
McGuire family?
**Binx's romance, KIND OF A BAD IDEA
releases August 2024!**

Subscribe to Lili's newsletter HERE **to keep up to date with all new releases and sales!)**

About the Author

Author of over fifty novels, *USA Today* Bestseller **Lili Valente** writes everything from steamy suspense to laugh-out-loud romantic comedies. A die-hard romantic, she can't resist a story where love wins big. Because love should always win. She lives in Vermont with her two big-hearted boy children and a dog named Pippa Jane.

Find Lili at...
www.lilivalente.com

Also by Lili Valente

The McGuire Brothers

Boss Without Benefits
Not Today Bossman
Boss Me Around
When It Pours (novella)
Kind of a Sexy Jerk
When it Shines (novella)
Kind of a Hot Mess
Kind of a Dirty Talker
Kind of a Bad Idea

The Virgin Playbook

Scored
Screwed
Seduced
Sparked
Scooped

Hot Royal Romance

The Playboy Prince
The Grumpy Prince
The Bossy Prince

Laugh-out-Loud Rocker Rom Coms

The Bangover
Bang Theory
Banging The Enemy
The Rock Star's Baby Bargain

The Bliss River Small Town Series

Falling for the Fling
Falling for the Ex
Falling for the Bad Boy

The Hunter Brothers

The Baby Maker
The Troublemaker
The Heartbreaker
The Panty Melter

Bad Motherpuckers Series

Hot as Puck
Sexy Motherpucker
Puck-Aholic
Puck me Baby
Pucked Up Love
Puck Buddies

Big O Dating Specialists
Romantic Comedies

Hot Revenge for Hire
Hot Knight for Hire
Hot Mess for Hire
Hot Ghosthunter for Hire

The Lonesome Point Series

(Sexy Cowboys)
Leather and Lace
Saddles and Sin
Diamonds and Dust
12 Dates of Christmas
Glitter and Grit
Sunny with a Chance of True Love
Chaps and Chance
Ropes and Revenge
8 Second Angel

The Good Love Series

(co-written with Lauren Blakely)
The V Card
Good with His Hands
Good to be Bad

Made in the USA
Middletown, DE
04 May 2024